Til Kingdom Cay

Other books by Craig MacIntosh

The Fortunate Orphans
(Beaver's Pond Press, 2009)

The Last Lightning
(Beaver's Pond Press, 2013)

McFadden's War
(Pugio Books, 2015)

Wolf's Vendetta
(Pugio Books, 2015)

Wolf's Inferno
(Pugio Books, 2016)

Wolf's Baja
(Pugio Books, 2017)

Wolf's Odyssey
(Pugio Books, 2019)

TIL KINGDOM
CAY

ISBN: 978-0991361182

Cover design by Kent Mackintosh
Book design by Belldog Media and typeset in Janson Text

Printed in the United States of America
Second Printing: 2020

9 8 7 6 5 4 3 2 1

Published by Pugio Books
13607 Crosscliffe Place
Rosemount, MN 55068
www.cjmacintosh.com

ACKNOWLEDGEMENTS

With each succeeding book I am reminded of how much of a team effort is required to go from a story idea to the printed word. My wonderful editor Cindy Rogers kept me pointed in the right direction at all times during the writing. Proofreader Marcia Herbster cleaned up my manuscript, and Jeff Wechter formatted the final version. Designer Kent Mackintosh produced another of his eye-catching covers, and along the way to the first printing my wife Linda added her proofing skills and encouragement.

With my gratitude to others thus acknowledged, I want to say a word about the setting for this book.

Seasoned travelers to the Bahamas will know not to pore over nautical charts looking for Jericho Island and Kingdom Cay. These two islands will not be found—they do not exist. They are a blend of experiences gained from my twenty years of visits to the Bahamas. Thankfully, the art of writing fiction affords authors wide leeway in creating a narrative. Though the settings, characters, and outcomes of *Til Kingdom Cay* may remind readers of places they may have visited, or people they met in the Bahamas —that would be a serendipitous outcome based on an imagined familiarity—not reality.

"The wages of sin is death."

—Romans 6:23

For Dennis Hackett

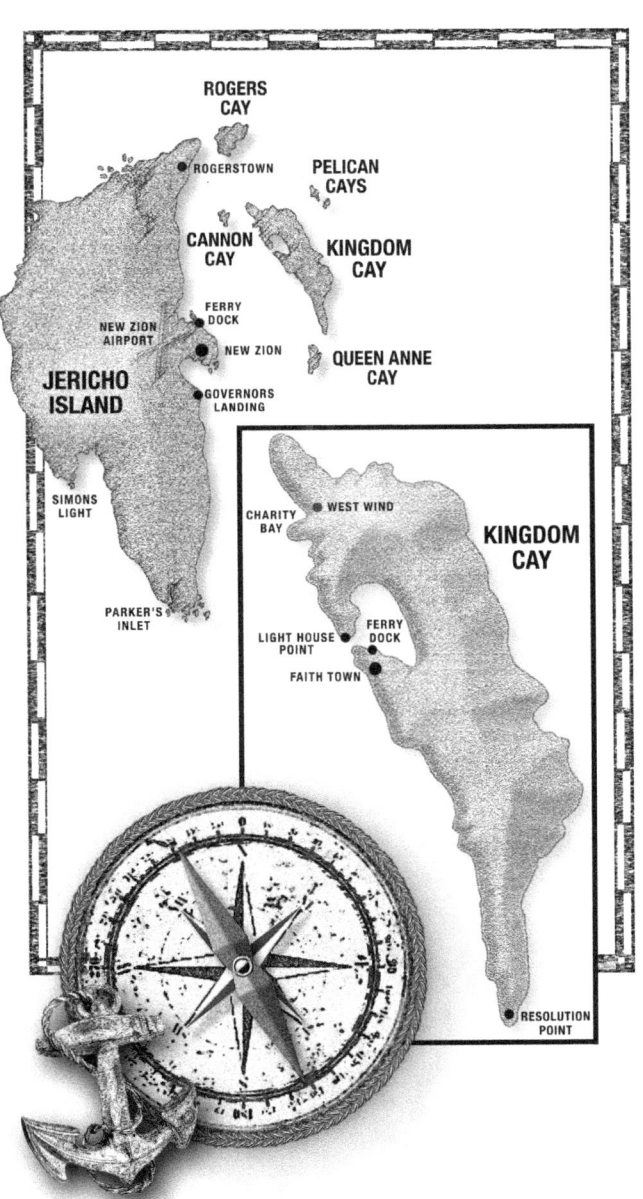

ROGERS
CAY

● ROGERSTOWN

PELICAN
CAYS

CANNON
CAY

KINGDOM
CAY

FERRY
DOCK

NEW ZION
AIRPORT

● NEW ZION

QUEEN ANNE
CAY

JERICHO
ISLAND

● GOVERNORS
LANDING

SIMONS
LIGHT

CHARITY
BAY

● WEST WIND

KINGDOM
CAY

PARKER'S
INLET

LIGHT HOUSE
POINT

● FERRY
DOCK

FAITH TOWN

RESOLUTION
POINT

Chapter 1

A fifteen-foot whaler with three men skipped across the evening sea like a flat stone thrown by someone with a strong arm. On the bow rode a bare-chested charioteer, his jeans drenched in spray, a taut line gripped in his left hand, his right-hand waving. Each time the boat went airborne over the waves, the yellow-haired rider shrieked in exhilaration.

Another young man with caramel-colored skin and a mass of unruly brown curls sat in front of the pilot's tinted windshield watching the crazy white boy making a fool of himself. Gusts of wind sent the man's shirt billowing up around his neck obscuring his view of the horizon where breakers exploded in white against the dark sea. He grinned at the pale buffoon and wrapped a towel against his bare legs, a futile effort, for everything was soaked from the spray.

It didn't matter really. He didn't know it, but he was a dead man. Had he known; he might have paid more attention to what his companions were doing.

A shirtless, muscular black man, older than the other two, stood at the controls in a pair of rubber reef shoes that kept him balanced on the slippery deck. His shaved head glistened from the salt spray pounding the cockpit's windshield. Peering through smeared, gold-framed glasses, he dropped his speed. Ahead, furious waves hammered a ragged ledge of sharp black coral, surf smashing and booming the length of the reef.

The sound was just what the pilot wanted—nature's cooperation.

The boat bobbed toward the cut in the rocks. The dead man looked back at the pilot and held up his hands as if to ask why they were here. The black man bellowed over the windshield. "We're meeting another boat." He drew closer. "Should be through the cut any minute now."

Shrugging, the youth braced his feet against the bucking deck and pulled his sodden towel tighter as the whaler fought the current sluicing through nearby rocks.

"Zeke, take the wheel." A stupid, salt-soaked grin spread across the blonde's thin face as he staggered back along the gunwales to the controls. "Hold her into the wind!" roared the pilot as the boat pitched in the chop. His menacing look sobered the youth as he crouched behind the spray shield. Leaning over the plexiglass screen, the leader barked at his other companion. "Get ready to anchor."

The youth rose.

"Keep your eyes on the horizon! Don't anchor until I tell you to! You got that?" He jerked his thumb toward the bow and sent the youth forward.

Crouching in the bow, his hand gripping the anchor, the young man squinted back over the coiled line, waiting for his signal.

The leader pulled yellow marine binoculars from a bag and circled the horizon. No other boats in sight. He caught the youth watching him. "Eyes on the horizon!" he yelled, lowering the binoculars.

"Wait for my signal."

The dead man snapped his head back over the bow.

At the helm, the white boy watched transfixed as the older man set down the glasses and pulled a sawed-off shotgun from his bag. Crouching to absorb the pitch of the whaler in the swells, the man crept forward.

The boom of the shotgun was lost in the waves, but the blast slammed the youth's body against the bow, his lifeless hands still gripping the anchor. Blood and bits of bone and brain splattered the muzzle of the smoking gun and the murderer's forearms.

The killer peeled the dead youth's fingers from the anchor and heaved the body over the bow. The corpse drifted from the boat as the assassin dipped his arms up to his elbows in the chop and scrubbed himself clean. He crabbed his way to the console, wrapped the gun in a towel and stuffed it in the bag. He glared at his companion.

"Snitches."

The body drifted toward the cut.

One last sweep with the binoculars was assurance enough that they were still alone on the sea. Satisfied, he threw the glasses in the bag and took over the helm. He urged the throttle forward to make a tight turn away from the coral.

The pilot ordered Zeke to wash the bow and deck with buckets of salt water. Only when bloody water began sloshing around his ankles did the pilot pull the drain plug and accelerate, putting the bow in the air. The saltwater poured behind them, quickly emptying the boat. When it gained calmer water, the process was repeated. The whaler shot forward, the water drained, and the executioner was finally satisfied. What light remained thinned and then night dropped at once over the island as the solitary boat aimed for the dim silhouette of an island on the horizon.

CHAPTER 2

Southeast of the Abacos sits Jericho Island, a rough dagger-shaped fragment aimed south. It is blessed with spectacular beaches, two wide bays on its eastern side, great stands of Casuarina pine and handsome coconut palms along its beaches. Halfway down its southeast coast, New Zion, the island's biggest town, boasts a modern dockyard and a new airport, capable of handling small jets. Farther up the east coast sits Governour's Landing, a collection of modest homes and small hotels overlooking a crescent of white sand that shelters a bay in its arm. Farther north of that is Black's Bay, a natural anchorage since pirate days and home to the lethargic village of Rogerstowne, both a watercolorist's paradise and a developer's lustful dream. Here, ramshackle homes sprawl the length of the beach in faded pastel coats of pink, yellow and china blue while gossamer curtains of fishing nets dry in trade winds.

Roger's Cay, a seven-acre island home to the boat building Cameron clan, lies just off the settlement and can be reached on foot during extreme low tides.

From New Zion's harbor, Kingdom Cay's low outline is visible three miles east, just inside an offshore reef running northwest to southeast on the Atlantic's edge. Faithtown, the island's settlement, is known throughout sailing circles for its slender white concrete lighthouse guarding the harbor mouth.

Kingdom Cay, a small island, runs seven miles long from eastern most Resolution Point to West Point on its opposite end and barely a quarter mile wide at its most narrow point. Smaller fragments—tiny cays with names like Cannon, Queen Anne, Pelican and New Light Cay—are strung around Kingdom Cay's perimeter.

The island shelters three hundred souls year-round in Faithtown, plus a scattering of private homes along its windward side where estates of American expatriates dominate. Time here is as warped as clapboard siding on Faithtown homes, and visitors and locals alike move as if in a dream. Sweet water is collected in cisterns for, as one of Faithtown's founders penned, "God hath not seen fit to provide fresh water among His abundance, thereby sorely testing us."

At low tide, a small bronze plaque commemorating the founders' landfall is visible near Lighthouse Point at the harbor entrance. The raised letters read, "Here, on May 15, 1790, in the year of our Lord, seventeen souls, transported by the sloop Trinity from Nassau, first set foot on Kingdom Cay, establishing the settlement of Faithtown. Among the party, seven gentlemen, five womenfolk and five children." That fourteen household slaves, who suffered the same privations, did not get equal mention was an oversight that has irked New Zion's black Bahamians ever since the tablet's 1949 installation ceremony.

Wheeling high above Faithtown harbor, a solitary gull began a long, lazy glide toward its favorite dock that always promised better pickings. Swooping down, the bird braked in a wobbly landing and swaggered the length of the weathered planks, picking and discarding tiny shreds of trash. Strutting inland, the gull skirted the edge of the harbor walkway where it encountered a lone figure moving in its direction.

Jeremiah McKay, Kingdom Cay's only policeman, eyed the feathered scavenger with contempt. He hated seagulls. A childhood encounter with an aggressive flock intent on stealing a crust from his toddler's hand had instilled a lifelong dislike for the waddling, scolding scavengers. To McKay, seagulls represented disorder and cocky arrogance. He also resented the birds' inborn laziness, which, ironically, acted as a constant reminder of his own failings.

Feigning menace, he moved directly at the gull, which ignored him. McKay picked up a small stone, skipping it at the gull. Wings flapping in panic, the squawking seagull backpedaled toward the water. Satisfied with the bird's retreat, McKay resumed his course.

Forty-one, Jeremiah McKay, *Mac* to his closest friends, was six feet and athletic, with a strong swimmer's shoulders and muscular forearms. McKay's thick, sandy-colored hair crowned blue eyes and a nose tinted pink more from alcohol than the sun. Postcard handsome, McKay always obliged visitors who asked for posed pictures of themselves with him and the lighthouse in the background.

At the foot of the public dock, McKay turned up an uneven street of broken cement. A rattling bicycle, pushed by a thin, unkempt crone in a faded blue sundress crossed his path.

"Morning, Jeremiah," sang out the old woman.

"Morning, Miss Emily."

"Fine morning, isn't it, Jeremiah?"

It was a ritual for both. They crossed paths at the same time each morning. Miss Emily wandered after sunrise, sometimes lucid, more often not. Usually conversing with herself, she never failed to greet McKay on his morning walk.

"An exceptional morning," he responded. "Are you in better health today?"

Nursing a persistent cough that had robbed her of sleep for over a month, the spinster appreciated his concern. "I'll be going into New Zion for medicine today."

McKay smiled and waved as he moved up the sidewalk.

She let him go and then called after him, "Oh, and Jeremiah..."

He paused.

"Let the seagulls be," she said. "They're God's creatures, you know."

Embarrassed, he shrugged, his best charming smile flashing at her. Miss Emily waved him on and guided the old bike ahead of her, already lost in conversation with an unseen companion.

Faithtown stirred from its morning lethargy. Miami radio forecast flawless skies and brilliant sunshine with two-foot seas. Another day like the day before, and the day before that one. Even with the official start of hurricane season only a month away, cruise line operators and tourist ministry officials worshipped days with the promise of this one. Yet, McKay loved to see the clouds come boiling over the horizon in purples and menacing grays. "It gives variety. Challenges the week, doesn't it?" he'd say.

Strolling the length of the main sidewalk, McKay felt the harbor come to life. Twelve sailboats had put in the day before. Their crews were starting morning rituals. Breakfast dishes clattered in the Harbor Lodge's kitchen on the far side of the bay. A lone inflatable purred between moored boats. Somewhere in town, hammering began. A handsaw soon joined the carpenter's chorus.

McKay reached his office, a large, two-story coral block structure topped by a rusting corrugated metal roof. At one time in the building's life it had been plastered, but most of the original coat had retired along with the colonial government a generation ago. Only two rooms on the ground floor were used now—McKay's cramped office faced the town's post office across a narrow-arched entryway.

Postmistress Sarah Cameron was already at work on a thick stack of mail. Short and stout, like all middle-aged Cameron women, she wore her long gray hair in a bun and shunned make-up except for badly done slashes of deep red lipstick across thin lips. Her small brown rodent's eyes— eyes that rarely missed a thing—scanned envelopes in front of her. At her elbow, a small, corroded fan whirred, already in a losing battle with morning humidity.

"Morning, Sarah."McKay fished in his pocket for keys.

The postmistress nodded without looking, "Morning, Jeremiah."

Turning a large silver key in the ancient lock, McKay opened a thick, wooden door and flicked the light switch several times until a fluorescent ceiling fixture kicked in. The light buzzed, flickered and died. Grabbing a wooden yardstick from the corner, McKay stretched, tapping the bulb into life. He hung his saucer cap on a wooden peg and snapped on his VHF radio. He coaxed a desk fan into life and settled into a creaking swivel chair.

McKay's official domain was small—a spartan, pale, plastered room, twelve-foot square with a ten-foot ceiling and a battered wooden desk jammed against one wall. A large, single-paned window, cut into the two-foot thick coral-block wall, bathed the room in light. From his desk, McKay could turn and watch the harbor and ferry landing. A faded portrait of Queen Elizabeth II, dusty, dour, and draped in ermine, looked down on him. Beside her majesty, a smaller glossy picture of the Bahamian prime minister smiled from a cheap frame. A miniature Bahamian flag hung limply between the two heads of state. McKay's police academy graduation picture topped a narrow glass-lined bookcase stocked with manuals and stacks of note pads. Three stuffed filing cabinets bulged with inherited paperwork.

McKay plugged in a dented metal pot for the first of many cups of weak, sweetened tea. Plucking a manila file from a desk drawer, he placed it in front of him, snagged a ballpoint pen from a forest of pens jamming a pewter mug by his phone and scanned a dull directive from Nassau headquarters. His day had formally begun.

CHAPTER 3

Three hundred steps from the constable's office sits Faithtown's Assembly of God Church, a white, one-story clapboard building straddling low coral blocks that once supported St. George's, an Anglican house of worship. Long ago, Kingdom Cay's Anglicans, like the sponging and sisal trade, had fallen on hard times. A fire in 1939 had finished off what the collapse of the economy had started. Anglicans who remained drifted reluctantly into the larger Methodist Church or ceased church-going altogether. A few parishioners moved to New Zion or Nassau in search of work, and St. George's was eventually erased from diocese rolls.

In 1954, with mission money in hand, Assembly of God elders from Nassau came calling and discovered a faithful handful still meeting in homes. Though they would not publicly admit to the charge, the visiting committee took perverse delight in reclaiming what had once been Anglican ground. Faithtown's Assembly of God Church was dedicated on a burning hot Sunday in August, in the year of Our Lord, one thousand nine hundred and fifty-seven. Since that date, seven pastors had taken the Faithtown pulpit. The current one, Pastor Samuel Josiah Burton, was the eighth, and longest serving.

The elders had drafted Burton—son of James and Abigail Burton, both descendants of Faithtown settlers originally from Abaco. It was, in effect, a homecoming for the preacher. His mother, a Cameron, had bequeathed him a rugged profile and stubbornness. From his father, Samuel Burton inherited a thick thatch of hair, a toothy smile and unyielding integrity with a heart for his un-churched island brethren.

While in New Zion, Burton had asked for the hand of Lillian Lowe, the red-haired, blue-eyed daughter of the Faithtown Lowes. She had agreed to share the young minister's frugal existence, seeing in him a sense of purpose other suitors lacked. When the call to Faithtown's pulpit came, Lillian was pleased to return home. Her younger sister Felicity had remained on Kingdom Cay, eventually marrying the island's newly appointed constable, Jeremiah McKay.

At the age of thirty-seven, the pastor's wife gave birth to Jonathan David Burton, a blessing and only child. She poured her love into the youngster and, as befits a Lowe woman, never once complained of life in the Out Islands. On Kingdom Cay, the Burtons gradually prospered. Using a small inheritance of his wife's, Pastor Burton had purchased a New England-built, thirty-foot hull powered by twin diesels. He outfitted the boat with an enclosed cabin and, with the New Zion commissioner's encouragement and a charter from Nassau, inaugurated the first regular ferry run between Jericho Island and Faithtown. Growing tourism fed his family from the ferry profits and allowed him to begin construction of a second home for rental.

His church, though faithfully attended by a core of Faithtown believers, lagged far behind the congregation of the Methodist Church with its pull on the American expatriate community. Even tourists seeking an island worship experience bypassed Burton's church in favor of the larger, whitewashed building with its slender steeple and narrow stained-glass windows facing the sea. Envy however, was something Burton would not entertain, a result of not only his Christian calling but his personality. His Cameron blood compelled him to stay with his small flock while his Burton traits drove him deeper into his Bible and its uncompromising truths.

Until 2009, Pastor Burton's small congregation included Felicity and Jeremiah McKay. But a malignancy, spawned years before, steadily sapped the strength of the constable's wife until she succumbed in November of the following year. In trying to forestall his sister-in-law's death, Burton mustered every theological argument he could present for God's hearing. He drew on every comforting Psalm he knew by heart, but it was not enough. His brother-in-law was shattered by the experience of watching his wife waste away in "God's very presence."

McKay, bewildered by his sudden widower's status, bolted from the church, weeping. For three days he drank himself into oblivion, ignoring meals his wife's sister sent with her son. Scourged by alcohol, McKay began a self-imposed exile from

Burton's church and a long intimacy with the bottle. He was, as he had bellowed to Burton during a drunken bout, "Done with you, your church and your God."

At first Burton gave wide berth to McKay, thinking the distance, which the policeman created, would one day cease. But the gulf yawned wider with each year. McKay angrily rebuffed every overture Burton made, railing against the preacher's "Unjust, uncaring, unfeeling God, who watches his children suffer in agony." It was an illogical argument that Burton, like all pastors, could not win.

Eventually, McKay tempered his bitterness towards his wife's family and allowed a seed of civility to grow. The preacher gave God the glory, while McKay credited time as the agent. There was now a formality about their conduct with one another. The village was too small, the island too confining, to permit a wall of silence to stand forever. But the adjustment had been made on McKay's terms.

"Good morning, Jeremiah," and "Hello, Samuel, how are you?" were as close as the constable would allow his former kinsman. Fond of Lillian, McKay found time for young Jonathan, but could not bring himself to close ranks with Burton.

Close by the church, the Burtons had purchased and enlarged an existing home. Built in 1900, the house, blindingly white clapboard with tasteful gray trim, was filled with Lowe family antiques, lovingly restored by Lillian.

On this brilliant clear morning, while his brother-in-law, McKay, busied himself with paperwork in the heart of Faithtown, the Reverend Samuel Josiah Burton was bent over the outlines of his sermon. Though he had been at it since six that morning, a fitting conclusion eluded him. He turned to find his wife standing in the doorway.

"Still struggling, Samuel?"

He pushed away from the desk, annoyed. "Yes, I can't end it."

"Let it simmer for a while," Lillian suggested.

"You're probably right. You usually are, luv." He glanced at the ship's clock above his writing desk. "I've got to make the eight o'clock run. Jonathan ready?"

His son served him as crew aboard the ferry, a boy who loved the ocean and had a genuine nautical grasp.

"He's been ready for the last hour. You know him." Lillian smiled.

"Well, I'll finish this tonight." He set the sheaf of papers aside.

"Let the Lord write it, Samuel. He always does."

"Right you are."

Snatching a large straw Panama hat from a wooden rack, Burton bent to kiss his wife. She lovingly touched his shaggy head, brushed back a strand of hair and stepped back. Burton poked one arm through a bright green nylon windbreaker and hurried down the backyard steps.

He would make two runs. At eight o'clock, Burton would promptly pull away from Faithtown's public dock and head for New Zion's harbor. The morning run carried older school children bound for secondary school, residents with business on Jericho Island, and occasional tourists with a day planned for the larger island. At eight-thirty, the crowded ferry would nose against its mooring in New Zion and discharge its cargo. Fifteen dollars one way, or twenty for a round trip, covered Burton's expenses and provided a small profit. A government contract covered school children and the daily mail run.

Precisely at nine-thirty, they would retrace their route to Faithtown, bringing tourists, residents and produce for island restaurants. At five o'clock, the last trip of the day was made with an immediate five-thirty turnaround from New Zion. The Burtons provided a dependable link to New Zion for residents and visitors alike, regardless of weather.

Occasionally, Burton ran charters to smaller cays or made special drops during his regular runs. On Sundays, Burton made just one trip, a two o'clock departure from Faithtown with an afternoon return at three. For Burton, the lone Sabbath run was a compromise. The steady traffic of those depending on his water taxi made his tenure at the church easier. Parishioners knew the Burtons would not allow a member of the flock to suffer privation and many of them had been the beneficiaries of a card in Lillian's neat script with several bills folded inside. Ferry money made the difference. Lillian kept tidy books for the service and ran their rental home as well. Jonathan's earnings built steadily and allowed him a sense of independence. He relished time with his father on the water and never missed a run between the islands. Surrounded by his family, at ease in his study among Bible commentaries, or preaching to fellow believers, Burton was content. Only estrangement from McKay nagged at him as unfinished business.

CHAPTER 4

At its eastern end, Kingdom Cay tapers to a spade-shaped ledge of rock. A lone white obelisk set in concrete provides a reference point for boaters and marks the tip of the island. Despite danger from razor-sharp coral there is good snorkeling here. Fifty yards from the post, swimmers who anchor in twelve feet of clear water on calm days, often explore the reef.

Low tide exposes wide expanses of sculptured rock, great clumps of turtle grass, and thousands of tiny marine creatures. Elk horn coral breaks the surface during low water, as though a great herd was about to surface. Just offshore, massive formations of coral, forested with purple sea fans, mark deeper water. Resolution Point, christened by a nameless Royal Navy cartographer in 1803, is an obligatory stop for visitors. Two-dozen homes line the last mile of pitted limestone road and several docks, sheltered by the island's southern shore, jut into the sound. Tide pools, created by the receding ocean are an amateur biologist's delight, the rocks regularly swarming with vacationers gingerly probing for souvenirs.

The theater of this morning's tide was deserted save for a couple moving slowly over glistening rocks, their heads bowed, shell bags at their sides. They were retired North Carolina teachers who were renting, as they had for fifteen years, a beach house at this end of Kingdom Cay. Even on this small island they preferred Resolution Point's solitude to foot traffic in Faithtown.

Walking the sandy beach each morning, they scouted the point at low tide. The couple had not missed a sunrise stroll in all of their years on the cay and rarely passed on opportunities to examine this edge of shore. Only threatening storm-tossed waves exploding against Resolution Point's jagged reef could intimidate their daily ritual.

Outpacing her husband this morning, Arleen VanDeWalker approached the limit of the ledge, her eyes distracted by something floating close to the rocks. Not sure of what she had spotted, she moved closer. Movement on the uneven coral was tedious and her rubber shoes offered little protection against the sharpest rocks. On closer inspection, she gasped, horrified by the sight of a bloated human body gently bobbing face-up in offshore swells.

"DEAN!" she screamed, turning away, stumbling toward her husband. At first cry, the crouching man lifted his head, thinking she had some delightful shell in hand.

"Dean! Please! Come here," she pleaded, pumping her arms.

Vaulting a tide pool, her husband nimbly leaped the rocks to his wife, who was clinging to a large wet boulder. He reached for her hand. "Are you all right?"

Shaking her head, she waved an arm toward the ocean. "In the water. Over there."

Turning where tiny waves gently slapped at the rocks, he spotted the floating shape. He edged closer. He had seen a body once before, in a river near their city. An old man had leaped to his death from a bridge upstream.

This corpse was a young, light-skinned black man, floating on his back, unseeing, opaque eyes glazed by the sun, a slight swelling buoying the body. The arms, locked at the elbows, rocked in a macabre waving gesture.

Wading forward, the schoolteacher yelled over his shoulder. "We've got to get him ashore, Arleen." His wife didn't move. "Arleen, give me a hand."

She shook her head vigorously. "I can't."

"Dammit, I need your help," he said. "The woman was paralyzed. "Then get to the radio and call the police," he commanded. She turned and jogged toward the distant house. The dead man wore only a pair of thin khaki shorts. VanDeWalker snagged a belt loop and tugged his burden towards a small crescent of sand. Mercifully, the tide was dropping and with it, the wave action. Had the body washed ashore earlier it would have been shredded into bloody ribbons on the coral.

Sharks, thought VanDeWalker, *let this one get away.*

Gaining a sliver of beach, he eased the corpse over on its side to prop it higher, away from the water. It was then he saw the wounds across the upper back and head. A large chewed area exposed the base of the skull and several dorsal nubs of ivory spine. Dropping to his knees in the shallows, he vomited. Pushing himself from the body, he settled himself on smooth rock and cupped his hand with saltwater. Swishing the brine in his mouth, the retired teacher spit in the ocean.

The sun climbed higher. The sea continued to drop. VanDeWalker's wife returned to the distant deck, yelling, her words unintelligible. Waving, he returned her signal. "I'll prop the body here," he mumbled, "and let the police deal with it." Grabbing a six-foot plank of driftwood wreathed in seaweed, he worked quickly to jam the wood against the corpse's buttocks, wedging the lumber against a rock to anchor the body. "There. That should hold you." He stooped to fan his hands in a tide pool, rinsing off seaweed, sand, and the feel of dead flesh.

From the home's wide sun deck Arleen watched her husband picking his way across the flats. Beyond him, she glimpsed a pair of outstretched arms marking the body's sandy niche.

At the bottom of the steps, Dean paused to catch his breath. "Did you call?"

"I couldn't get a cell signal, so I radioed the inn. They said they would relay the message." He nodded and climbed the stairs. She offered him a glass of ice water. "Oh, Dean, it was horrible wasn't it?" Grateful for the cool glass in his hand, he settled into a canvas deck chair.

"I wasn't much support, was I?" she said. "I...I'm sorry, I just couldn't..."

He forgave her with a wave. "It's all right, Arleen. Couldn't be helped. Someone had to call the police." She sighed, grateful for his understanding. "Any idea..." she began.

Finishing her sentence, he said, "Who he is? No clue. He was only wearing shorts."

"A drowning, Dean?"

"Hard to say. Something obviously got to him on one side."

A hand went to her mouth. "How horrible! I'm so sorry."

Downing the water, he leaned forward in the chair. "I need to rinse off. Shower. I feel...clammy, unclean."

CHAPTER 5

A plume of steam rose from an ancient teapot on a single burner. McKay fussed over a late lunch. Paperwork had delayed his mealtime, putting him in a cranky mood. Tourists were missing three pieces of luggage a New Zion cabdriver had put on the wrong ferry the previous day. The visitors had done what they thought proper when confronted with the problem—they had contacted the police upon arrival. The elusive baggage was still somewhere between Jericho Island and Faithtown. It was a few minutes after noon, and the wayward suitcases had defied McKay's best efforts.

His radio, squelch button turned to maximum, crackled into life. "Faithtown Police, Coco Palms calling."

Most island homes and shops had call signs. Coco Palms was a six-room hotel perched on a rocky crest just east of Faithtown, along the south shore. Since most residents would have simply used his first name, this call was business. Thirteen McKay's lived on Kingdom Cay, but only one was named Jeremiah, and he was seldom called in the middle of the day. Most people simply stopped by his office if they needed advice or wanted to tempt him with a morsel of news. His chair legs scraped against linoleum as he leaned in to pluck the radio from its hook. He keyed the handset. "McKay here, go to channel one-four."

"Right," the voice answered. "Meet you at one-four."

Initial calls were made on sixteen, but follow up conversation took place on other channels, freeing sixteen for important contacts. It was a courtesy among islanders and anyone lingering on sixteen would be scolded onto another channel.

He keyed fourteen. "McKay here, go ahead."

"Jeremiah, this is Ruthie. We have a problem. A body washed up on Resolution Point this morning."

Ruth Webster, an American, was part owner of the small inn. McKay frowned. News like this meant work. There would be reports to file, paperwork to complete and interviews. Lunch and the missing baggage would have to wait. *Very inconvenient.*

"Still there?" the voice inquired.

"Yes, I got it." Running a calloused hand over his forehead, he pinched his eyes shut as he answered. Thinking on his feet, he rose from the chair. "What's the location of the body?"

"On the point. Couple from a rental home found it while walking this morning."

McKay said, "Right. I take it you're relaying the call, so get back to them and ask that they keep an eye open for me on the road, please. Oh, and what's the couple's name? What house are they in?" There were not that many homes at that end of the island, but it would save him some time to know exactly which one.

"Yellow Bird. Dean and Arleen VanDeWalker."

"Thanks. I'll be out that way shortly, Ruthie." McKay paused before signing off.

"Anything else?"

"That's it. Back to one-six." Her call ended.

"Right, one-six." He twisted his dial back to the main channel.

Drops of water hissed on the burner. Tea would have to wait. McKay flicked off the hotplate and sank into his chair, cradling the microphone in his fist. His boat would be impractical in the shallows and his thick-wheeled bicycle was ill fitted to the task. Normally, it would be a pleasant ride to the point, the route shaded with palms and graceful pines, but for a body he needed a truck.

To contain the news, he opted for the telephone. Lines ran to half the homes in town and there was a cable to New Zion, but for dependable communication, everyone relied on VHF radios. Today, McKay was grateful for the phone. *No need to broadcast unpleasantness,* he thought. *By evening, everyone would know.* He dialed Faithtown's clinic, with its staff of one, a retired nurse from the states who volunteered her services three mornings a week. With no patients to tend, she agreed to meet outside his office.

Martha Thomsen, a forty-something nurse from New York City, had moved to Kingdom Cay five years before. Divorced, childless, long-legged and tan, she wore her auburn hair in a boyish cut that gave her a youthful look. To McKay, she was a refreshing all-American green-eyed beauty and they had grown fond of each other since she had taken over the clinic.

She arrived with a wide smile at the constable.

"Bit of a problem, Martha," McKay began. "We've got a body on Resolution Point. Probably a drowning. No details yet. I'm going out to look it over. I'll see if I can use my cousin Robert's truck." She grimaced, nodding at her own memories of bloated corpses fished from New York's East River. "Once I get him back here, I'd like you to take a look. Nothing formal of course, just for my report."

She agreed. "Better have someone bring several blocks of ice to the storeroom at the back of the clinic. In this heat, things get sticky fast. And depending on how long he's been in the water, well..." She left the rest unsaid. McKay pointed her toward the clinic, his hand at her elbow.

"Right. I'll ring Robert now and arrange for the ice." He paused. "No need to let on about this. Bad for visitors, you know."

Understanding him perfectly, she smiled. Tourists want no unpleasantness when they visit, especially the likes of a body washing ashore on picturesque Kingdom Cay. They parted, and McKay slipped into his office to dial his cousin at Faithtown's grocery store. His mother's nephew ran Faithtown's largest store and was notorious for both Irish-Scotch frugality and a prickly personality.

"Robert, it's Jeremiah," he said. "I need your help. Official business of course."

"Go on," his cousin groused, bracing for what was coming next.

"There's been an accident on Resolution Point." McKay was a policeman now, skipping details. "Seems we have a drowning victim, washed up this morning. I need your truck to fetch the body if that's all right with you."

Cornered by the request for help, Robert McKay said, "I suppose. I'm closing for lunch anyway." He paused. "You have help?"

"It would be good if you came along. Tides almost out. Baking in the sun all morning won't do our lad any good. Oh, and Robert, I'm going to need ice, say five or six blocks until I can make arrangements with New Zion."

Ice was a precious commodity. McKay waited for the request to sink in.

"At government expense, I take it?"

"Absolutely," McKay assured him.

"Better call the marina," said the grocer. "They have more ice than I can spare. I'll be at your office in ten minutes."

"Perfect." McKay appreciated efficiency. "And thanks, Robert."

McKay quickly dialed Faithtown's harbormaster, Abner Russell. He outlined his request. "I need a large sailcloth bag or something like it. Got anything on hand?"

"For the body?" Abner gloated in his reedy blunt voice.

Well, McKay thought, *you didn't waste any time eavesdropping, did you? With the news out there is no need to be diplomatic.*

"Yes. Robert and I are heading to the point. We'll bring the body back to the clinic's storeroom. Be a good citizen and drop off a bag to Martha would you?" McKay imagined Abner pouting at the request. "And I'm going to need a half-dozen large blocks of ice, can you do that?"

"The ice won't be easy," whined the harbormaster, "but I suppose I can get it for you. As for the sail bag, I'll do it, but mind you don't ruin it, Mac. They're not cheap and I might have need of it again."

Russell had a point. McKay had no idea of the body's condition. "We'll wrap it in plastic and surround it with ice when we get back."

"Make sure you do," grumbled Russell. "I'll have my boys bring the bag and ice."

"Thanks, Abner. Appreciate your help." McKay turned to find his cousin's truck nosing into view. "Well then, I'm off. Martha will be expecting your boys. Thanks."

The grocer's truck idled outside the office, a large plastic tarp spread across the bed and a pile of black garbage bags tucked under a gas can. McKay slid in beside his cousin, carefully placing his cap between them.

He said, "Thoughtful of you to bring the tarp, Robert."

"Just being practical Jeremiah. I like to take care of my things," he growled. McKay ignored the rebuke. His cousin said, "You didn't mention what your cadaver looked like, but I can guess."

Passing the public dock, he shifted gears as they ran the pothole gauntlet on the edge of Faithtown. A cloud of limestone dust trailed the little truck as they drove along the south shore.

CHAPTER 6

McKay braced himself as the truck dodged gaping holes. He had forgotten just how bad a driver Robert was. With the exception of two Haitian day laborers pedaling toward the harbor, there was no one else on the road. Both cyclists returned McKay's wave and were immediately swallowed in the truck's cloudy wake.

To McKay, this noonday investigation was an inconvenience that promised an official headache. Even his policeman's soul, which should have risen to the occasion, was irritated at the thought of the routine that would inevitably follow.

From above, the truck was a child's toy spinning a whirlwind of limestone dust on a crooked ribbon of road. The pockmarked highway cut through skimpy patches of shade cast by pine and palms lining the road. At midday, even this lush foliage gave scant relief from the sun. As they neared a rise, Robert slowed to take a sharp turn past the Coco Palms Inn. Glancing at his watch, McKay figured driving time to the point. They would be there in ten minutes, perhaps less, the way his cousin was driving. The truck whined in protest as Robert downshifted. Hugging the road's one good side, he avoided a string of washouts and rocks big enough to puncture the Toyota's muffler.

Suddenly, the ocean appeared. From this point the road narrowed to a rock-strewn path running along the coast where homes faced the water. Crimson splashes of bougainvillea broke walls of green hedge. Sunlight sparkled off a turquoise horizon, seemingly brighter at this end of the island.

"There, Robert." McKay pointed.

A stocky, pink-faced man in a loud shirt stepped into the roadway a hundred yards to their front and waved for their attention. "Right, I've got him." The truck slowed.

McKay waved the pedestrian over. He opened the door and snatched his policeman's cap from the front seat. Tucking his hat under an arm in an official pose, McKay extended his right hand. Both men were enveloped in choking dust.

The man clasped McKay's hand. "Dean Van DeWalker. Thank you for being so prompt."

"Constable McKay, at your service, sir. We'll try to make some sense of all of this," he said soothingly. "Now suppose you tell me all about this morning."

McKay followed the American to the rented house. The nervous man waved his arms wildly as he babbled excitedly about his discovery. "It was just horrible." He paused, trying to remember the policeman's name.

"McKay," the policeman reminded him.

"Yes, Constable McKay, sorry, I seem to be having trouble concentrating. One doesn't find a body every day."

Nodding sympathetically, McKay waved his cousin's truck slowly into the driveway, the tires carving a trail in the carpet of sand and pine needles. At the front door, McKay met Van DeWalker's wife, a short, blonde woman who confirmed his image of retired teachers. Her husband gestured to the officer as his wife extended her hand.

"Arleen, this is Constable McKay."

"Thank you for coming," she said. "It was a horrible way to start the day."

"Yes ma'am, I'm sure the deceased would agree," commented McKay.

The woman's broad face flushed, and she stepped aside.

The rental home was comfortable. Built for casual living, it commanded eight hundred dollars a week for its Faithtown owner. Arrangements like this were common throughout the cays. Bahamians built and rented second homes for extra income. McKay followed the couple onto a sun-washed deck overlooking the ocean. Robert called to him. "I parked the truck. We should take the tarp with us."

McKay introduced the couple. "This is Robert McKay. He was kind enough to lend me his truck for the task."

Exchanging handshakes with the grocer, Van DeWalker's wife said, "We've shopped in your store for years."

"Yes, I thought you looked familiar," said the storekeeper.

"Well, let's have a look," said McKay as he twisted on his cap. "Where exactly is the body?"

The teacher identified the coral cleft where he had left the corpse. Squinting at the spot, McKay headed for the stairs. He paused. "Robert, no need for you and Mr. VanDeWalker to come at the moment. I'd like to have a look at the scene first."

Shrugging, the two stayed behind. Folding the tarpaulin, the grocer put it aside and settled into a chair. VanDeWalker and his wife stood watching the policeman's progress toward the rocks.

For the first fifty meters it was slow going in the soft sand. When the rocks began, McKay moved deliberately toward the body, sixty feet to his front. Small tide pools had evaporated, leaving the rocks slippery. McKay stayed alert for dabs of marooned tar.

No need to ruin a perfectly good uniform in the line of duty.

The beach was alive with small alarmed crabs scuttling out of harm's way. McKay stopped at the water's edge. The body was wedged against the coral by a driftwood plank. Moving slowly, McKay made a mental inventory about the scene. Pulling a small red leather book from his breast pocket, he penned notes in sloppy handwriting.He spoke to himself as he scribbled.

"Black male, early-twenties, light colored shorts, no shoes or shirt. No tattoos or jewelry visible. Victim discovered south side of Resolution Point, possible drowning. At least one day in the sea."

Breaking his concentration only once, he glanced at his watch and kept writing.

McKay sat against a large rock, resting his left leg, which had begun its normal dull throbbing after prolonged standing. Crawling randomly across the dead flesh, one dozen flies roamed the body. McKay fanned them away with his hat. The insects ignored him. Crouching to examine a ragged wound where skull and neck joined, he made more notes. Satisfied, he stood up, his eyes sweeping along the shoreline and sea. Nothing. Not expecting any clues, he had looked out of habit. Turning, he raised his hat and waved.

From the deck, the constable looked like a man awaiting rescue. "He wants us, Mr. McKay," said the husband. Grumbling, the grocer rose from his comfortable perch and gathered the tarp. The two descended the stairs and worked their way to the shore.

Once on site, McKay ordered, "All right, gentlemen, let's bundle him up to the truck. Robert, you bring up the rear." He nodded at VanDeWalker. "You and I each take a corner."

Discarding the driftwood, they rolled the stiffened corpse into the canvas. McKay plucked bits of stray seaweed from the dead man's clothing while instructing his companions. "We needn't carry him the entire way without stopping." He went on, injecting some relief into the situation. "I don't know about you, but I'm far too old to be doing this sort of thing."

Grunting in agreement, the other two took up their corners.

It was laborious going in soft sand. The trio made four stops to catch their breath as they struggled toward the house. Twice, the body's left arm poked through the shroud and McKay called a halt. Calming the horrified teacher, he stuffed the wayward limb back into place. Hustling the improvised stretcher up the stairs sapped their energy.

Once the body was placed in the truck's bed, grocer McKay arranged the plastic and fought off swarming flies while policeman McKay questioned the couple on the deck. Arleen VanDeWalker appeared with a tray of glasses filled with iced tea. She called for the storekeeper to join them. Putting away his notes, McKay held a chilled glass against his forehead. After a minute of silence, he stood and thanked the couple.

"I appreciate your cooperation and your willingness to get involved," he said. "Bad business to have him wash up on your beach, but these things just happen sometimes." The group moved from the deck toward the driveway. "If you remember any further details, or if you think of anything else I might need to know..." McKay paused.

VanDeWalker finished for him. "We'll call you."

"Good. We're off. I have business to take care of and Robert's needed at his store." McKay gave his official smile, touched the brim of his hat, and went to the truck.

"Sorry to keep you so long, Robert," he apologized.

Flashing a toothy grin, his cousin started the engine. "No problem, Constable. Margaret will handle things until I get back. She's done it before."

"And she'll have to do it again, I'm sure," McKay said, smiling.

With one arm draped over the steering wheel, the storeowner peered out the back window to judge how the corpse would take the jostling. Satisfied the body was secure, he accelerated in a shower of gravel.

CHAPTER 7

"Don't you have some reports to do?"

Martha Thomsen was at her nurse-in-charge best, annoyed at McKay's hovering. She was trying to finish her preliminary autopsy in primitive conditions. The body lay on six immense blocks of ice. Though the temperature outside hovered at eighty-five the clinic's back room felt cool. Scant light filtered through a set of unwashed windows and a single bulb provided minimum illumination for her makeshift morgue. Brushing away a stray lock of hair with the back of a gloved hand, she sighed in exasperation.

Shrugging, McKay moved out of her way. "A case like this comes with its own paperwork, you should know that, Martha." Heading for the door, he paused. "How much time do you need?"

Looking up from her work, her green eyes angry, she murmured under her breath.

"All right," he said. "I leave you in charge. But I'm going to have to move our friend to New Zion and turn him over to their police. They can do the official routine. After all, they have overall jurisdiction. Two hours enough?"

Martha nodded, without looking up. "Plenty of time."

A glance at his watch told McKay it was close to two. He backed out slowly.

Faithtown harbor baked in an indolent, deserted air. Most sailboats were out taking advantage of the day. The incoming tide was slowly covering a pile of bleached conch shells at the base of the public dock. A watercolor class of retirees camped nearby, its students in rapt attention as their teacher demonstrated the finer points of a wash. Small boats tugged gently at mooring ropes and ever-present gulls strutted on waterfront sidewalks.

Strolling to the dock, McKay checked on his boat, a twenty-two-foot V-bottom with center console and a sleek, black two hundred twenty-five horsepower Yamaha engine. The motor was tilted forward, its prop well out of the water, the boat's nylon top rippling in a slight breeze. Trailing fifteen feet from the stern, an anchor rope guarded against drift. Reflections played against a row of fiberglass hulls and a small school of translucent fish cruised under the boats. McKay inspected his mooring knot, stepping on the tethered line to check its tension. Satisfied, he headed for his office, bracing himself for Postmistress Cameron's snooping.

"Good afternoon, Jeremiah," she challenged as he tried to slip past.

"Ah, Sarah," he began. "I suppose you've heard."

"Most certainly. I saw Abner earlier."

Gaining his office by promising her more news, McKay said, "I've got to start my report. Seems we have a drowning. Likely a Jericho Island boy. Didn't recognize him."

He heard her rustling; imagined her shuffling a stack of mail, then folding her plump freckled hands to await more detail. Sarah Cameron was persistent, much quicker at gossip than her mail chores. When McKay wasn't forthcoming, she waddled into his office and parked her fleshy bulk against the doorjamb, determined to sniff out a bigger morsel of news.

"That's all there is to it?" she said.

Waiting for his laptop's computer screen to light up, McKay said, "Looks like it. Probably just too much to drink. Maybe he fell off a freighter working the islands." He began stabbing keys with the index finger of each hand.

"I'm supposed to be satisfied with a morsel of news like that?"

He hit the S key instead of the A and silently blamed his detractor. "Sarah dear," he scolded, "if there was more to tell, I'd let you know. And if I had told someone else, you'd know by now anyway."

Ignoring his remark, she shifted her perfumed bulk and snorted. "Huh, what's Martha doing with your corpse then?"

McKay sighed. *The woman misses nothing.* He said, "An autopsy for my report to the New Zion Police." He threw her a scrap. "Stop by tomorrow morning," he said as he stopped typing. "We'll have tea and gossip. I'll let you know what my findings are." He paused, letting his offer sink in. "Good enough, Sister Cameron?" He paused, fingers poised above the keyboard.

"Very well, Constable McKay, I'll hold you to your word." Satisfied for the moment, she returned to her office to wait on a tourist couple that wanted stamps.

From his perch on the marina docks, Abner Russell had seen McKay inspect his boat, then head to his office. Seeing the postmistress ambush the policeman in his office made the dock master smile. He scrawled a note to himself about the six blocks of ice and sail bag his sons had delivered to the town clinic. Ice didn't come cheap, even for the government. Tomorrow he would settle his books.

"Hey, Abner."

Nosing against the fuel dock at the wheel of a new 22-foot day cruiser, Zeke Cameron waved. He threw the throttle into neutral as the boat glided to the pumps. Russell whistled at the glistening hull, impressed by its newness and promise of speed. The blade-shaped boat was sculpted from cream-colored fiberglass and trimmed with a thin chrome railing highlighting a maroon candy stripe running the length of the deck. Even in neutral, the powerful outboard throbbed impatiently in a wreath of bluish fumes. Grinning, the boater goosed the engine in a raw display of power before cutting its power.

"Whadaya think of her, Mister Abner?"

"It'll do, Zeke."

Pretending insult, Cameron climbed up, rope in hand. He quickly looped the line around a piling and folded wiry arms across his muscled chest. Zeke Cameron wore his blonde hair long with curls spilling from under a blue baseball cap. His pale blue eyes, an upturned nose and perfect white teeth gave him an attractive adolescent look.

"It'll do?" He laughed. "This is probably the newest, fastest, most beautiful boat that will stop for fuel this entire year."

Russell nodded. She was beautiful, he granted young Cameron that. "Whose is it?" he asked as he unhooked the nozzle and flipped the power switch. The pump hummed into life and he handed the hose to Zeke.

Poking a thumb at his chest, Zeke crowed, "Mine. I picked her up last week."

"Boat building must pay well, Zeke. That's at least twenty thousand dollars worth of boat."

Cameron shrugged. "It pays okay, but I pick up extra work in New Zion."

Russell let the conversation die. He topped off the boat's tank and shut down the pump. Cameron snatched two quarts of oil from the shelf and added them to the gas. He wiped a stray drop of oil from the seat as he replaced the gas cap.

"You hear anything about a missing person in New Zion, Zeke?"

Cameron looked up, puzzled. Russell continued. "Somebody washed up this morning, out on Resolution Point. Might be someone from Jericho."

"Haven't heard a thing. Been in New Zion all day, too. Black or white?"

"What?"

"I said, black or white?"

"Don't know. McKay found him. That is, some visitors found him, and McKay brought him in. He'll probably end up in New Zion anyway. Police will have to look into it. Bad for business, right?"

"Yeah, people oughta be more careful." He waved. "Put it on my tab." He gunned the motor into life and untied his line. Backing from the pier, Cameron headed for the harbor.

Abner Russell added Zeke's bill to a clipboard filled with receipts.

CHAPTER 8

New Zion's uncrowned king is Hamilton Sawyer. Jericho Island is as much a private fiefdom for this former washerwoman's son as Nassau is for politicians and lawyers who excel at manipulating Parliament. As senior partner in the law firm of Sawyer, Sawyer and Russell—the extra non-existent Sawyer added to impress clients—Hamilton Sawyer has a hand in everything that turns a profit.

An Out Island godfather, Sawyer dispenses favors, justice and gossip on a brick veranda under an ancient banyan tree shading the bricked backyard of a bungalow office. Between sips of sweetened iced tea, the porcine attorney alternately works a cell phone, VHF radio, and Veronique, a curvaceous young secretary with questionable office skills.

Sawyer's legal partner Isaiah Russell carries the workload for most of the firm's court appearances as well as the voluminous paperwork, a legacy of Britain's colonial system. Sawyer prefers handshakes, nods, and the occasional stuffed envelope. He favors the dollar for debts owed, although on this afternoon he was entertaining thoughts of barter in relation to a fee due his two-man firm.

Their debtor, Thomas McIntosh, a lanky young dreadlocked stonemason with an arrest record for drunkenness, squirmed in a wicker chair before a lecturing Sawyer.

"The way I see it, Thomas, you in over your head on this thing, mon." Letting his assessment sink in for a few seconds, the lawyer added, "Let's see how we can help each other."

Sawyer's mahogany moon face, framed by huge mutton chops and topped with oiled, straightened hair, showed a trace of smile as he dropped his gaze to a letter in his right hand. He had his man exactly where he wanted him.

"You got a Hobson's choice, mon."

Sawyer was working him hard. Lifting his eyes from the ground, McIntosh clearly had no idea what the lawyer meant.

"A Hobson's choice," Sawyer repeated. "Means you out of options, Thomas."

The young man nodded. "Police say I'm going to jail, Mister Sawyer. Said I hurt a man real bad this time."

Sawyer waved Veronique forward to refill their tea. "Leave the pitcher, my dear, and please ask counselor Russell to join us."

Placing the iced tea on a large silver tray near Sawyer, the young woman retreated, hips exaggerating her exit. Sawyer followed her with a wolfish grin and winked at his visitor.

He continued, "Brother Russell, now he's real good in the courts, mon."

On cue, Isaiah Russell strolled onto the veranda. As thin as Sawyer was corpulent, Russell sported prematurely graying hair ringing an ebony face cut with deep, sad lines. With a head too large for his wiry frame, a slight palsy gave him an unsteady, distracting nodding when he talked. Jaundiced eyes hinted at a failing liver and a suit coat flapped against his frame.

"Did I hear my name taken in vain, Solicitor?" said Russell.

Chuckling at a line he had heard a thousand times, Sawyer said, "Thomas here has a bit of a problem, Isaiah. Seems he's too fond of the grape. Got into some sticky business last weekend."

"Yes, I've read the report." Russell pulled a wicker chair up close to Sawyer and faced McIntosh. "Argument over a woman, wasn't it?"

Nodding, the stonemason stared at his feet as Russell took over the conversation.

"The authorities be asking after you, Thomas. You may have gone too far this time. Man you hurt is a constable's cousin. A distant cousin, but still family."

Sawyer put out his bait. "Well, Isaiah, do you think you can make some sense out of this mess for young Thomas here?" The youth looked up, his eyes searching for some good news.

This is almost too easy, thought Sawyer.

"It's not hopeless, Hamilton," said Russell in a silky voice. "I think I can make an impression with our police, maybe get the charges reduced." Setting the hook deeper, Russell turned to Sawyer.

"I have business with the sergeant this evening. I'll chat him up a bit and see what we can work out. Informally of course."

"Of course." Sawyer beamed, then put on his serious face and waved at the nervous young man. "Do what you can for our friend here."Sawyer turned his gaze on McIntosh.

"Now, about compensation. You got no real money. I know that for certain."

"That's true, Mister Sawyer. My mother say she help me a bit."

"Thing like this can get expensive, you know," observed Russell. An awkward silence descended. He spoke again. "I hear there's some work needs doing at the Island Imports warehouse. Isn't that true, Brother Sawyer?"

"Yes, I've heard they are short of workers right now. Why do you ask?"

Breaking into a sly grin, Russell said, "Well, that's it. Say Thomas here works out our fee that way. Would my honorable colleague agree to that?"

Their client sat upright, waiting for Sawyer's answer.

"Hmm, yes, your esteemed colleague would agree to that arrangement."

Russell turned to Thomas. "What do you say?" McIntosh nodded eagerly.

"Done then," pronounced Russell. Rising, he faced his law partner and a suddenly relieved Thomas. "If you'll excuse me, I've business to finish." He shook hands with McIntosh, cocked an eyebrow at Sawyer, and ambled toward the bungalow.

Sawyer swiveled in his chair. "And as for you, Thomas, be at the warehouse Saturday at three. You know it, don't you?"

"Sure, everybody knows it, Mister Sawyer."

"Good."Plucking a business card from his vest, he scribbled on the back. "See Mister Key, he'll put you to work."

"Thank you, mon. You won't be sorry you give me this break."

"I sincerely hope not, Thomas. I don't like to be disappointed."

Their meeting finished, both men rose. Sawyer stood a full head shorter than the young man. The barrister held out his fleshy mitt and the pair shook hands. Sawyer walked the mason to the end of the patio. "Okay, mon, we'll let Mr. Russell work his magic with the police, all right?"

"Oh, sure, I do appreciate the help." McIntosh paused at the gate.

"What is it?" said Sawyer.

"Well, I been looking at your veranda, Mr. Sawyer, and I got to tell you..." He paused, apologetic, waiting for permission to speak.

Sawyer was curious. "And?"

"Well, them bricks, they need tidying up a bit, you know."

Sawyer glanced down at the uneven space. The mason was right. The veranda was in need of repair. "Okay, mon, you straighten this out for me and maybe we give you a break on your bill. Maybe cut some warehouse time, eh?"

"Sure, I'll fix you up good, Mister Sawyer."

"Excellent. And Thomas..." he added as he ushered him out the gate, "stay out of the bars until we get this mess cleared up. You understand, mon?"

"No problem, Mister Sawyer." The young man smiled, turned and headed to the road. Sawyer watched him go, unaware of Veronique gliding up behind him.

"Mister Sawyer," she cooed, hand on jutting hip, waiting for him to face her.

"Yes, my dear, what can I do for you?"

"A boy brought this note while you were meeting." She handed him a piece of paper folded in half. Sawyer flipped open the folded paper and quickly scanned the message, his eyes betraying nothing.

"Ask Isaiah to meet me out front, please."

Sawyer picked up his VHF radio, waddled through the garden gate to a blue golf cart, unplugged an electrical cord and arranged his bulk in the cart. Rounding the corner of the building with a lurching, whirring hum, Sawyer ground to a halt at the front door. He handed the note to Russell.

The thin man's eyebrows shot up. "What you gonna do, Hamilton?"

"Going to find out what this is all about."

"You think that's wise?"

"Always got to know what's going on, mon."

Russell shrugged, his head bobbing. "Be careful. I don't trust his kind."

Forcing a smile, Sawyer sighed. "Yeah, well, we meet all kinds in our business, eh? Main thing is to keep the ears open. Folks get surprised by what they don't know. I'll be back soon, but don't wait on me, Isaiah."

The golf cart accelerated down the blacktop toward New Zion's harbor.

Russell told Veronique to finish her work and take what was left of the day for herself. "I'll close up," he said with a wink. "You go about your fun."

Delighted, the secretary cleared her desk. Russell turned back to some nagging correspondence and did not look up when she left. His thoughts were with his partner's meeting at the harbor. He pulled the note from his pocket and, with a flutter of bony fingers, unfolded the paper to read the crude handwriting. Worry gnawed at him; an emotion Russell seldom allowed himself. Taking a lighter from a drawer, he held its flame to the note and dropped the burning paper into a large brass ashtray. Leaning back, hands laced behind his head, he watched the penciled words curl into ash.

CHAPTER 9

Stabbing steadily at his computer keyboard, one finger at a time, McKay produced his official report. Satisfied with his effort, he printed three copies and scrawled his signature at the bottom of all three.

A glance at his wall clock told him that he had five hours of daylight remaining. In the tropics, ice was a stopgap measure for a modern morgue and the sooner New Zion authorities got involved, the better.

Let them sort this out on their watch, he thought. *I've done all I can on this end.*

He picked up the radio and called the harbor. "Faithtown Marina, McKay here."

"Go to channel One-Four, Mac."

McKay switched frequencies and keyed his mike. "Abner, I'm set to move the package to New Zion. Can your boys give me a hand with a cart?"

"I'll send them over now if you want."

McKay paused. "Give me ten minutes. I need to make a call to the ferry first to make sure I can get our package on board."

"Sure, we're refueling a couple of boats. Call when you're ready."

"Thanks, Abner. Back to One-Six."

McKay turned to the main channel and tried to raise Samuel Burton.

"Faithtown Ferry, this is McKay, over."

He repeated his call three times before Jonathan David's voice responded. "Faithtown Ferry."

"Meet me at One-Three, Jonathan."

"Right. One-Three."

McKay asked for the young man's father.

"This is Samuel, go ahead."

McKay explained the situation and asked his former brother-in-law to stop at the fuel dock ten minutes before the afternoon run. That would allow them time to stow the body out of sight in the bow compartment.

"Be better if visitors don't pick up on this, Samuel. You understand."

"Of course," Burton agreed. "We'll be there."

"Good. Pull in at Abner's pumps. Thanks."

It was only a request for help from a policeman to a ferry captain. To McKay, any contact with the pastor was awkward. To Burton it was an opportunity, an opening. Their conversation had been polite, business-like, yet McKay knew his brother-in-law coveted the conversation. He picked up his phone and dialed the New Zion police. Through bursts of static, he heard a high, singsong voice.

"New Zion Police, Corporal Simmons here."

"Constable McKay, Faithtown calling."

"Yes, Officer McKay, how may I help you?"

"Had a drowning this morning. I have the body. Male, black, early twenties. Unidentified. I would like to turn it over to your office since we have no facilities here. Can you help us out?"

There was a long pause. Another voice, older, came over the line. "McKay, this is Sergeant Newton. What's this about a body?" McKay repeated his story and when he finished, the New Zion officer grunted agreement. "We'll meet you at customs. Tell the pilot to swing by after he drops his passengers. Will that take care of your problem?"

"Much appreciated, Sergeant. Your doctor can look him over for the record." McKay checked his watch again. "See you in about forty minutes. I'll have a report for you as well."

"Very good, McKay, until then."

The receiver went dead in McKay's hands. *Well*, he thought, *Newton hadn't added any social graces since their last encounter.*

He replaced the receiver and made one copy of his report for his files and another for New Zion. Kneeling before a scarred steel safe, he cracked the heavy door and tossed one copy of his report inside. A quick glance confirmed both handguns were still there. His armory consisted of the police-issued nine-millimeter Smith & Wesson and a nickel-plated, snub-nosed .38 a yachtsman had donated during a search for drugs aboard his sloop. In exchange for a warning, McKay demanded a promise of good behavior and a gift of the weapon.

Fringe benefits of the office, McKay had joked at the time.

Locking the safe, McKay grabbed his VHF radio and stepped outside. "Sarah, I'm off to New Zion," he said, twisting a key in the lock. For once, the nosy postmistress barely stirred as he slipped past her door.

At the foot of Faithtown's public dock, McKay whistled to catch Abner Russell's attention. When the harbormaster poked his balding head from the refueling shed, McKay mimicked pushing a wheelbarrow while pointing to the clinic. Russell waved and sent his boys on their way with an aluminum cart.

McKay met them at the clinic. An envelope with his name in Martha's handwriting fluttered in the doorframe. He took the note and opened the door. The nurse was nowhere in sight.

A single bulb burned in the back room. Ice packed to keep the body cool had melted, leaving behind pools on the floor. A makeshift body bag of black plastic garbage bags had been slipped over the corpse and bound with strips of duct tape that accentuated the body's shape.

How like tidy Martha, thought McKay.

Russell's teenaged sons stepped into the room. "Where's your cargo?"

"Right there, boys," he said, waving them inside. McKay pointed to a large canvas roll.

"We need to put the load into that sail bag in the corner. Mind you're careful, your daddy wants it back." Circling warily in the dimly lighted back room, both young men let their eyes adjust to the gloom. The faint scent of decaying flesh filled the room.

They froze, mouths agape, eyes wide. "A body? Daddy didn't say nothing about a dead person." The two youngsters looked at each other, uneasy.

"What, you two never seen a body before? It's just a shell. Let's get him into the cart shall we, boys?" His reluctant helpers shuffled forward uneasily. McKay's voice echoed in the small room, galvanizing them into action. "Well, c'mon, we haven't got all day. I've got the ferry coming for our friend here. Let's get a move on."

Each boy hesitantly took an end of the plastic covered burden as McKay spread the canvas pouch near the door and ripped a zipper the length of the sail bag. Even with three of them muscling the body into the open bag, the corpse was a tight fit. McKay sealed the bag and the boys carried it to the cart. They hurried to the docks with their odd baggage. A tourist couple passed by, ignoring the boys and their cart, preferring instead to engage McKay in small talk. After exchanging pleasantries, he begged off and caught up with Russell's sons as they maneuvered to the end of the dock where Burton's ferry idled, engine exhaust bubbling in the shallows.

"Afternoon, Jeremiah." Burton waved politely.

McKay nodded. "Samuel."

Burton's son and the two Russell boys wrestled the bag from the cart to the ferry's bow storage. To break its obvious shape, Burton threw spare life jackets and coils of rope over it.

"Thanks, boys." McKay slapped each on the back as they climbed the ladder.

Abner Russell joined him on the dock. "Don't forget my bag, Mac. They don't grow on trees."

McKay smiled. "I'll bring it on the return trip. Thanks for the loan. Your government is grateful for such prompt cooperation."

The little man barked, "Shove off, I'll handle the lines."

McKay climbed onto the stern and stood with hands braced against the overhead. Jonathan held the ferry against the dock as his father went forward to the wheel. Burton shifted into reverse to clear the dock, then eased the throttle forward, plowing slowly toward a knot of passengers waiting on the public pier. McKay took a seat in the cabin as they drew abreast of Faithtown's main landing. Poised on the bow, Jonathan stood, line in hand, as his father jockeyed into position. At the younger Burton's urging, helpful tourists looped the line around a piling and Jonathan worked his way to the stern to supervise loading.

An elderly woman timidly descended the ladder. "Good afternoon, welcome aboard. Watch your step please. Yes ma'am, this is the New Zion ferry." Twelve people were heading to Jericho Island. McKay nodded at the visitors, exchanging greetings with regulars and smiling, wondering how passengers would feel about riding with a corpse.

"Something amusing our constable?"

McKay glanced at storekeeper William Bethel. "Hello, Bill. I'm just enjoying the afternoon. Being on the water. Conversation. That sort of thing, you know."

Bethel slumped down as the ferry cast off. "Business in New Zion?"

"You could say that. Just paperwork. You know government."

Grunting in agreement, McKay's seat-mate folded scrawny arms across his chest.

Once clear of the harbor mouth, the twin diesels pounded and the bow rose with a sudden surge of energy, sending green water slapping against the white hull. When they passed the last channel marker, Burton's son went forward to stand beside his father at the wheel. With the engines at maximum power, conversation became impossible and passengers were soon lost in their own thoughts.

McKay dozed against an obliging William Bethel who sat staring at the horizon.

Midway between Faithtown and Jericho Island, a gust of wind added a vicious chop to the waves and the boat rolled, slamming against an angry turquoise sea.

CHAPTER 10

"Hey, mon, why you messing with those fish?"

Pushing back from his boat's gunwales where he had been poking at a school of milling grunts, Zeke Cameron groused at Hamilton Sawyer.

"You took your sweet time coming down here." Sawyer glowered in resentment and the boy backed off and tried another approach. "How about going for a ride? You won't be disappointed."

The thought of descending the dock's ladder into the young man's boat did not appeal to Sawyer and he ignored the invitation. "Let's talk in the shade," he said, jerking a thumb at a small bench beneath two palm trees. Sawyer waddled along the wharf, expecting the youth to follow him. Zeke took a last stab at the hovering fish and scaled the ladder as commanded. Lowering his bulk carefully, Sawyer loosened his tie and told the blonde-haired youth to sit beside him.

Zeke, the youngest of Cannon Cay's boat building Cameron family, was uneasy in the older lawyer's presence and easily manipulated without knowing how to combat it. Like many on Jericho Island, Zeke knew only that he owed his sudden affluence to the overweight lawyer's favors.

"Your note," sighed Sawyer impatiently, "complete with misspellings, said you had important news. What is it?"

"Abner Russell said they found a body this morning on Kingdom Cay."

Sawyer's eyes showed boredom. "So? Probably a drowning, huh?"

Zeke continued. "Everybody was talking about it this morning on their radios. He washed up on Resolution Point, east side." The lawyer pursed his lips as Cameron babbled. "Maybe it's like you said, Mister Sawyer. Might be a drowning. Renters found it."

Zeke paused, waiting for the fat man's response.

"This is why you called me away from important legal work?"

"You always say you want to know anything that happens, Mister Sawyer."

"Who's taking care of it in Faithtown?"

Zeke stared at his hands and recited the list as he knew it.

Sawyer mused aloud. "All right, Constable McKay handled the initial inquiry, so what? That's what policemen do. He'll pass it on to New Zion from what I know about him. You say the nurse knows, and McKay's brother-in-law, and the visitors, of course. I suppose the town's gossips got nothing better to do, huh?"

Sawyer's listener nodded. A minute passed, the lawyer deep in thought. "Where's the body?"

"McKay is bringing it to New Zion. I saw Abner Russell at the marina. He gave the constable a sail bag to bring it over."

Sawyer glanced at the sky. "Probably on the afternoon ferry. Can't keep meat overnight in Faithtown."

The youngster grinned malevolently at the barrister's crudeness.

"Here's what you do, mon." Clamping a vise-like grip on Zeke's shoulder, he spoke softly. "Just keep an eye on things. You listen to what folks say, got that?" He stared Cameron in the eyes and the youth nodded solemnly. Sawyer stood up, pulling Zeke with him, their meeting over. Tugging a wad of cash from his coat pocket, he peeled off three twenty-dollar bills.

"A little something for gas money. It must cost a bit to run that boat."

Zeke eagerly accepted the money and stuffed it in his jeans.

"Remember," Sawyer admonished, "you just watch, you don't do nothing. Next time try to bring me some real news. Something I don't know. But don't ever come to my office."

Zeke tapped his hand to his forehead in salute and scrambled down to the dock. Sawyer huffed to his golf cart and heaved himself into the seat, out of breath. He turned into the road and was gone in a cloud of dust.

Leaping to the bow of his runabout, Zeke untied the line and fired his engine. Threading his way through nearby rental boats in New Zion harbor, he ignored the *No-Wake* sign and skirted the stone breakwater, pushing his throttle forward. Bracing for acceleration as he headed for the channel, Zeke skirted a large orange marker buoy and kept well to the port side of the incoming Faithtown ferry. Once the two boats passed, Zeke's boat became a blur of white and red as his motor carved a furious wake toward Roger's Cay. Eyeing a squall in the northeast, Zeke figured his current speed would get him home in twenty minutes. He made it in ten.

CHAPTER 11

Lingering by a soft drink machine on the porch of New Zion's police station, two small boys parked their bikes against low coral blocks used as parking dividers. Engaged in an adolescent bragging contest, the boys' high voices and laughter floated through the building's open windows, breaking the late afternoon silence.

At a bank of radios behind a waist-high counter, Corporal Theodore Simmons' concentration was interrupted by the children's shrill banter. Tossing down an incomplete crossword puzzle, Simmons sauntered to the door, pushed open the screen and thrust his best disapproving face outside.

"Don't you kids have someplace to be?"

Both youngsters stopped chattering and stared at the policeman leaning in the doorway. The older of the two defended himself. "Just playing, Theo. Ain't bothering nobody."

Simmons was unmoved. "Well, you bothering me. I'm trying to get work done. Go play in the park or something, eh? We got a police station to run. This is not a playground, you know."

Shrugging, the boys reluctantly retrieved their bikes.

"And don't call me Theo," yelled Simmons, folding arms across his chest.

Kids, he said to himself, *they'll play anywhere they can.* His watch read five minutes after four and the station clock confirmed it. He and Sergeant Newton were due at the New Zion customs shed.

The radio barked. "New Zion Police, Faithtown Ferry."

Retreating inside, Simmons grabbed the handset. "Come up to one-two."

McKay's voice crackled through the static, alerting Simmons that the ferry was now unloading passengers and would go directly to the customs dock as arranged. He asked about transportation and Simmons assured him it had been taken care of. McKay signed off.

Simmons timidly knocked on his sergeant's office door. "Faithtown Ferry just got in. They're unloading and will have the body at customs in ten minutes."

Newton's voice boomed from the office. "Be right out, Simmons." The door to his superior's office opened and the corporal respectfully stepped back, allowing room for the sergeant's portly visitor.

"Simmons, how's your family?" asked Hamilton Sawyer.

"Oh, fine, sir. My wife, she's working the Shell Gift Shoppe now."

"Yes, I know," deadpanned Sawyer. "I hired her, remember?"

Simmons blushed. "Of course, Mister Sawyer, good thing too. Nice to have that extra paycheck."

All three laughed. "Well, think kindly of me then, Simmons," Sawyer teased.

"Yes sir, we surely do."

The attorney turned to the senior officer. "Thank you for your interest in this matter, Sergeant Newton. I leave it entirely in your hands then."

The policeman drew to attention. "No problem. I'll get right on it and keep you informed."

"Good," Sawyer grinned. "I appreciate that. Good day, officers."

The lawyer settled in his golf cart. When Sawyer drove off, the officers headed for a dusty brown station wagon with faded government seals on both doors. Simmons held the door for his sergeant, then slipped behind the wheel.

"Better roll up the windows and crank up the air conditioning. Make this car earn its pay, eh Simmons?"

"For the body?" Newton kept his eyes on the road ahead.

"Very astute, Corporal. You're going to make sergeant yet."

Missing the sarcasm, Simmons smiled. The air conditioner wheezed into life and by the time they turned onto the harbor road, the interior was thoroughly chilled. Newton spotted McKay standing on the stern as the Faithtown ferry spread a gentle wake toward the customs dock. Simmons pulled into the parking area as the ferry glided to the dock.

Newton got out. "Back it in as close as you can to the customs shed, Simmons."

The corporal parked and left the motor running as he took his place behind his sergeant.

Stepping on the dock, McKay gave a lazy salute and shook the policeman's hand. "Sergeant Newton, good to see you. Appreciate your coming."

"Good afternoon, Constable McKay," nodded Newton. He gestured to his subordinate. "You know Corporal Simmons, I'm sure."

McKay nodded at the officer. After a few minutes, Samuel Burton joined them. Newton ordered Simmons to help the minister's son move the body to the idling car. As the two younger men muscled the sail bag to the dock, the three made small talk.

"Well, Pastor Burton," said Newton, "is the Lord treating you well?"

"Can't complain, Sergeant. Although I wouldn't mind his calming the sea a bit. Little bumpy for visitors on the way over."

McKay excused himself to help with the body. When the cargo was inside, he slammed the door shut. "One moment," said McKay. "I promised Abner Russell I'd get his sail bag back to him tonight."

Simmons shrugged, looking to his superior for orders. Newton nodded and within minutes the bag had been stripped from the corpse and returned to McKay.

Newton, hands clasped behind his back, rocked gently on his heels. "Well, that's it. We'll take our friend here to the funeral home and have it looked at by the doctor first thing, eh? What do you say, Constable, will that do it?"

"Yes, that's why I called," replied McKay. "You have more experience with this sort of thing." He smiled, adding, "We just don't see much of this on Kingdom Cay. Thanks again for your help." He offered his hand to both policemen. Burton said his goodbyes and retreated to the boat to join his son for the return trip. He cranked the engines into life and told Jonathan to let go of the lines. As his final act of duty, McKay took a folded report from his left breast pocket and offered it to Newton.

"Here are my notes on the body's discovery, witnesses and the like."

Without speaking, Newton opened it and began to read as McKay joined the others on the boat. Burton backed the ferry from the customs dock and circled back for waiting passengers. McKay stood on the stern, gripping a handrail as the New Zion officers slowly drove away. His eyes followed the car's route along the waterfront until it turned up a side street and disappeared.

Five people paced the public dock, anxious for the day's last run to Faithtown. As Burton tied up, two more taxis arrived and added another six paying passengers. After piling luggage, coolers and assorted bags of groceries in the middle of the cabin, Jonathan signaled that everyone was on board.

McKay sat alone on the fantail, warmed by the fading afternoon sunlight. He winked at Jonathan as the youth helped stow a fussy matron's luggage. Young Burton clapped the policeman on the shoulder as he crept forward along the outside rail of the ferry to coil a line. Burton looked fore and aft and then eased his diesels into a slow pull from the dock. The wind was dropping and wave action around the breakwater had lessened since their arrival. He silently praised the Lord for calmer seas.

The afternoon passengers, all tourists, chatted happily among themselves as the boat picked up speed past channel markers. Hoping for handouts, a quartet of gulls followed as far as the breakwater before turning back. Both engines throbbed in perfect rhythm, producing a pleasing rocking sensation as they skimmed the waves. A wide foaming wake trailed back to New Zion. The crossing was uneventful.

After the ferry entered Faithtown's harbor and dropped passengers, the Burtons shuttled McKay to the marina dock where he returned the sail bag to Abner Russell. As a gesture of thanks, McKay helped top off the ferry's tanks for the next day's run and then waved good night.

Daylight lingered for another hour, but once twilight retreated darkness swallowed the cay. Laughter from restaurants along the harbor's edge echoed across the water and reggae music pounded out a beat from somewhere in town. Sailboats, marked by lights, tugged gently at buoys, their glowing cabins echoing with the chatter of bridge foursomes and backgammon.

McKay looked up at a vast dark heaven scattered with stars and waited for the Faithtown Light to probe the inky night with its beam. Pungent floral scents floated on the evening air and a concert of breakers crashed against the barrier reef. Dry palm fronds rustling in a light breeze was the only other sound along the narrow main street as McKay walked home.

CHAPTER 12

"McKay! McKay!"

An urgent voice filled the dozing policeman's head. Groaning, McKay rolled on his side, trying to shut out the world. His mind swam in a sea of rum and fatigue, but the voice was insistent, rousing him from his hangover. Squinting with bleary eyes at his visitor, McKay mumbled, "Uhh, Martha."

He tried unsuccessfully to rise to a sitting position on the couch. Plucking an empty rum bottle from the floor, the nurse disappeared into the kitchen. She filled a kettle at the tap, set it on the stove to boil, measured out coffee, and marched back into the living room to run up the blinds with as much noise as she could make.

Sunlight flooded the room. McKay rubbed a rough paw across his puffy face and tried to smooth his hair. "What brings you out so early?"

"You call this early?" she scolded. "You're going to cut years off your life if you keep this up."

McKay sank back against the couch and held up a protesting hand. "Martha, my love, you're a wonderful nurse and a good friend, but you're not my anointed keeper. You know that I answer to no one but myself, thank you very much."

Shrugging, she pulled up a chair opposite the sagging couch. She wore a sleeveless red pullover and a pair of tan pants. Her brown hair, wet from an early shower, was pinned back with a gaudy pink barrette. Though Martha wore little makeup she had a weakness for deep red lip-gloss that accentuated her full lips. Though a beautiful woman, her appearance this early was wasted on an oblivious McKay.

She arched her dark eyebrows at his disheveled appearance. "I'm not a part of this little ritual of yours, Mac. I'll have nothing to do with it, but as a friend." She paused to emphasize her next point by waving a graceful hand in the air above his unshaven face. "AND as a nurse, it's my duty to warn you of your slow, willful, self destruction." She waited for her reproach to sink in, but he remained focused on the floor and she abruptly changed the subject. "Did you read my note?"

"Sorry, forgot all about it." He fumbled in his shirt pocket.

"I gathered as much," she said, "or you would have come to see me as soon as the ferry got back." She got up to check the coffee and called over her shoulder from the kitchen.

"What did they tell you in New Zion?"

She poured two strong mugs and waited for his answer. McKay scanned the crumpled note. "Says here I'm to see you as soon as I can," he recited. "That you have interesting news for me."

"That was yesterday," she said caustically.

Leaning against the doorway, she offered him coffee. McKay cupped the mug in both hands and inhaled the steaming fragrance. He sipped timidly, one eye on the nurse like an errant schoolboy. She drank her coffee, her green eyes boring holes in his back. When he finally realized she was not leaving, McKay rose from the sagging couch and shuffled past her into the cramped yellow kitchen. He set his mug on the small table, stripped off his shirt and draped it over the chair.

"Show time, constable?" teased the nurse.

McKay managed a smile and leaned over the sink to let cool tap water flow over his head and neck. He splashed cold water against his face and rubbed his eyes, trying to match Martha's alertness. After cutting the water, he leaned over the sink, little better for the effort. She handed him a towel. McKay buried his face in terrycloth and backed against the counter. After an eternity, he began vigorously rubbing his head to join the living. He sat at the table; the towel draped around his neck like a woozy boxer who'd just gone fifteen rounds in a loss. Smiling at his rumpled image, she raised her mug.

"To a new day, Mac." Chastened, he tapped her mug with his and took a long draw of coffee.

Sobriety was slowly returning. "Your note," he mumbled.

She interrupted. "Just facts. It didn't say WHY you should see me."

"Right. Continue," he urged. McKay yawned and blinked his red-rimmed eyes, trying to focus.

"Well, your corpse first appeared to be a drowning," she said, excitement rising with each word.

He sipped quietly, listening to her lengthy description of the autopsy. He set his mug down and rubbed stubble on his chin. "You're saying the man was shot to death? That's a pretty serious charge."

She was taken aback. "You don't believe me?"

He held up a hand. "No, I didn't say that. I'm just saying such a conclusion, short of an official finding, is a pretty serious claim."

"So how do you explain this?" She dug in her pocket and handed him a small plastic bag. McKay opened it, dropping six small lead pellets into his cupped palm. He stared at her.

"Shotgun, most likely," she announced, folding her arms.

"Who's the policeman here, Martha?" he groused.

"Mac, this man was shot to death, executed if you will. Point blank or close to it. One shot at the back of the head. Powder burns near the base of his skull. Just like a pro hit." McKay gingerly fingered the lead shot. "And did I mention that there were no defensive wounds or water in his lungs?" He glanced at her. She said, "That means he likely knew his killer or was surprised. It wasn't robbery."

He studied the pellets quietly. "New Zion's got to know about this," he said.

Martha said, "Let them do an autopsy report first, please."

He looked up, puzzled. "Why?"

"Because, if I'm right, they'll confirm it. The autopsy, I mean." She let the gravity of her remark sink in. A clock's ticking broke the silence.

"And if they don't?"

"I may not be a medical doctor," she said, "but I served enough time in New York emergency rooms to know a shotgun wound when I see one. This was no accident, Mac. This was..."

He finished her sentence. "Murder? I don't know Martha. This puts a different light on the whole thing. It's too big for me to handle. Besides," he said, "it's out of my jurisdiction now. New Zion's involved."

She leaned back in her chair. "But you were the first one on the scene. It's your investigation." Martha added, "And you asked for my opinion."

McKay stood up to pace across the tiny kitchen. "Out of curiosity, just to satisfy my..."

"Copper's instinct?" she said.

"You know, Martha, you have an annoying habit of finishing my thoughts."

She could tell he agreed with her. Smiling, she drank her coffee as he walked back and forth, his policeman's mind sorting the pieces. He joined her at the table but said nothing for a full five minutes.

She slid a large index card across the table at him. "Here's another ace up your sleeve, Mac."

A set of ten fingerprints, swollen black ink images, lined the white card. She tensed, waiting for his reaction. His brow furrowed. Delicately turning the card in his hands, he held it by the edges, and then stared at her for a long minute. "You missed your calling, Martha."

She beamed, triumphant.

"All right," he said. "I'll wait to hear from New Zion before sharing your findings with them."

Patting his arm, the nurse mouthed a thank you.

"If their conclusions don't match yours," said McKay, "then we'll have to let them know what we think. Agreed?"

She nodded. McKay lifted his coffee mug. "To forensic medicine."

CHAPTER 13

New Zion's only mortuary boasts a large neon sign promising loving care, courtesy of Hamilton Sawyer. The cross-shaped stucco building consisted of a one-story chapel, two viewing rooms forming the arms and a modest office and prep room at the rear.

Sawyer's bank had foreclosed the business ten years before, and he had since transformed it into a prosperous concern. Although New Zion's churches do most of Jericho Island's burials, it is understood that the deceased are to be prepared at Sawyer's funeral home. Like New Zion's bank, warehouses, new waterfront condo development and his law practice, the undertaking business had solidified Sawyer's clout on the island. His funeral director, also New Zion's reigning unofficial coroner, was Doctor Bernard Singh, formerly of Trinidad. With his characteristic eye for a man in need, Sawyer had rescued the good doctor from a dispute with Nassau authorities and had installed him in the funeral business.

One man's misfortune—in Singh's case a series of botched abortions in the capital—was Sawyer's gain. Short and soft looking, with smooth brown skin and great dark pouches under his eyes, Singh owed his freedom to the lawyer.

On this Saturday mid-morning, Singh was repaying his benefactor by conducting a cursory autopsy on a decaying corpse. A medical conclusion, already determined by Sawyer, had been relayed along with the body the previous day, courtesy of Sergeant Newton of the New Zion Police. It had been a drowning, according to the officer, and that's what Sawyer expected the autopsy report to say.

Even with the body's rapidly deteriorating condition, Singh knew drowning was the least of the victim's problems. But the doctor shrugged off his concerns and filled in the report exactly as Sawyer wanted, and then made preparations for the dead man's burial.

"Ah, doctor, if I might interrupt." Sergeant Newton filled the doorway. "Just thought I'd stop by and see how the work is going."

Singh pulled a mask from his face. His small mouth, with its thick lips, seemed too small for his teeth and he was not in the habit of smiling. The physician stepped from the porcelain table with its decaying burden.

"Huh, come for the report, I'd guess."

Tucking his hat under his arm, Newton flashed a tight grin. "Yes. Thought I'd tidy up the report, get it into the files and close this case. Mister Sawyer, he likes things tidy here on Jericho. Likes to keep short accounts, you know."

Grunting, Singh peeled latex gloves from his slender, feminine hands. Neither man liked the other. The physician thought Newton an opportunistic toady and the sergeant judged Singh a hack who had fled his native Trinidad for some odious reason only Sawyer knew. Indians were rare on the Out Islands, and Singh's solitary ways only added to his mystery. The doctor plopped in a chair behind his desk and opened a manila folder. Propping wire spectacles on the bridge of his prominent nose, he scanned the paper with huge, sad ebony eyes. He peered at Newton.

"Very unusual case, Sergeant."

"How so, Doctor?"

"You say it was a drowning, but there's no water in the lungs. Even in this advanced state of decomposition it appears our victim suffered other trauma besides being unable to swim."

The officer leaned over the desk. "Doctor Singh, I am only a policeman who follows orders. And you," he nodded, "are only a funeral director who prepares bodies for proper burial."

Newton spoke in a menacing tone. "So let's each do our proper job as asked. I handle my end of the case and you take care of yours. Agreed?"

Shifting slightly in his chair, Singh laced his fingers together. "Very good, Sergeant. Very correct. But I remind you, as a medical doctor, I am a bit reluctant to sign a report putting me on record as saying this was a drowning when in fact, it appears to be something quite different."

He added a thought. "Nassau authorities will have to be alerted to this contradiction, Sergeant."

"Don't trouble yourself. Counselor Sawyer asked me to handle the details. He believes this young man deserves a speedy Christian burial."

Staring at the papers on Singh's desk, Newton asked, "Did you sign it, Doctor?"

"Oh, I signed it, Sergeant, because I was asked to. But I did so reluctantly."

Newton's tone turned icy. "Doctor Singh, this conversation is over. I came by for the report and you gave it to me. When can you put him in the ground?"

Singh stood in defeat. "I have a few things left to do, but we should bury him tomorrow, quickly. Perhaps in the afternoon, after the church has cleared."

"Excellent. I'll tell Mister Sawyer he can be assured you've done your part." Newton ran his hand along a rack of glass bottles. "Do you have a spot for him?"

"Don't touch those," rebuked the doctor, his pen poised over more paperwork.

Newton withdrew his hand and began drumming his fingers on the edge of Singh's desk. Ignoring the calculated irritation, the doctor pretended to study the sheet in his hands.

"Yes, Mr. Sawyer always has a couple of plots open," Singh assured Newton without looking at the policeman.

"Good," Newton said, plucking the autopsy report from Singh. "I'll send Simmons over to see how things go. There will be no family, no friends, as far as we know."

The doctor sighed in resignation. "I have no idea who this man is—or was."

Newton ignored Singh's comment. "Good day, Doctor. I'm due at Mister Sawyer's home. I told him that I would personally deliver your report along with a small pile of paperwork from some of his other businesses."

After Newton left, Singh slipped on gloves to put finishing touches on the mysterious body in his workroom. Wrapping the corpse in a clean sheet, he wheeled a cheap, felt-wrapped plywood coffin next to the metal table. He stepped outside in the sunlight and called to his groundskeeper.

"Nathaniel, I need your help," he said.

Propping his rake against a palm tree, Nathaniel Rolle followed Singh into the preparation room. The two of them lifted the body into a narrow felt-covered wood casket and fastened the lid. Singh broke the silence. "Please move our client into the side room and turn the air conditioning on high. Then close all drapes." Rolle obediently began rolling the casket to the small viewing room.

"Will there be a viewing, Doctor?"

"No, Nathaniel. No funeral. He's a stranger. Probably off a freighter or charter boat. No one's missed him as far as we know."

Straining as he wheeled the coffin, the old man asked, "Will that be all, Doctor?"

"Yes, Nathaniel." As the caretaker guided the cart down the hallway, Singh hosed down the autopsy table. When finished, he stood at the stainless-steel sink and scrubbed his hands long and hard under a running tap as if he could wash away his confrontation with Newton. Stripping off his lab coat, he threw it in a large laundry tub. Singh went into his office, got a bottle of cheap cologne from the shelf and splashed the perfume over his hands, rubbing the fragrance into his palms and smooth brown forearms. Unrolling his sleeves, he carefully buttoned them and then swept paperwork off his desk into a drawer.

Singh glanced up to find the aged groundskeeper waiting. "Yes, what is it?"

"It's like you say, Doctor. I close the drapes and turn on the air conditioner."

"Thank you, Nathaniel." Singh stepped toward the old man and touched his arm. "I'm done for the day. I'm going into town for dinner as usual. When you finish, make a note of your time. We'll settle on Monday as usual."

Rolle bowed slightly and left through the laboratory door. In a few minutes, Singh heard the old man's rake scratching through the sparse grass. The physician turned out the office light and shut both chapel doors to ease the air conditioner's job. He settled a large straw hat on his balding pate trimmed in wiry gray hair and stepped into the evening heat, lost in thought.

By the time the weary physician settled into a chair at his favorite New Zion cafe, Sergeant Newton was turning into Hamilton Sawyer's driveway. For a man of considerable means, the lawyer lived in rather simple surroundings. Sawyer's one concession to wealth was a large living room in the center of the house where he entertained. A cedar deck offering spectacular views of the city spanned the back of the house. On clear nights one could see Faithtown's light blinking at five-second intervals across the channel. An invitation to Sawyer's house was coveted in what passed for New Zion society.

Newton glided to a stop in Sawyer's driveway. Any summons to Sawyer's home made him nervous and he smoothed his uniform blouse to project an air of authority. Holding the autopsy report in his right hand, Newton mounted the steps to Sawyer's porch. Wearing a white, open-neck shirt and dress slacks, the lawyer waited impatiently at the top of the stairs.

"Good evening, Counselor."

The portly lawyer disarmed the officer. "Good of you to come, Newton." Sawyer snapped his fingers and thrust out a chubby hand. "The report, I trust?"

Newton surrendered it and smiled. "Ink still wet. I watched Doctor Singh sign it not more than ten minutes ago."

"Good," grinned the barrister. "Any problems?"

"No, sir, no problem. The doctor say they gonna bury him Sunday. I scheduled Corporal Simmons for duty down there to be sure. Keep the curious away, you know."

Sawyer waved away the officer's suggestion. "Tell Simmons never mind. Better to go yourself. Less chance of something going wrong."

Newton frowned. "I told my wife we'd visit her brother over the other side, Mister Sawyer. She be pretty upset if I cancel."

"It won't be all day, Sergeant. We have to make sure the boy is buried properly. I want someone I trust there." Newton started to protest, but Sawyer cut him off. "We wouldn't be doing this now if this person had family to take care of it. Besides, if any of his people turn up, you can handle it, mon."

Newton swallowed his disappointment. His wife was sure to bristle at the cancellation of the Sunday plans. He, not the overweight lawyer who had just rearranged his family outing, would suffer verbal assaults at home tonight.

Sensing the policeman's unhappiness, Sawyer quickly defused it. "Can you stay for something cold? I'd like to read over the report with your help. Get your opinion." He grasped Newton's elbow and urged him toward the back deck. Sawyer was at his unctuous best and it worked.

Newton beamed at the impromptu privilege. "Of course, Mister Sawyer, I guess I do have time."

"Will iced tea or lemonade do, Newton? I know you're still on duty."

The two men laughed loudly as they walked outside. The lawyer served iced tea and they talked on the shaded deck for half an hour. By the time they had finished their drinks and discussed the autopsy report, Sawyer knew Singh was due a stern lecture on loyalty to his employer.

Thoroughly charmed by the attention, Newton volunteered to stay for the entire graveside service on Sunday. Sawyer was pleased and let the sergeant know it. Exuding oily charm, the corpulent attorney escorted the officer to the door and shook hands. When a beaming Newton finally left, Sawyer went directly to his study to read Singh's report again. He drew wooden blinds shut, snapped on a reading lamp, and poured himself a tumbler of light rum before sinking into his favorite chair.

Sawyer was not one to let a detail like Singh's report pass unexamined.

CHAPTER 14

In Faithtown, wooden docks baked bone dry in the sun and a falling tide revealed barnacle skirts around the pilings. Moon jellyfish drifted in the shallows, their translucent saucer bodies pulsating in the current. Schools of tiny, striped fish darted nervously from the shadows and the ever-present gulls worked hard to stay aloft. Morning breezes swept away clouds and sunlight played on a deserted harbor. Most charter boats had sailed to take advantage of wind off Jericho Island. A weekend charter from New Zion had docked earlier and small groups of tourists strolled Faithtown streets, peeking in shops and clucking over village children who reacted with their usual indifference.

McKay ambled painfully down to the main dock. Martha had suggested a day on the reef as a hangover antidote. He agreed, partly out of contrition for the previous evening's drunkenness and because he enjoyed her company. Martha lifted McKay's spirits with her combination of sarcasm and humor. He also admired her independence, her enjoyment of life. McKay suffered the sniping of Sarah Cameron and her gossiping friends for his attention to the American nurse, but he counted the cost worth it. His head had cleared a bit, thanks to coffee and conversation. McKay waved to a niece who was roaming with a group of girls. A honeymooning couple on bikes passed him in the narrow street.

Martha was already at the pier, guarding a red cooler stocked with sandwiches and drinks. She waved as he shuffled toward her. "You're late, Constable."

"So report me to someone in authority," he joked.

"Oh, I already have, Mac," she giggled.

Lowering himself onto the bow of his boat, he pulled it to a nearby ladder. Martha passed the cooler to McKay and joined him in the boat. He lowered the prop into the water and cranked the Yamaha into life. As the boat idled, he hauled in the stern line and stowed the anchor. Shifting into reverse, he backed from the dock and kept his throttle low as they chugged slowly through the harbor.

Uncapping a bottle of sunscreen, Martha began oiling her arms and legs. She smiled at him and he grinned back. She painted a streak of oxide on her upturned nose, daubed her cheeks, and playfully added a swipe of lotion at McKay's nose.

They passed the Faithtown ferry. Jonathan was mopping the boat's deck.

McKay bellowed. "We're off for a picnic on the reef." He laughed as they glided past. Samuel Burton was coming down the winding steps, bright green windbreaker tucked under his arm, his face shaded by a brimmed straw hat. The ferry would begin its afternoon run in one hour. Martha stood beside McKay and pointed at the lighthouse when they neared the harbor mouth. At the top, visitors leaned against the railing, signaling to less adventuresome friends below.

Laughing, Martha infected McKay with her joy. She took a seat behind him as they left the harbor mouth. Accelerating past two inbound boats, they picked up speed, the boat's bow rising over the swells. Outside the harbor, McKay made a lazy sweeping turn south, leaving a foaming wake. Wind whipped through the canvas top, snapping at straps holding it in place. His head felt completely clear. They flew over the green surface. McKay glanced down at Martha and she grinned with a wet smile.

He set a course for Queen's Cay, a scrap of scrub-covered rock just south of Resolution Point, a smudge of blue gray on the horizon. Staying parallel with the southern coast of Kingdom Cay for twenty minutes took them skimming over great stretches of pale turquoise shallows broken only by large purple-green swatches of turtle grass. Occasionally, they skirted mottled clusters of rock and coral. McKay twisted a faded blue baseball cap tightly on his head and donned a pair of sunglasses. Martha leaned back to revel in the sun and spray.

A quarter mile from the point McKay slowed, studying the surf. He nodded, satisfied. "It's almost perfect," he said over the engine's growl.

She corrected him. "It IS perfect."

McKay handed her the free end of the anchor rope. "Tie this off forward. We'll anchor just past the point." She went forward as ordered, slipped a thick noose under the cleat to secure the line and, braced herself at the bow.

"Okay, pick a spot," she said.

He nosed toward the reef, his wary eyes on the thin line of breakers marking the Atlantic. Martha urged him on and then signaled for him to kill the engine. They drifted, the hull rocking in small waves. As they drifted over a large rock that would hold them, she lowered the anchor to avoid damaging the surrounding coral. When the flukes caught on the boulder, Martha pulled it snug and played out fifty feet of line before the boat held firm.

"Good job, mate," he beamed.

"Practice makes perfect, Mac."

Only one other boat, a deserted fifteen-foot rental, was anchored on the reef.McKay spotted three snorkels poking above swells fifty yards away and pointed. Martha nodded. He tilted the motor forward and unfolded a small aluminum diving ladder off the stern. She pulled a diving mask, snorkel and fins from her bag. She stripped to a green one-piece suit and glanced to see if he was watching.

McKay was grinning.

"Is that a lustful smile?" she coyly asked. He reddened. She threw her shirt at him, and then sat on the bow, long tanned legs pulled up, her arms in a mock seductive pose. He pretended to ignore her and peeled off his shirt, replacing it with a ragged, striped T-shirt.

She shook her head. "I can't believe you still wear that."

He gripped the ragged hem. "This happens to be my lucky diving shirt. Caught the biggest crawfish I ever saw while wearing this shirt. And, I might add, you were fortunate to dine on that same catch. So don't be so quick to judge. Besides," he continued, "you say the same thing every time I wear it. So why should I take your comments seriously now?" He rambled on as she swung her long legs over the gunwales. "A man has to have a few sentimental things in his closet."

She laughed, grabbed a white T-shirt from her bag, slipped it over her head, and went over the side with a splash. After she reappeared, he continued his lecture while he donned mask and fins. "It's true. Check any man's wardrobe and you'll find at least one item of clothing that may be worn through, but it still holds a particular meaning for him."

Mocking him as she treaded water with lazy kicks, she yelled, "If that's true, then your entire closet, with the exception of government-issue uniforms, is an exercise in sentimentality."

His response was a perfectly timed cannonball swamping her.

They both surfaced laughing. Martha turned on her back and stroked from the boat. Ten yards from the bow, she treaded water and adjusted her mask before submerging. McKay tugged his own mask tighter and joined her.

Sunlight streamed down, flooding an underwater canyon beneath them. They drifted over a huge mass colony of brain coral; each wrinkled mound bigger than its neighbor. A white sandy bottom, groomed in a corduroy pattern by underwater currents, was thrown like a wide pale quilt around the base of the reef. They floated into deeper water where great towering pillars of shaggy coral thrust toward the surface. Purple sea fans waved in unison and a magical forest of spiky elk horn coral suddenly appeared. Fish were everywhere. A school of yellow and black striped sergeant majors detoured around the approaching swimmers and an adult green turtle glided by, its wizened eyes staring. McKay dove and settled gently on the sand ten feet below. Martha hovered to watch as he squatted on the bottom, arms at his side. He pushed off in a cloud of sand and broke the surface in front of her. Treading water beside him, she asked, "How's the head, Mac?"

"Still there. I feel quite human again." He lay back with his arms spread wide and floated.

She said, "A little fresh air does a body good. Let's circle back around those large coral heads and then picnic on the boat."

From under a rock ledge, a four-foot barracuda studied their approach, its silver body hanging motionless in the shadows. The fish eyed the intruders as they glided toward its hiding place. Spotting the barracuda, McKay tapped Martha on the shoulder and pointed to their shadow. She waved away his caution. Shrugging, he swam, occasionally looking back to check on the curious fish. Apparently satisfied they posed no threat, the barracuda let them go and returned to its post beneath the rock.

They swam above a narrow, twisting divide varying in depth from five feet to fifteen, its walls bristling with fused stag horn coral and legions of fish weaving between branches.

A curtain of blue tang parted on cue for the swimmers as they neared the end of the fissure.

McKay and Martha finished within sight of their anchor, still tightly snagged against the half-buried boulder. Small butterfly fish darted around the taut line, curious about this alien addition to their favorite rock.

Martha swam to the small stern platform. McKay followed. By the time he stepped into the boat, Martha had toweled off and switched to a sweatshirt. She handed him a towel and a cup of punch.

"Such service," he said. "It's enough to make me give up diving alone."

"Man is not meant to dive alone, Mac. You should know that."

"And neither was woman, Martha." He raised his cup and drained it. She promptly refilled it.

"I can't believe how hungry I am," he said. "What did you pack?" McKay went forward and sat on the life jacket locker. Martha opened the cooler and held up two sandwiches.

"Ham and cheese, or cheese and ham?"

He laughed and grabbed one. They ate in silence, enjoying the day.

Coral heads poked above the surface. Breakers dropped to occasional whitecaps. Their boat rode high in the sea, the canopy shading them. McKay waved his half-eaten sandwich at the horizon.

"They left."

Martha realized the other boat was gone. *Good*, she thought, *we have the reef to ourselves.*

She sat closer, her legs propped on the bow next to his. McKay greedily devoured a second sandwich. His headache was gone. She packed away the scraps and collected their cups while he sat quietly watching the water.

After a long interval, she said, "I'm glad we got away today. I've been waiting for a chance alone with you. There's something I want to ask you."

"Ask away."

"Why do you keep drinking?"

Wearing a sheepish look, he avoided her eyes for what seemed an eternity. "Why am I a cop?" he said. "Why do I stay in Faithtown?" He faced her. "Why did you come down here to live?"

He shrugged. "I don't know Martha. It seems like the thing to do, I guess."

"Does it have something to do with Felicity's death?"

He fell silent again, his focus trained on the ultramarine horizon. "I really don't want to talk about that, Nurse Thomsen."

"Okay, I'll leave that subject alone. But seriously, why the drinking?"

He shrugged again, avoiding her probing eyes. He knew she would stay on the subject as long as she could. "Ever think about quitting?" she said.

"Oh, I've quit." He laughed. "Hundreds of times."

She pressed him. "No, Mac, really. Why not stop? I mean, for good."

"Someday I just might. You know, Martha, you're a terrible scold at times. I know you mean well, but..." His voice trailed off.

Reaching for his hand, she said, "If I didn't care for you, you big dumb Bahamian cop, I wouldn't say a thing. You know that don't you?"

Smiling, McKay put his arm around her. "Yes, Nurse Thomsen, I know that. And, like all drunks, I appreciate it."

"You know, it's like ancient history," she said. "We sound like some old Katherine Hepburn-Spencer Tracy movie, you and I. Mac and Martha." She chuckled at her joke and pulled her sweatshirt tighter.

McKay kissed her forehead and drew her close. They sat like that for almost an hour, gently rocked by the waves, mesmerized by the turquoise water. Martha finally broke the spell, sighing. "If we don't get back, Sarah Cameron will send out her card-playing cousins to look for us."

McKay snorted. "She'll hold off judging us if I promise to tell her what we were up to."

He went forward and hauled in the anchor. Martha fired the engine and throttled forward, the hull leaping from the surface as they turned toward deeper water. Bracing her feet against the pounding deck, she set a course for Faithtown.

CHAPTER 15

A slim, muscular black man in immaculate pressed khakis, paced in front of a towering stack of concrete blocks. Dictionary Key, manager of Hamilton Sawyer's Island Imports warehouse was questioning Thomas McIntosh, the wayward stonemason. "You ever lay block before, mon?"

"I worked lots of jobs. New Zion, Nassau. Even in Florida. A big job."

Key pivoted to face the dreadlocked stonemason. "I got a job needs doing, Thomas. Big job. Need a skilled man. Got one chance to do it. Got to have it done right."

Thomas drew himself up. "I'm the man to do it."

Key smiled. "Plus, you working off a debt to Mister Sawyer, right?"

The young man deflated. "Sure. He said to see you about a job. I'm supposed to work it out."

"Okay," snapped Key, "no shame in that, mon. Let's put you to work."

He led McIntosh toward a large excavation adjacent to the Island Imports warehouse. A backhoe sat idle, its extended claw buried in a pile of rough limestone chips. Large interlocking vertical strips of rusty steel formed a cofferdam across one end of the hole and heavy wooden beams reinforced the metal wall around the newly dug crater. The two peered into the cavity. Brackish water from the saltwater inlet on the other side of the steel seeped into the site, adding to puddles in the muck.

Spreading his arms over the hole, Key explained, "What I want is a crew to pour footings here. Then we can lay block." He glanced at McIntosh. "You following me?" The mason nodded.

Key continued. "We build up the walls good, like a huge garage, okay? What we want, mon, is a big boathouse structure, you see. Once she sets up, we backfill and pump the water in slow like, so she won't come rushing in and smash it."

The young man chimed in. "Then you deck it over and you got yourself a place for boats, right?" Key smiled as McIntosh paced off the length of the crater. The mason whistled. "That's a lot of block, Mister Key. That's one big boathouse."

Key laughed. "I got plenty of block, mon. More coming all the time. Don't worry about block, Thomas." He removed his gold spectacles and wiped them with a white handkerchief as he spoke in low tones. "Now, I got three rules about this job, Thomas."

"One. You working for me, no one else. I know you here to pay a debt to Mister Sawyer. That's between you and him. But you be working for me regardless of what you owe him. Understood?"

McIntosh bobbed his head.

"Good. Second rule, you start here at the end of the regular workday." Key donned his glasses and continued.

"I got too much business to run during the day, I don't need to watch you, too."

"How much time I got to finish this, Mister Key?"

"Seven days. Can you do it?"

Peering into the hole, McIntosh let out a long sigh. "That's a pretty big job for one man. I'll need at least two other brothers to help."

Key nodded. "All right, you can pick them. But you pay them from the money I give you. Same conditions for them."

Thomas added, "And I'll need to pay them an extra hour every day to do this."

Key didn't like the suggestion. It was a long time before he answered. "Okay. Come at four o'clock every day but Sunday. Pick your helpers. You start on Monday."

McIntosh had one more question. "You say you got three rules."

Dictionary Key let a grin spread across his face. "Very good. You paid attention. I like that." He walked McIntosh from the excavation. "You don't say anything about what you're doing for me. Nothing. Understand?" Key explained as they walked along the pier. "People get nosy in business around here. We got to keep the competition guessing all the time. Anybody ask questions, you say you work for me, right?"

"Sure, mon," answered McIntosh. "But Mister Key..." He stopped and pointed back at the hole. "Why build such a big boathouse? Makes more sense to just tie up like everybody else."

Key folded his arms. "Because we're not like everybody else, mon. There's big money to be made, but you got to expand. That's what we be doing."

The men reached the gate. The sun was starting its long afternoon slide. The two stood in the warehouse's lengthening shadow. Key unlocked the front gate. "From now on you just do your job and let me ask the questions," he said.

McIntosh extended his hand and Key grasped it. "I expect you Monday, Thomas."

"Yeah, mon, Monday."

McIntosh flagged down a passing pickup truck and leaped into the bed beside an upturned wheelbarrow straddled by two laborers. Key locked the gate and headed back to his office. He thought about the prospect of actually having the boathouse finished on time and allowed himself to feel delighted.

CHAPTER 16

Reaching Faithtown's channel, McKay and Martha joined a caravan of boats slowly making their way into the harbor. The reason for the bottleneck was obvious— a day-sailor, its sails sheathed in bright blue covers, was timidly motoring past exposed mud flats flanking the harbor mouth. Lining the sailboat's railings, the novice crew kibitzed their nervous helmsman as the procession of runabouts and whalers politely waited for the sailboat to negotiate the entry. The process added fifteen minutes to McKay's return. While he jockeyed for position in the traffic jam, Martha tied the anchor line to a stern cleat. They finally reached the main dock and secured the boat.

"I'm having Michelle and her cousin for cards," she said. "Will you join us?"

McKay scowled. "The thought of facing those two chatterers across a table is enough to drive a man..." He looked up and smiled, waiting for her to finish his sentence.

Martha didn't disappoint him. "To drink?"

"Well, if you insist, Miss Thomsen."

She was not amused. "It won't be a long evening, Mac. Besides," she pleaded, "you can come for dinner and leave after cards."

"Sorry, Martha, some other time." He busied himself with last minute tugs on his line, trying to ignore her on the pier above him. He handed her the cooler. "Don't be so downcast. We can see each other tomorrow, I promise."

She sighed. "I'd prefer tonight."

McKay scaled the ladder and joined her on the dock. "Carry your parcel, Miss?" Stomping off, she didn't answer. Cradling the cooler under an arm, he hurried to catch up with her. They walked to town without speaking, Martha pouting. From the corner of his eye, McKay spotted Sarah Cameron's approaching. "Trouble off the starboard bow."

Intercepting them on the sidewalk, the postmistress stood in a judicial pose, her fleshy, dimpled arms folded across a sagging bosom. "Good afternoon, Martha, Jeremiah."

The short chase had winded Sarah and she gulped air like a landed fish. Waving an envelope under his nose, she panted. "From the New Zion police. Came in on the one o'clock ferry."

Hiding his eagerness, McKay took the envelope. "Thanks, Sarah."

The rotund woman's expression fell. She had perched reading glasses on her nose expecting him to share the letter's contents. "Don't you want to see what's in it?"

He nodded. "Of course. But first, I've got to walk Martha home and clean up. I'll get to it eventually. It's probably just routine business."

The postmistress peered at the envelope just out of reach.

"Official business," he cautioned, "but routine, nonetheless." He stuffed the letter into a shirt pocket and turned away.

She huffed through painted lips. "I thought you were expecting some sort of important news from New Zion. I thought I would be doing you a favor by finding you as soon as I could."

Knowing he would have to pacify the postmistress, McKay said, "Martha, would you excuse us for just a moment?"

"Of course, Mac. I can go on alone," she offered.

"No, this shouldn't take long," he reassured her. She nodded and stepped out of earshot. McKay leaned into Sarah Cameron's face to deliver a gentle rebuke.

"Sarah, I appreciate your taking the time to personally deliver the letter. But all in good time. I shall get to it when I have discharged my other duties. Said duties at the moment consist of escorting Martha home where I shall deposit her and this cooler."

He continued. "Then I shall return home and freshen up a bit. There, I will open the letter and see if it's business that needs attending to." He went on, his arm now around the postmistress. His patient manner and the possibility of news disarmed her. She reminded him of his earlier promise when he had found the body. "But there was nothing to add, Sarah," he protested. "If I had discovered something I would have told you."

The postmistress threw a suspicious look over her shoulder at Martha.

McKay layered his flattery. "Martha hasn't a nose for police business the way you do."

He bent down and picked up the cooler. "So, now, if you'll excuse us, we'll be on our way."

Wagging a finger at him, the postmistress warned. "Don't forget."

Winking conspiratorially at the portly woman in the flowered dress, McKay rejoined Martha.

"What was that all about, Mac?"

"Oh, you know Sarah. She's so hungry for news, gossip, anything, really."

"Well, "said Martha, "she leads a rather boring life, wouldn't you agree?"

McKay nodded and they walked without further conversation.

Martha Thomsen lived in a light blue clapboard house with white shutters and a wraparound porch trimmed in struggling ivy. Built against the lee side of a hill, her home was sheltered from the Atlantic by a tangled hedge of sea grape and stunted pines.

At the gate, McKay balanced the cooler on a post and pulled the letter from his pocket. He held it up against the sun. "Think it might be important?"

Making a playful grab for the envelope, she squealed. "You're impossible. Of course it's important. It's probably their autopsy report." Opening the gate, she glanced around before whispering, "Let me put on some tea and we can take a look."

In the kitchen, Martha filled a small blue kettle and set it on a burner before disappearing into her bedroom. "I'll take a quick shower. Make yourself at home. Keep an eye on the teapot."

McKay barely heard the hiss of the shower as he pulled up a chair and tore open the envelope. Inside was a hand-written letter on police stationery signed by Sergeant Newton. In addition to the note, there was a copy of the official autopsy report. He read the letter twice before he heard the kettle scream. Turning off the burner, he settled in his chair while staring at the report.

"Well?"

McKay looked up. A barefooted Martha, in a thick, white terrycloth robe, fished for tea bags in a painted tin on the counter. Her auburn hair, wet from the shower, curled against her neck. He stared at her for a long time, enjoying her beauty.

Breaking his spell, she cocked her head to one side. "Well? The letter. Good news or bad?"

He offered her the note and report. While she read, he fetched two cups and saucers. As he set the cups down, she grabbed his left wrist.

"I was right."

McKay was troubled. "You are absolutely sure that your original examination was correct?" Knowing how she would answer, he asked anyway.

"I'm positive! No doubt whatsoever. Your body, whoever he is, was shot to death. They had to know that." Picking up the report, she waved it at her guest. "Singh's a quack. He's a has-been."

"But he's a doctor, Martha," protested McKay.

"And I'm not?"

He held up a hand. "Don't put words in my mouth."

She dropped two tea bags in the pot. "Mac, this report says your man drowned. We both know that's a lie. And this note from the New Zion police says they agree with the autopsy. Lazy excuses for policemen. For them the case is closed. How convenient."

McKay didn't argue with her logic. She hammered at his silence. "Your victim has no name, no identity, no loose ends. How very tidy." She stood over him, hands on her hips. "You've got to find out who he was and why he was killed."

"I wouldn't know where to begin, Martha."

"You're a detective, it's your job."

"Policeman," he corrected her. He poured tea and timidly sipped for several minutes, avoided answering. He finally said, "I need to think about this whole bloody mess. I'm going to go home and clean up. Then I'll weigh my next move."

Martha pursued him, "What would that be?"

He shrugged his broad shoulders. "I really don't know." He patted her on the arm and headed toward the front door.

She asked, "Will you be coming by tonight?"

McKay shook his head. "Not tonight, thanks. I need some time with this."

She watched him amble down her walkway and wave as he shut the gate.

Thick hedges along his route were casting shadows across cracked concrete sidewalks by the time he reached home. His left leg ached. His skin was raw from ocean salt. At the back of his cottage, McKay disrobed for a quick outdoor shower in the privacy of a lattice stall off his kitchen porch. He let the water run longer than usual and dried slowly, thinking through his options.

After changing into an old pair of slacks, McKay fixed himself a sandwich from leftovers. While eating, he read the New Zion letter again before tucking it between two thick volumes of Dickens on his bookshelf. He sat in a threadbare wingback chair for hours without moving. On the mantel, a tarnished brass timepiece punctured his solitude with its measured ticking. After announcing the hour, the clock's chimes echoed in evening's fading light. Another hour slipped past. The Faithtown Light awakened to begin its vigil. With night's approach, McKay stirred. Padding barefoot into the kitchen, he reached into a cupboard above the sink. Retrieving a bottle of smoky rum, he retreated to the darkened parlor, settled in his chair and proceeded to get very drunk.

CHAPTER 17

In Reverend Samuel Burton's tidy world, church begins at nine-thirty and concludes at noon.

His ferry was moored at the main dock, poised for the Sabbath's afternoon run. The clergyman had showered, shaved and had paused briefly for a spartan breakfast of orange juice, toast and tea. After eating, he donned a fresh white shirt, knotted a pale blue silk tie and slipped into neatly creased gray trousers and polished Sunday shoes.

Stepping into the hallway, Burton looked lovingly at his wife sitting quietly in the parlor bathed in morning light. Eyes closed, and wearing a beatific smile, Lillian sat with open Bible on her lap. Leaving her undisturbed, he returned to the bathroom, brushed his teeth, and ran a comb through his thinning hair.

The conclusion to his sermon, which had eluded him all week, had fallen into place the night before, as his wife had predicted. The ending had written itself as Burton had pored over the gilt-edged pages of the Book of James.

Returning to the front hall, he called to his son in the kitchen. "Jonathan, I'm off to church. I'll see you and Mother there. Everything taken care of on the boat?" His son nodded; his boyish smile smeared with jam. "Good," Burton said, satisfied he was free to go. "Until church, then."

He stepped into a flawless Sunday morning. High edges outlining his front yard sent cool morning shadows stretching across the pavement. Despite the day's beginning, he knew the weather promised stifling heat. Burton paused to pluck a fiery blossom from the mouth of a crusty, blackened smoothbore cannon crouching like a petrified pit bull outside the front steps. Lillian detested the ugly artifact and had argued against its installation. Burton loved the relic, a find from his earlier days diving on offshore wrecks. "Come, let us reason together," the pastor had laughingly teased. They reached a compromise. The old cannon stayed, and Lillian faithfully stuffed the gun's mouth with bursts of red petunias.

Threading the flower into his lapel, Burton headed
for church.

It was a quick ten-minute walk and Burton enjoyed his
privacy. Faithtown's harbor was absolutely still. No outboards
cut the quiet. Pennants hung limply from sailboat masts.
Empty dinghies tethered at the sterns of the moored boats
barely moved. Across the harbor, the lighthouse keepers had
gone to bed, leaving freshly laundered clothing drying on a
railing at the base of the tower.

Bible tucked under his arm, Burton moved briskly. A
sleeping cat, its body an unkempt ball of charcoal fur, curled
in the morning sun, ignoring the approaching footsteps.
Rounding a cement pathway where a stunted tree festooned
with orphaned floats marked the water's edge, he passed
Robert McKay's shuttered grocery store. Burton glanced at
his watch. Forty-five minutes until services.

Framed by palm trees, the church's white clapboards
shone against the blue sky. Burton skipped up broad coral
steps to weathered wooden storm doors. Fishing in his suit
jacket for a large brass key, he unlocked the chapel,
flooding the church with sunlight as he pinned the doors
against the clapboard siding.

A heavily varnished wooden stand dominated a raised
platform covered in cheap blue carpet. Burton stuffed
his Bible and notes on a shelf beneath the lectern and
opened two small side doors on opposite walls of the
stage. After propping open both doors with conch shells,
he scuttled along side aisles flinging open shuttered
windows to let in more light.

Cousin Adele McKay would soon arrive with her flower
arrangement, faithfully thinned from her own flower garden.
The woman was clock-like on Sunday and her selection of
color for the altar brightened an otherwise bare sanctuary.
Reaching behind the wooden altar table, Burton retrieved a

large well-used CD player, uncoiled the power cord and set the box at the front of the small electric organ at the rear of the platform. He selected a collection of instrumental hymns, popped in the disk, flipped the play button and adjusted the volume. Background sounds of horns and piano pumped *How Great Thou Art* throughout the sanctuary. A walking flower arrangement bustled through the front doors. Burton couldn't help smiling as he stepped into the center aisle to welcome Adele McKay.

"Good morning, Cousin. Your flowers look wonderful."

The older woman beamed. "Well yes, Pastor, they are as fresh as I could get them, what with the heat yesterday." Her reedy voice trailed off as she negotiated the steps to set the bouquet in the center of the altar. He steadied the old woman's arm as she tottered backward to admire her work. She adjusted the arrangement twice before she was satisfied. "There," she said, "that will do nicely, I do believe."

Burton nodded in appreciation. "You do have an eye for color, it's true. It brings the glory of the garden indoors." Reading his watch, he excused himself to ring the bell for worship. In the entry, Burton grasped a knotted rope and tugged vigorously to produce a clanging that managed to be both charming to visitors and annoying to Faithtown's unchurched who lived nearby. He would ring for five spirited minutes to signal start of services.

Angus McKay, minutes behind his wife, the florist, was always ready with a critical comment about church property. "It needs oiling, Pastor."

"Yes, Angus, but I need a wiry fellow like yourself to scramble up there and take care of it." Burton followed the script and the thin little man in the ill-fitting black suit responded on cue.

"Not likely, Samuel."

Marching down the aisle to join his wife in the third row to the left of the platform, Angus McKay took his usual seat. Several other parishioners straggled in, some with reluctant children in tow. The pastor greeted all with a smile. Burton's wife and son were among the last to enter. Releasing the rope, he flipped a wall switch, stirring two sluggish ceiling fans into life. Filling only a third of the pews toward the front, his congregation scattered themselves as twos and threes in their usual places. The count was twenty-one. *No visitors today*, Burton noted.

A young, plump woman in a plain blue dress, her dark hair pulled into a bun, took her seat at the organ and propped a folder of sheet music above the keyboard.

With the exception of Angus McKay, widower Montgomery Lowe and his own son, Burton's congregation was mostly older white women. A lone, black Bahamian family who worked at Faithtown's dive shop had recently begun attending services and Burton was grateful for the addition. Reaching down, he shut off the CD player and stepped to the pulpit. Opening with a loud but short prayer, he then yielded the next twenty minutes to hymn singing led by the organist. The open, whitewashed rafters reverberated with reedy, uneven voices. The people sang with heart, if not attention to key and Burton's scratchy tenor could be heard above them all. At the end of the singing, an offering was taken, and obligatory thanks given.

After a few announcements, Burton rose to speak. Launching into his text on James, he spoke non-stop for forty-five minutes before his wife discreetly coughed. It was their private signal and he trusted her timing. He closed with a short boyhood story that brought smiles to his flock's faces. The aged Montgomery Lowe gave the benediction. Rising as one, the congregation waited for the expected blessing.

With his crown of white hair, ruddy face and pale blue eyes, Lowe could easily have been a nineteenth-century New England elder in a tiny Vermont church.

"Lord, give us this day and this week as you would have it unfold without our meddling. And don't let us be found in opposition to your plan. Amen."

Burton nodded. "Thank you, Brother Lowe. Don't forget tonight's service. Sister Bethel will be charming us with her vocals. God Bless," he added.

The service broke up in a cacophony of goodbyes and promises of lunch or trips to New Zion in the coming week. Worming his way to the front door, Burton joined Lillian in shaking hands. When the last parishioners were left chatting on the sidewalk, Burton shut down the power and asked his son to help shutter the windows. As he turned his key in the lock, Burton noticed his wife talking to an elderly black man at the end of the walkway.

"Who's Mother talking with?" asked his son.

"Don't know. Can't say I recognize him. Let's join her and find out."

Burton and his son descended the wide coral steps together and when they reached the end of the walk, Lillian turned to her husband. "Dear, this is Nathaniel Rolle. Don't you remember?"

Burton held out his hand to the smaller man. "Forgive me, Brother, your name is familiar, but I've forgotten your face."

Flashing a forgiving smile, the old man said, "I live on the big island now, Pastor. Used to be in your congregation when you first get the call."

Burton placed him. One of the first to worship in the early church he and Lillian had pastored in his younger, leaner years. "Yes, Nathaniel." He embraced Rolle, clasping the thin body to him. His former parishioner smiled politely.

"Well, it has been a long time, Pastor. About twenty year by now."

Burton's wife interrupted, tugging on her husband's sleeve. "Jonathan and I should be going. We'll be at home." The pair turned to leave.

"Jonathan can take the afternoon ferry run if you need him to." volunteered Lillian.

Rolle spoke up. "I won't be long, ma'am. Just need some time to catch up with the pastor."

"Nice to see you again, Nathaniel," she said. "Please come back."

"Maybe I do that, Miss Lillian, thank you." He bowed as the pair left.

Burton said, "How'd you come over, Nathaniel? Will you need passage back?"

"No, Pastor. I have a small rig. Good enough, thanks."

Burton motioned to a low stone bench in the churchyard's only shade. They sat together, the old man waiting politely as Burton questioned. "What are you doing now, Nathaniel. If I remember, you ran two boats for fishing, didn't you?"

Rolle nodded. "Yes, but it got too expensive, you know. And then my oldest boy died." The small man paused.

Burton remembered the tragedy. "Yes, I did the funeral, Nathaniel. A tragic loss. The sea..."

He swept his arm toward the harbor. The awkward moment passed. "And now, Nathaniel? No boats?"

"Just the small one, Pastor." Averting his gaze, Rolle shifted his feet on the stones. "I do odd jobs. I take care of the funeral home in New Zion. Know it?"

Burton nodded. "Hamilton Sawyer's place, isn't it?"

The little man's eyes flashed. "Yes, that's it. That's why I come to see you, Pastor. You know what to do."

"I'll try. What seems to be the problem?" Burton listened as Rolle poured out his story. The sun rose. The shade retreated.

The two men talked. In the end, Burton embraced his visitor and prayed softly with him, his lips barely moving. He walked Rolle to a scuffed fifteen-foot whaler tied at the grocery store dock and shook hands. Burton stayed until Rolle had wound his way through the crowd of moored boats. Near the harbor mouth, the tiny black figure turned to wave, and then Rolle's boat accelerated into swells at the edge of the channel.

Burton knew exactly what he needed to do. Patting the small envelope Rolle had given him, he returned home. His son would need to take the afternoon run after all. That would give Burton time to visit with McKay. They needed to talk.

CHAPTER 18

In the middle of a weedy backyard, a rusting machete thrust into a pile of dead palm fronds was a sign of the owner's neglect. Blistered yellow siding, dulled from years of salt air and sun, gave the once handsome house an air of indolence, like an aging mistress coming apart at the seams.

Surrounded by overgrown shrubbery, Jeremiah McKay, architect of the neglect, lay sprawled in a huge rope hammock. At the rear of the house, an outdoor stall with a leaking showerhead dripped precious drops. Serving in lieu of the needed repair, a plastic pail caught the overflow. Faithtown's only policeman, wearing a weekend uniform of old trousers and T-shirt, slept between two spindly coconut palms. A straw hat with chewed brim shaded his face. His right hand dragged the ground near a plastic milk jug long since converted to hold rum. The empty container had fallen from his grasp.

McKay's slow, deep breathing was punctuated by an occasional snort. Even much-despised harbor gulls could have strutted through his backyard with impunity.

At the cottage's front door, Burton stood patiently, rapping bony knuckles against wood. No answer. He stepped away, let the screen door slap into place, and slipped around back where he spotted McKay in the sagging hammock.

Asleep? Likely a hangover. Stooping to retrieve the empty jug, Burton sniffed it.

"Goombay Smash, Samuel."

Burton dropped the jug, embarrassed. "Didn't know you were awake."

The policeman yawned. "That wouldn't have stopped your snooping."

Burton let the insult land unanswered. Lifting his straw hat, McKay cocked a bloodshot eye at his visitor. "Well?"

Shrugging, Burton attempted a smile. "May I join you?"

McKay gestured to two weathered rattan armchairs. "Help yourself."

Picking the best one, Burton dragged it close to the constable's perch. McKay swung his weight forward and sat upright, rocking slowly in the netting. "You making a friendly call or is this professional?"

"Maybe both."

"I'd offer you a drink, but..." He kicked the empty jug aside. "I've made a pig of myself again." Before Burton could reply, McKay rose and ambled to the outdoor shower, removed his hat and knelt to thrust his head into a plastic bucket brimming with water. He blew a small explosion of bubbles as the overflow splashed on concrete.

"Ah, that feels bloody marvelous," roared McKay as he raised his dripping head and groped for a towel. The big man buried his face in the cloth and draped it around his neck. Studying his face in a round mirror hanging from a rusty nail, McKay ran a comb through his hair. Satisfied with his efforts, he sloshed water in his mouth and shot a stream at the bushes. Grooming complete, McKay returned to his hammock.

"All right, Samuel, what's so important as to merit a visit from you?" Before Burton could answer, McKay added, "And don't you have a ferry run?"

"Jonathan's taking the run for me Jeremiah. What I have to say is important."

McKay shrugged. "I'm all ears."

"I had a visit from an old friend today, after church. I knew this man many years ago. He's honest, Jeremiah. I trust him."

"Go on."

"My friend lives on Jericho Island, knows a lot of people. He hears things."

"Samuel, get to the point."

Fishing a small white envelope from his pocket, Burton carefully removed an old photograph with peeling edges and handed it over. "You recognize this man, Jeremiah?"

McKay studied the photograph of a young black man sprawled on a couch, his arms thrown across its back, a cocky, arrogant smile spread across the face.

He had seen that face before. But where?

McKay's eyebrows knit together. "Hmm, he does seems familiar, Samuel, but...I just can't place him." He handed the photo back. "Who is he?"

Instead of answering, Burton pulled another photograph from the envelope, a color Polaroid of what looked to be a sleeping young man.

McKay jerked upright, planting both feet on the ground. "Where did you get these?"

Burton remained calm. "As I said, from someone in New Zion." He handed the first photograph to McKay. "Look at them together."

Cradling both pictures in his right hand, McKay let out a short sigh. "No question, it's the same man." He turned policeman again. "Do you know what you have here, Samuel?"

Burton nodded. "It's him, isn't it? The body that washed up."

McKay nodded as he scanned the pictures. "Yes. Who is he? Did your friend give you a name?"

Burton nodded. "Virgil Livingston. Hails from Parker's Inlet. You know it?" McKay did not.

"It's not much more than a half-dozen houses on the south tip of Jericho," Burton said. "The boy's aunt lives there. Up until three years ago, he stayed with her. He spent a lot of time going back and forth to Nassau apparently."

"These photos are evidence, Samuel. The ones I took are worthless compared to these."

Burton agreed. "My friend said we could keep them."

Carefully replacing the photos in the envelope, McKay got up to pace, hands jammed deep in his pockets. "How did he come by the photos of the boy?" Before the minister could answer McKay followed his question with another. "And does he know anything else? What did he tell you?"

Burton held up a hand. "You'll have to ask him when the time is right. I'll introduce you at some point." Rolle had insisted on anonymity and despite McKay's curiosity Burton had to honor his agreement. He continued. "As far as the rest...well, I understand until two months ago, Virgil Livingston bumped around New Zion doing a variety of odd jobs. Spent some time in construction with those new condos going up. He hung around marinas. Spent some time as crew on *Green Turtle Two*."

"You sure about that last one?"

"My source was positive about his information."

"Anyone else know about this?"

Burton shook his head. "No one."

McKay pressed him, "Not even Lillian or Jonathan?"

"No one."

"Good. I'm speaking as a policeman. Keep it that way, Samuel." McKay resumed pacing. "That means there are three of us who know about this. And they know, of course."

Burton was puzzled. "They?"

"Whoever's involved. You might as well know. Martha's convinced our boy was murdered. He did not drown." Burton was dumbstruck. "Yes, Samuel, murder. I need to do more work to confirm that and make a connection. I want your absolute silence on this, agreed?"

"You have my word."

"Good. I'm not telling you this because I have this sudden need to renew family ties. It's just that you've given me some crucial information and you at least deserve some light on the situation."

"Jeremiah, I..."

McKay cut Burton off. "Don't say it. Maybe some other time. Can you stay for a bit? I want to talk to someone else about this."

"Of course. Jonathan took the afternoon run for me, remember?"

McKay headed inside. "Good. Sit tight. I'll make a call."

CHAPTER 19

Burton settled into a lawn chair and McKay disappeared into his house. When he returned, he was dressed in clean slacks and shirt. He carried a wooden tray with a pitcher of iced tea and three glasses. As McKay poured two glasses, Burton discreetly studied his host. The policeman seemed animated by the revelations. To be sitting in his former brother-in-law's backyard and sipping tea as a guest was an unexpected turn. The information he had delivered must be important.

Miracles do happen, he thought.

The two men sipped in silence for ten minutes when suddenly, Burton looked up to see Martha Thomsen strolling across the weedy lawn.

McKay and he rose to greet her. Martha offered her hand. "Samuel, good to see you. I thought you'd be pulling out for New Zion about this time."

Burton smiled apologetically as McKay answered for him. "He's got more important business than carrying a few spoiled tourists."

Making herself at home in the hammock, Martha smoothed her skirt and rearranged several ragged pillows behind her. McKay pulled up a rattan chair and poured her a glass of tea. Tilting her head at him, she asked, "How much does he know?"

"Until a half-hour ago, more than either of us."

Martha threw the pastor an admiring look as McKay laid down some ground rules.

"Let's get some things straight between the three of us. Nothing about this case that we discuss is to go outside of this group, understood?" His visitors agreed. "Good," McKay said with finality. He took a long swallow of his tea while Martha eyed him over the rim of her glass.

"Samuel, it's like this. I asked Martha to do an autopsy for me before I sent the body to New Zion. Just for my satisfaction as the on-site authority, you understand?"

Burton nodded, "Of course."

"Martha, tell him what you found."

She put down her drink and laced fingers together across her knees. "Well, the victim did not drown. He was definitely shot. Murdered."

"You're absolutely positive?" said Burton.

"She's right, Samuel," said McKay. "Even with the body being in the water, it was obvious to me he had been shot. Martha confirmed it."

"Probably a shotgun blast at close range," she added. "Sloppy, but lethal."

McKay nudged Burton's elbow and handed him a small plastic sack holding a dozen shot pellets. "She picked these out of our lad."

"That's it," Martha finished. "Murder, pure and simple."

Burton handed the bag back to McKay. "How did he end up in the water?"

McKay rubbed his jaw. "Obviously, someone wanted the sharks to finish him off or at least obscure the wound. Martha thinks he hadn't been in the water long. Someone just botched the job."

"That's true," Martha added. "The body didn't appear to have been adrift for more than a day."

"How can you be so sure?" said Burton.

She bristled. "I worked enough shifts in a public hospital in New York City to know how long a body has been in water. You'd be surprised how many people are fished out of the river each year."

"Well, then tell the New Zion Police what you've discovered," suggested Burton. "They'll take it from here, don't you think?"

Martha rolled her eyes. McKay cleared his throat. "Here's the rub, Samuel." He passed the New Zion Police department letter to Burton who read in silence.

Folding the letter, he said, "Something's wrong here. They are either mistaken or Doctor Singh's incompetent. Could he have missed the wound, Martha?"

She shook her head. "No, an amateur would have spotted it. Even the folks who found the body on the point mentioned it to Mac."

McKay turned deadly serious. "She's right, Samuel. It was a deliberate call. It's as if they didn't want it to go any further."

Burton was incredulous. "But how can they refute your findings?"

Martha said, "They don't know we did our own autopsy."

Burton sagged. The news was not what he had expected.

"Now do you see why it's important to keep this under wraps?" said McKay.

Burton said. "Now what, Jeremiah?"

McKay had a plan. "First, I'll drop in on the aunt at Parker's Inlet for a positive identification. Then I'll visit the Winthrop place. He's the American owner of *The Green Turtle Two*. Maybe I can get permission to question his crew. Then I'll tell New Zion's finest what I've found."

"You may shake things up a bit, Mac." Martha suddenly looked apprehensive.

McKay smiled. "I'd like to do exactly that. And you, Samuel," he said, pointing at Burton. "If you're willing, I'd like you to ask around the marinas and check with your friends in New Zion. See if anyone places this boy."

Burton was willing. "I can do that."

McKay offered an out. "You've already done quite a bit. Don't do this if you feel uneasy."

Burton was adamant. "No, I can certainly ask about for you. No harm in that."

"Good, but don't make it so bloody obvious, Samuel. Be discreet."

Martha, annoyed at having been left out, asked, "What about me, Mac?"

"Would you be willing to make a special trip to Florida? You had mentioned going over in two weeks anyway. Could you schedule it sooner? There's someone I'd like you to meet."

Martha thought for a moment. "I'm supposed to fly over with Emilie Russell and her husband for her chemo treatments at Mayo's in Jacksonville. It's already set." She was apologetic. "It took us weeks to get the appointment, Mac. I can't just change it overnight."

Waving a hand at her, he said, "No, no, you're right. Keep the appointment. Matter of fact that might be better. You could raise suspicions by making a special trip. It's better to just go about your routine. Once you've got Emilie at the clinic, you'd have time." Rubbing his hands together, McKay warmed to the chase. "Tomorrow I'll send an email to my contact in the States."

He pulled the fingerprint card from the envelope. "He's a friend with the FBI who owes me a favor or two. I'd like to run the prints through the Feds or Interpol. Officially I'd have to go through Sergeant Newton, maybe even Nassau, but that would tip the game. Make sense to you both?"

McKay's newly won co-conspirators agreed.

"Good." He smiled, raising his glass of iced tea. "Let's toast to good old-fashioned detective work." Martha grinned at Burton, who managed only a weak smile. Clearly the pastor felt carried along in the intrigue but was anxious.

CHAPTER 20

Monday dawned with a rich blue sky swept of clouds and a sea stretching to the horizon like a sheet of turquoise silk. Faithtown's reef showed a feeble line of breakers and the harbor was a mirror. Up early, McKay fixed himself a light breakfast. He estimated he could make the run to the big island and be back in the afternoon without arousing suspicion. He packed a small cooler with a sandwich and a gallon jug of water.

To avoid announcing his morning visit to Parker's Inlet, McKay donned civilian clothes—khakis and a dark baseball cap. Like any cop, he knew people sometimes talked more

freely when not confronted with a uniform. Besides, he would
be a complete stranger in the small settlement.

At seven o'clock, he left the house and let himself into
the community library. He made a dozen copies of the
photographs Burton had furnished. He dropped a handful
of coins on the main desk along with a note explaining his
use of the machine. Locking the door behind him, McKay
walked to his office and rummaged in his desk for a
laminated boating map of New Jericho Island.

Scribbling a message about errands in New Zion, he taped
it to Sarah Cameron's door. He knew the postmistress would
corner him when he returned, but the note would buy him
some good will.

He called Martha to let her know he was leaving and then
headed for the harbor.

While the Yamaha warmed, McKay checked the fuel and
stowed the canvas top. The boat's tank had enough gas for
the trip to Jericho Island and back, but he planned to top
off in New Zion. He cast off and weaved his way through
moored sailboats towards Burton's ferry landing. Father
and son were readying for their morning run. The pair
waved as McKay glided alongside the ferry. Throwing his
engine into neutral, he leaned over to grab the larger
boat's gunwales.

"Samuel, I have something for you." The two hulls gently
kissed, the rumbling of McKay's engine made conversation
difficult. He took several of the photocopies from a nylon
bag and handed them to Burton. "I'm off to Parker's Inlet.
Thought you might use these in New Zion," he said. "Only,
don't spread them around too much."

Burton nodded. "I know, be discreet."

McKay laughed. "Right! Discreet it is." He cupped his
hand against the minister's ear. "Still interested?"

Burton nodded. McKay gave him thumbs-up and pushed from the ferry.

Starting the ferry's engines, Jonathan coaxed the ferry from the dock as his father pocketed McKay's copies. School children bound for Jericho Island were gathering at the main dock and the ferry was running two minutes late, something Burton would remedy in the channel between the two islands. With the morning's glassy sea, any lost time would be regained before they reached New Zion's harbor.

Jonathan jockeyed the big boat toward the dock as McKay cleared the harbor. By the time the ferry wedged its fantail against the pier's ladder for loading, McKay was a tiny dot at the end of a wide, spreading wake.

When the last fare had boarded, Burton gave the OK sign and his son pulled from the pier at wake speed until they left the harbor. Jonathan eased the throttles forward and the bow lifted from the water in a powerful lunging motion. A pair of low rooster tails rose from the stern and Burton's young cargo squealed with delight at the increase in speed. Glancing at his watch, the minister smiled and patted his son on the back. They had already recaptured one of the lost minutes. The ferry crossed traces of McKay's wake and began carving a frothy path toward the low silhouette of Jericho Island.

Twenty minutes into his own crossing, McKay began a slow turn south along Jericho Island and closed to within one hundred meters of shore, on a parallel course with the beach. Tapping the throttle back, he spread the boater's map in front of him. Along this edge of the island the sea floor became a wide, light-green stretch of sand and dark rushing blurs of turtle grass. According to the chart, it ran like this until the extreme southern tip where rocks and sandbars made a wide turn out into deeper water mandatory.

McKay glanced at this watch. *Making good time*, he thought. He studied the map to memorize a landmark—an abandoned shack perched on jagged headland where the rocks began. Scanning the low banks, he found the skeletal ruin amid a field of scrubby bushes and began a slow turn seaward.

In fifteen minutes, McKay reached a large curving bay. Parker's Inlet was at the end of a short creek emptying into the bay. Fifty meters from shore, he pulled back on the throttle to search for the inlet. Three skinny poles poked six feet above the surface, marking the channel. Piloting between the sticks, McKay spotted the creek mouth.

The sandy bottom was crisscrossed with long, ugly prop scars. Mounds of bleached conch shells covered the inlet's southern shore and scrawny mangrove roots crept into the water on the opposite shore. Dropping speed, McKay glided into the anchorage.

Parker's Inlet was a long, crescent-shaped mud bank with houses at the north end. The map warned boaters no gas was available, and that low tide would strand any boat drawing more than a foot.

The sun blazed down as McKay entered the sheltered anchorage. He headed for a long wooden dock leaning noticeably to one side. Four forlorn boats floated in sluggish brown water. An orphaned sailboat, pathetic without rigging, was beached near the pier's base. A once handsome cruiser lay heeled over, its cannibalized innards strewn about. Two scavengers, ignoring McKay's arrival, bent over machinery, picking through what looked like scattered diesel intestines.

Cutting his engine, McKay drifted silently to the only available ladder. Climbing the rickety steps, line in hand, he was surprised to be met by a small boy with rust-colored hair and a swollen stomach at the top of the dock.

"Good morning."

"Morning" the youngster parroted.

McKay looped the line around a post and stretched. Even on smooth water, muscles tend to cramp and it felt good to be back on land. He knelt to face the boy. "You know where Virgil Livingston's people live?"

"Top the hill. Blue house." And then, "Whar you from?"

McKay stood up. "Over Faithtown way."

"I been there afore," bragged the boy.

McKay smiled and patted the boy's shoulder. "Watch my boat for me?" He held up two shiny Bahamian quarters.

The boy brightened. "Sho. You want me show you the house?"

"I'll find it." He strolled along the tilting pier toward a collection of homes and several crumbling coral block foundations huddled against a gentle limestone slope. Gardens dotted the home sites. Gnarled pines struggled for life on high ground above the houses. Surrounding the clapboard hovels, wild clumps of coconut palms competed with head-high brush, sea grape and refuse. The garbage was clearly winning.

McKay paced himself up the broken rock steps serving as a road from the beach. With the exception of the child on the dock—and the pair working on the beached boat— he saw no signs of life. His destination was a house squatting on short concrete pilings with a commanding view of the little harbor. Painted blue at one time, now only a few boards of the cottage wore the faded color. Even McKay winced at the tangerine-colored door assaulting the eyes. A rusting motorcycle, missing its seat and rear wheel, leaned against the side of the house. Three skinny chickens strutted in the scrubby plot, ignoring both a sleeping dog and this latest visitor. McKay stopped in the yard to admire the view.

He could make out the northwest coast of Jericho Island where reef met deeper water in a ragged skirt of breakers. The southern shore was marked by shallows and hazards of rock and sand. Beyond the hill where he stood a carpet of low foliage rose and fell in a series of thirsty brown waves. Near the blue house, the pitted limestone road widened and ran toward the coast in twenty miles of tortuous turns and ruts. Somewhere north of this tiny village, New Zion bustled with tourism and everyday life. McKay found it hard to believe he was on the same island.

"You lost, Mistah?"

McKay turned to find a thin, bowed woman peering at him from the orange doorway. Her light brown skin contrasted with black, waist-length hair streaked with gray. A diapered child, propped on the woman's bony hip, was held in place with her large, rough hands.

"Good morning, ma'am. Name's Jeremiah McKay from Faithtown."

He stepped towards her. "I'm looking for Virgil Livingston's aunt."

"You found her," she said, "but Virgil...he hain't around anymore."

"Yes, I know. Can we talk?"

"Come in." She gestured. "We can talk."

Pulling off his cap, McKay stepped inside the house.

CHAPTER 21

Samuel Burton leaned forward with one of the photocopies McKay had given him. "Brother Hollis, you ever see this person before?"

The elderly cabbie with a face like a brown ferret studied the blurry photograph for a long time. Squeezing his face into a mass of wrinkles, he caressed the picture as if trying to coax a memory.

"Naw, Pastor, never saw him before. Lots of folks coming and going these days, you know."

Burton sighed in disappointment. "Thanks for looking just the same." He slipped from the station wagon's back seat and poked his head in the driver's window. "If anything refreshes your memory you know how to find me."

Left standing in the heart of New Zion's business district, Burton's plan was to talk to cab drivers, dockworkers and charter boat crews—anyone who would listen. Those he questioned were polite but not helpful. For two hours, Burton collared occasional passersby in hopes of finding someone who knew the dead man. McKay had warned Burton to be discreet, but caution wasn't working. If the young man's name didn't jog a person's memory, Burton produced the deceased's picture and asked those he stopped to study the face.

At noon, he introduced himself to a skinny black teenager sprawled in the shade of a mammoth boat repair shed and covered in fiberglass dust. Sounds of sanding and sawing drifted from the cavernous building. Crews were putting finishing touches on upended hulls. Burton showed the reclining laborer the picture.

"Yeah, that's Virgil Livingston, mon. What's he done now?"

Burton sat down beside the marina worker. He probed, asking questions he thought McKay would want answered. "When's the last time you saw him, Brother…?"

"Pickering." The youth's brow furrowed as if the act of thinking hurt. "Maybe three weeks ago. Yeah, something like that, mon."

"Was he working, or did you see him somewhere else?"

"He was working about the warehouse." He waved his arm at a row of metal buildings. "You know, a job here, a job there, nothing for long."

"You remember where he worked last?"

A frown again. "Maybe Island Imports. Not sure, mon."

"Anything else?" Burton had an afternoon ferry run to make.

Offering empty hands as an answer, the man picked up a soft drink can and downed the contents. Knowing the interview was over, Burton said, "Thanks very much, Mister Pickering. You've been very helpful." He turned to leave.

"Hey, mon, you should ask Dictionary about this brother."

Burton paused. "I beg your pardon."

Pickering stood and stretched. "Dictionary Key. He run crews over Island Imports." Smiling, he lifted his empty can in a farewell salute.

Burton repeated the name. "Dictionary Key." He laughed to himself at the sound of it. *Dictionary Key would have to wait until tomorrow. McKay should hear this*, he thought, stuffing the photos back into his pocket, and heading for the marina's taxi stand. Along the way, he dodged a loaded forklift and worked his way past several crews lounging among unfinished fiberglass shells. Lunch breaks had slowed the waterfront's pace. Only tourists and taxi drivers moved at the height of the day. Crossing the road, Burton aimed for cars parked in the shade of a massive banyan tree.

"Hey, Pastor Samuel, you need a ride?"

The cabdriver Hollis and two cronies were holding court from the hood of his station wagon. Burton made straight for him.

"Yes, I overstayed," he said. "I need to get back to the pier without a speeding ticket to show for my time here."

The group laughed—speeding tickets were unknown and would have been ignored if issued. "Get in," commanded Hollis. "You as good as there, Pastor."

Burton settled in the back seat. Pausing at the edge of the road for oncoming traffic, the dusty station wagon wheeled into the left lane for the short trip to the harbor. Hollis radioed the ferry to wait for his fare and then glanced over his shoulder. "Any luck finding your man?"

McKay's warning about talking clicked in. Burton showed a patient smile. "No one seems to know him. Hard to believe someone could work around here and not be remembered." It was as close to outright lying as Burton dared go.

It worked. Hollis laughed with sympathy. "Yes. Well, you know these young people. They go here; they go there. Never stay in one place long enough to put the roots down." He chuckled, staring ahead as they circled a roundabout. Ten minutes later, the car lurched to a stop near the docks. Burton reached for his wallet, but Hollis held up his hand in protest.

"Hey, I'd be in trouble with the Lord if I take money twice from the same pastor in one day."

They both laughed, but Burton pushed two bills into the man's hand. "At least for gas."

That won the cabby. "All right, just this once. Remember, you need a driver, you call taxi Thirty-Six, Pastor."

"Thanks, Hollis, and God bless."

"The same, Pastor. See you again, eh?"

Burton waved and hurriedly walked to the public dock where the ferry sat. As soon as the minister hit the pier, his son cranked the big engines into life. Burton pulled the stern line in after him and apologized to the nearest passengers for his tardiness as he made his way forward. Several Faithtown residents chided him good-naturedly about being late. Backhauling a full load of tourists and locals meant a cabin piled high with luggage and groceries. Jonathan backed the big boat from the dock and spun the wheel to starboard. A flock of seagulls exploded into flight, anticipating scraps from the moving boat. "Clear astern?" yelled Jonathan.

"Clear," bellowed his father.

The ferry passed a long row of moored luxury yachts and sailboats. Once they skirted the tall white marker pole with its barnacle collar the ferry leaped ahead. There were whitecaps in the channel, but they would make good time. Jonathan eased the throttle forward. Burton doffed off his hat and leaned against the console. The engines' throbbing was comforting. Staring at the rippled, blue horizon, he wondered how valuable the information he'd gained in New Zion would be to McKay.

At the marina, the taxi driver Hollis got out of his car, casually strolled to a hotel's poolside bar, and hailed the waitress. "Cynthia, darlin, give me a cold beer to wash the dust from my throat."

He smiled at the voluptuous young woman in tight jeans and skimpy red halter-top. Swiveling on the stool, his back to chatting regulars lining the bar, Hollis tapped keys on his cell phone. He turned to wink at Cynthia who slid a frosted bottle across the polished bar. He toasted her and dropped his voice.

"Hey, mon, it's Hollis. There's a certain party been asking questions around town about Virgil Livingston." The voice on the other end erupted. The cab driver broke in to explain. "It was Pastor Burton from Faithtown. Yeah, Samuel Burton. I know him. He was wanting to know if anyone knew Virgil Livingston."

Pausing, Hollis rubbed his jaw. "He had some pictures. What you want me to do, mon? Yeah, I let you know if he come around again. Right."

Hollis snapped shut his phone and resumed flirting with the barmaid.

Whatever the pastor was looking for had upset the man on the other end, thought Hollis.

CHAPTER 22

At dusk, a four-foot nurse shark, its body a blur of brown velvet, glided in the shallows outside Faithtown Harbor in search of food. Normally, it would not chance the confines of the harbor, but hunger drove its brain and the fish rode eddies into the opening. A small, soft-shelled crab never sensed the shadow and with a slight yawning grin the shark devoured its first meal without stopping. Fish heads and tails, trimmings from the day's catch, slopped from a cleaning station at the north end of the harbor drew the shark. A school of jacks beginning to feed on the remnants scattered at the approach of the torpedo-shaped body.

Making a wide sweep of the anchorage, the shark broke the surface near the Faithtown ferry where Jonathan Burton was securing the boat for the night. Leaning over the port gunwale, he pounded on the hull with his fist, startling the shark. In a flash, the fish fled toward the channel. Jonathan broke into a grin at the shark's flight and returned to his chores. Daylight was fading and dinner waited. In the house, Burton helped his wife set the table.

"Lillian," he said, "I've invited Jeremiah and Martha for a chat after supper."

She looked up, pleased. "Well," she purred, "what a pleasant surprise. What's the occasion?"

He frowned. "Jeremiah thought it best to meet and compare notes. Find out how our days went."

She was puzzled.

"It's that business about the missing boy," he reminded her. "The one they found. You remember, don't you?"

"Yes, the man who spoke to you on Sunday, Nathaniel Rolle. Is he part of this?"

"In a way. He had some helpful information."

She corrected her husband's silverware placement as their son came in the door.

"Do change for dinner, Jonathan, and wash, please," she ordered.

Burton looked up at his son and winked. The young man smiled and stripped off his jacket before heading for the bathroom. His father called after him, "Everything fine with the boat?"

"Perfect," Jonathan replied. "Topped off, cleaned, and shut down for the night." Burton heard his son's voice above the sound of running water. "We may get some rain tonight, so I drew the tarp over the stern."

"Thank you," Burton said. "You probably knew I would ask about that."

Returning to the dining room, his hands twisting in a thick towel, Jonathan said, "Yes, I knew you'd ask."

Lillian carried in a steaming dish, the rich aroma of rice and peas filling the room.

"Smells wonderful, Lillian," said Burton.

She blushed at his compliment and took her place across from her son.

"Shall we pray?" said Burton. They joined hands around the table. "Father, thank you for your bounty and your day. Your blessings on the table and this family are an undeserved reward and we are thankful for them. In Christ's name, Amen."

"Amen," they chorused.

"Now," said Burton, "let me tell you both about my day."

Across town, McKay sat at his kitchen table in fading light, dining on a day-old sandwich and lukewarm beer. He ate without ceremony, a silenced VHF radio in front of him. McKay finished the beer and rose. In the bathroom, McKay stripped and showered. He dressed quickly and strolled to Martha's house.

The evening was soft, fragrant, touched by a gentle trade wind that rustled tall palms between the houses. From Martha's place it was an easy five minutes to the Burtons. McKay knew he would share what he had discovered at Parker's Inlet. Of the three, Martha was the most excited about the mystery of the case and he determined to keep her within bounds. Burton, he knew, would do as asked.

McKay reached her home and rapped loudly on the screen door. The living room light was on. He settled on the porch swing to wait, pushing gently, letting his shoes drag on the deck.

"Just a moment, Mac," she called.

McKay didn't bother to answer, knowing her moment would turn into ten. When Martha finally stepped on the porch, light from the doorway softened her silhouette and McKay thought her beautiful. Pirouetting in a light blue floral skirt and white sleeveless top, she said, "Like it? It's a little thing I picked up in West Palm last month."

He stood. "Very nice, Martha. Only it's just Samuel's house, not the governor-general's ball."

"Ugh, you're good at finding your way around a compliment. But thank you for noticing just the same. Shall we go?"

CHAPTER 23

The two walked in silence, enjoying the night. Martha didn't throw questions at McKay. She knew he was saving his words until Burton's house. Lillian met them at the door. "Hello, Martha, Jeremiah. Please come in. Samuel's in the parlor."

Taking Lillian's hand in both of hers, Martha exchanged small talk as McKay nodded politely and crossed the threshold ahead of her. He found Burton at his desk looking over some notes. Burton stood to greet him.

"Evening, Jeremiah. Martha with you?"

McKay jerked a thumb toward the hall. "She's catching up with Lillian. Martha's the polite one, you know."

"Tea?"

McKay laughed. "I'd prefer something stronger, Samuel. But no thanks. Perhaps some water." He settled himself on the sofa. Martha and Lillian appeared.

"Martha, how nice to see you again." Burton extended his hand.

"I have things to do," interrupted Lillian. "So, if you'd like anything for our guests, Samuel, let me know before I leave you on your own."

"Just a pitcher of ice water, dear, unless..." He looked at Martha, who nodded. "Just water."

Lillian returned with a full beaker of water and several glasses on a tray. Before she left the room, she turned to McKay. "Jeremiah, it's nice to see you in our home again." McKay managed an awkward smile, and then Lillian was gone.

Samuel filled three glasses. "Well, Jeremiah, the floor is yours."

McKay took a long swallow and set his glass on the tray. "Thank you, Samuel, for agreeing to host our little conspiracy." Martha and Burton chuckled nervously.

"I'll start," said McKay, "by giving you a rundown on who I saw and what I learned."

For the next fifteen minutes, he described his trip to Parker's Inlet and his conversation with the dead man's aunt. When finished, he invited questions.

"The aunt said Virgil was spending a lot of time in New Zion?" Martha said.

"Yes, she claims that she saw less of him in the last two or three months."

"Did she notice anything strange? Extra money? New friends? Did she know what he was doing, who he was working for?"

"He told her he was hiring on with *The Green Turtle Two*."

Burton was intrigued. "That's the Winthrops' yacht isn't it?"

"Hard one to miss. Biggest boat in New Zion."

"That's interesting," Martha mused. "I mean, the Winthrops have a big footprint in Faithtown, Mac. Maybe he was just trying to impress his aunt."

Burton chimed in. "Or maybe she's lying, Jeremiah."

"Possible, Samuel, but why would she lie? No, instinct tells me that she had nothing to gain by lying. She was honest with me."

"She know you were a cop?" asked Martha.

"I was out of uniform, but I told her who I was, and I kept the questions routine." McKay spread his hands on the low table in front of the sofa. "I didn't think there was much to gain from his people there. I just wanted to pin down the victim's whereabouts when he disappeared. I think this puts him in New Zion about the time he was killed." He paused for more water. "The aunt did say he stopped by two weeks ago and left some money with her before he fished up on the beach."

"I don't suppose she said how much, did she?" asked Martha.

"So young, yet so cynical." McKay grinned. "No, she did not. Why volunteer that to a government man?"

"Besides, it's irrelevant," added Burton.

"You're catching on, Samuel," said McKay.

Burton rose and stretched. "Are you going back?"

"No. I got all I need from her." McKay stood and paced behind the couch, glancing out the bay window at the harbor. "I want to talk with Winthrop about whether this boy worked aboard his yacht."

Martha shot a serious glance at Burton. "I've never met them, but to hear Sarah Cameron tell it, the Winthrops are the closest thing to royalty Faithtown has."

"True," reflected Burton. "They've poured a lot of money into our little town for three generations. I'll be surprised if you actually get an interview with Winthrop."

"It's worth a try," said McKay. "Now, tell us about your end of the investigation."

Lowering his glass, Burton recited his day in New Zion. When he mentioned his last-minute success, McKay was intrigued. "Did this handyman, this Pickering fellow, say he knew our man well?"

Burton paused. "No. He seemed to know who Virgil Livingston was, but not as a friendship thing. You know," he added, "this Dictionary Key fellow might be able to shed some light on the boy."

Martha laughed. "What an unusual name. I've never heard it before."

"That's what I thought," said Burton. "Not a name to forget. Apparently Key does a lot of the hiring around there."

"Where does he operate?" asked McKay.

Reading through his notes, Burton said, "Island Imports. It's one of New Zion's bigger concerns. I don't know much about the business."

"I've heard of it," said McKay. "Hamilton Sawyer could be involved."

Martha's sarcasm returned. "On Jericho Island what business doesn't he own?"

"Do you know anything about Island Imports, Jeremiah?" asked Burton.

McKay shrugged. "Not even positive it actually belongs to Sawyer, really. Big firm. Brings in most of the diesel fuel, gasoline, lumber, cement, stuff like that. Did you talk to Key?"

Burton apologized, "Sorry, Jeremiah, I was running late as it was and had to catch the afternoon run. Besides, this turned up at the end of the day."

"Could he go back tomorrow, Mac?" said Martha.

"I'm supposed to ask that," scolded McKay. The three laughed.

"Could you go back tomorrow, Samuel? Try to meet this Dictionary Key?"

"Of course, but what would I be looking for?"

McKay said, "For starters, find out if Virgil Livingston worked for Island Imports."

"Shouldn't a policeman ask those questions?" said Martha.

McKay frowned. "I'd ask myself, but New Zion is not my jurisdiction."

"I don't mind asking, Martha, really. But Jeremiah," said Burton, "how far am I to go with this?"

"I wish I knew, Samuel," said McKay.

Martha wouldn't be denied. "We've got to have some sort of plan. Some idea of where this is going. Eventually, we'll have to turn over the information to someone who can be trusted."

Burton said, "She has a point, Jeremiah."

McKay agreed. "Yes, of course, you're right. I'm stymied right now. I know we can't trust the New Zion police with this. At least not now. I'm not sure why. Call it a hunch. Maybe the best thing to do is keep picking up bits and pieces here and there." He sank back on the couch. "Maybe we can make sense out of it when we have more information."

"You can confront Sergeant Newton when you have enough facts," said Martha. "If he does nothing, appeal to Nassau or someone with clout in the police or attorney general's office."

She looked to Burton for support. "Don't you think that makes sense?"

Before Burton could answer, McKay held up a hand. "You're both right. Samuel, see if you can find this Dictionary Key fellow tomorrow and get his story."

Martha said, "You need my help, Samuel?"

McKay stared at her. "No volunteers. I don't think it's wise for you to be involved just yet."

Martha blushed at the rejection. "That's not fair, Mac. I did your autopsy."

"She's right," said Burton. "If it wasn't for Martha, you wouldn't know the boy had been murdered."

Outnumbered, McKay refused to give ground. "No. At this point, she should remain in the wings until this thing begins to take shape. We don't know what we're dealing with yet."

Sensing her disappointment, he tried to soften the blow. "Look, Martha, you and Samuel are the only two I can share this with. I've got no one else to turn to right now. Please understand."

"Perhaps he's right," said Burton. "It could get sticky."

She stood and faced the two, her hands balled into fists. "I've said this before but maybe you weren't listening. I spent fifteen years running an emergency room in a New York City hospital. I handled everything you could think of and then some. And I did it on my own terms."

She came round the couch, her eyes boring into McKay's back. "I've had Mafia capos bleed on me. I've stitched up so many gang members I lost count. I've seen my share of shootings, stabbings, and beatings. I've probed and prodded so many bodies that they all began to look like an endless line of so much meat. So don't tell me that it might get a little dangerous. I'm no innocent when it comes to a little adversity, so spare me the chivalry, gentlemen, please."

Martha sat down in the middle of the silence she had created.

Sipping his water, Burton shot a wary glance at McKay, whose demeanor was that of a chastened child. After a few tortuous minutes staring at the carpet, McKay cleared his throat. Avoiding Martha's eyes, he directed his gaze at Burton.

"Uh, Samuel, why don't you take Martha with you in the morning. I'll call the Winthrop place first thing and see if I can make a run up there. Maybe find out if our victim worked for him on *The Green Turtle Two*. If Winthrop agrees to see me, then I could go to New Zion and stop by his yacht in the afternoon."

McKay slapped his palms together. "One more thing. Let's stay in touch in case we end up in New Zion at the same time."

Martha hesitated. "Should we be seen together at this stage of the game?"

"It's okay," McKay assured her. "I won't be in uniform when I go to New Zion." They agreed to his plan. "Well, that's enough for tonight," said McKay sitting back. "Why don't we meet again tomorrow night?"

"My place if you like," offered Martha. "That all right with you Samuel?"

Burton nodded. McKay stood. "Thank you for the hospitality, Samuel."

"Of course, let me show you out."

"Don't bother," protested Martha. "We'll be fine." The two walked to the door. "Good night, Lillian," called McKay up the stairs. He held the door for Martha and followed her out into the night for the long, quiet walk to her house. It was one of the few times McKay found himself at a loss for words, reluctant to speak.

At her front door she turned to face him. "Good night, Mac. Thanks for an interesting evening." She read his pained expression and offered him an olive branch. "Don't take it personally. I was just standing up for myself."

Attempting a smile, he said, "Well, you certainly did that."

"It'll come out okay. You'll see. Samuel and I will get your information."

"Just be careful, Martha. I wouldn't want anything to happen to you."

"I'm more worried about you," she chided. "You've got to visit the mysterious Mister Winthrop. You're the one who'd best be careful."

He bent to kiss her on the cheek. "Good night. Until tomorrow."

Caressing his face with her hand, she said, "Until tomorrow, Mac."

She stayed on her porch until his outline melted into the night.

CHAPTER 24

In the morning, McKay dressed in his uniform, downed a pot of tea and ate a hurried breakfast. He was out the door by eight, a yellow rain jacket under his arm and a spare set of civilian clothes in a nylon bag. Stopping by his office, he radioed the Winthrop estate to ask if Spencer Winthrop would be willing to see him. After a long wait, the housekeeper told him the owner would receive him.

McKay timed his exit to avoid Sarah Cameron's questions. By the time the postmistress arrived for work, he was refueling at the marina. Few clouds and just a hint of rain promised smooth boating. He signed for his fuel and headed for the northwestern tip of Kingdom Cay. Once past the harbor mouth, he opened the throttle, pitching the bow above the surface. McKay braced himself against the wheel, turned on the VHF to monitor chatter, and settled in for the thirty-minute ride.

In Kingdom Cay, the Winthrop's had found splendid isolation. Using old money, the family carved out a pampered lifestyle on what had once been crown land. Built in part-New England, part-West Indies plantation style, the Winthrop home was a large house of fifteen rooms and six bathrooms, extravagant for the time. Enormous sums were spent to haul soil and plants to the site, transforming a wind-swept hillside into a terraced, groomed oasis. The founding patriarch died on his estate in 1920 and his son, Preston Junior, had succeeded him as a benevolent absentee landlord. Winthrop was said to have traded the respectability of Brahmin finance for a new venture—supplying rum and whiskey to the States during Prohibition. The islands had become a staging area where enterprising businessmen made enormous sums supplying alcohol to dry America. Stonemasons from Faithtown had whispered of chiseling one hundred steps and a large cavern in the secluded bay's limestone cliffs. On Kingdom Cay it was hard to keep secrets. There were legendary stories of all-night parties and boatloads of visitors. Those few old enough to remember recall hearing jazz drifting on the night air.

By the time of FDR's first term, Winthrop Junior had moved on, his fortune swelled by enormous profits from liquor. He began spending more time on Kingdom Cay and less time in Boston. He married into a banking family and his wife's enormous dowry added to his wealth. They produced one child, a son, Spencer Preston Winthrop III. When the father wandered into dementia in the late 1980s the son had already followed his father's example by marrying well. Wealth gains more wealth. His new wife, Elizabeth Lawlor, was a Vassar beauty with her own sizable trust fund.

Winthrop used his position and money to open the door of Massachusetts's politics, serving two terms as a state legislator until bored. In the late 90s, Winthrop had run for lieutenant governor and won. It had been too easy. He grew restless in the office and declined to run again. "Family business calls," he said, winking as he eyed a U.S. Senate seat. Pundits declared he was destined for the party's vice-presidential list. All things were possible for Spencer Preston Winthrop III. He assumed it and people expected great things of him.

On Kingdom Cay, Winthrop showered money on Faithtown in keeping with the family legacy. A new school with state-of-the-art computers had opened new worlds to Faithtown's children. Winthrop money rebuilt the public dock. A gleaming red fire engine had been shipped to the cay to replace an ancient jeep pumper. Almost singlehandedly, the Winthrop's endowed the Methodist church. Gifts like these were not taken lightly by the village elders and the Winthrop's, though fiercely private, were respected, almost loved in Faithtown. McKay knew it was only his role as Faithtown's policeman that had gained him an audience.

From the sea, *West Wind*, the Winthrop estate, is visible for miles. Pulling close to shore, McKay spotted a two-story house, its windows trimmed with bright green shutters, its coat of gleaming white paint reflecting the morning sun. Then the scene was gone, replaced by an abrupt shelf of limestone cliffs. He glanced down at his boater's map and followed the contour of the rocky wall until finding himself in picturesque Charity Bay. A wide crescent of perfect white sand created a beach ringed by rocks. Spotting a cement pier and stone stairs rising to foliage lining the cliff, McKay cut across the bay, heading directly for the landing where a small black figure stood motionless on the dock.

Probably one of Winthrop's rumored Haitian gardeners, thought McKay. He aimed for the landing; swinging his boat alongside the pilings, bow to the sea. Silently, the wiry black man in straw hat and work clothes grabbed McKay's line and tied off the boat against two rubber bumpers.

McKay climbed onto the concrete pad, jammed his policeman's hat on his head and stared down at the man who spoke with a thick accent.

"Mr. Winthrop, he be waiting, sah."

He motioned to the stairs and McKay followed the little man up the steps. At the top sat a gold golf cart with *West Wind* stenciled in black script across the front. McKay climbed in beside the driver, whose stoic expression remained unchanged. The electric cart whirred along a gravel road winding through lush corridors of sea grape. Low bushes gave way to taller pines and stands of stately coconut palms. The drive was meant to impress visitors with the estate's setting. It was working. McKay admired the effort, the maintenance of the place.

The cart began a slow loop around a circular driveway. In the center, a mound of flowers and bushes ringed a bronze sculpture of two leaping dolphins. Water rose in a fountain's spray, adding a soothing delightful sound to the setting. McKay stared at the fountain.

To use water this way, on an island that relied on cisterns, was evidence that the Winthrops had tapped the cay's only fresh water supply. Until now, he had thought the well a rumor. The cart stopped and the driver stared straight ahead, waiting. McKay dismounted and the cart purred down the curved driveway.

Greeting him was a wide porch of flagstones in an arched breezeway flanked by huge, colorful plants overflowing polished earthenware jars as tall as a man. He turned again to admire the landscape where not one worker was visible. McKay knew *West Wind* no longer employed Bahamians for jobs that willing Haitian immigrants did for a pittance. Even in Faithtown, the steady influx of Haitians was a problem. Illegal aliens had begun showing up in New Zion when the first wave of Haitian boat people had started washing ashore looking for employment. 2010's horrific earthquake had worsened the impoverished Haitians' plight. But all that was not McKay's problem—yet.

"Constable McKay, welcome."

Startled by a woman's voice, McKay spun to find a plain-looking, thin woman with brown hair tied in a bun. Her pale face was splashed with freckles beneath piercing gray eyes. She stood in a floral dress, hands folded patiently in front, devoid of emotion.

He said, "And you are?" The question hung between them.

"Joyce Russell, the Winthrop's housekeeper."

He remembered. A widow. Her husband lost while diving on a Civil War wreck with a group of tourists twenty years ago. Rescued from poverty by a job on the Winthrop estate, she was now dedicated to the family.

"Of course, Mrs. Russell. I believe Mister Winthrop is expecting me."

"He is." She ushered him to the door. "He'll be down shortly. I'll show you to the library. Is this your first visit to *West Wind*, Constable?"

He nodded. "Yes, and I must say, I'm impressed."

The widow barely smiled. "Most people are. It's a lovely home. The Winthrops have made it quite a showplace."

Removing his hat, McKay followed the woman into a two-story front hall, where a winding staircase rose beneath an immense brass chandelier. American, British and Bahamian flags hung above pictures of the Queen, America's president, and the islands' prime minister. Polished floor tiles echoed with the policeman's footsteps, as he glided past a pair of tall, narrow, carved mahogany doors.

"Mr. Winthrop will be with you shortly." Having said that, the widow Russell withdrew.

McKay found himself at the edge of a soft Persian carpet covering most of a parquet floor. Sunlight flooded the room through French doors opening to a covered, glassed-in porch. A polished grand piano sat near a set of overstuffed chairs flanking a long, silk-covered couch. Twelve-foot ceilings trimmed in carved plaster rose above pale yellow walls. Above a marble hearth, a tall, gilded framed painting of a man in a brown uniform with swagger stick and jodhpurs looked down in a solemn gaze.

Behind McKay, the doors opened and a six-foot patrician, with dark hair combed straight back, and wearing a linen jacket, entered. Spencer Winthrop III came forward, arm outstretched.

"Ah, the constable of Faithtown, I believe."

Winthrop's tanned face was unlined, his blue eyes set deep under bushy black brows. His wide grin revealed flawless white teeth. McKay felt himself admiring the man despite his wealth and power. Winthrop's long fingers fluttered at the portrait.

"My grandfather during the Great War."

McKay stared at the Winthrop painting, mentally comparing the man before him with the oil above the mantel. *A good likeness*, he thought.

"I love that painting, Officer McKay. My grandfather commissioned Sargent to paint him at the front." Winthrop chuckled. "Actually, he was a staff officer with Pershing in some French villa, but it was more romantic to put him in the trenches."

Quickly turning to business, Winthrop asked, "What's on your mind?"

He waved for McKay to sit. Each man took an armchair, a couch between them.

Clearing his throat, McKay said, "A young man was found dead two days ago out on Resolution Point. A couple renting a house discovered him along the rocks."

Winthrop's brow furrowed in sympathy. "Yes, I heard about it. Regrettable."

"Oh? How did you hear the news?"

Winthrop averted his eyes, staring at the portrait. "I believe our housekeeper mentioned it. Yes, of course. Mrs. Russell told us. Such sad news for the community."

"We're not sure who he is. We think he may have crewed aboard your yacht."

Winthrop leaned forward. "Really? *The Green Turtle Two*?" McKay nodded.

"Do you have a name?" Winthrop said.

"Virgil Livingston. That's all we know at this point."

"Doesn't ring a bell." Winthrop sat back again, one hand cradling his handsome chin. "But frankly, Officer McKay, I don't do the hiring for my boat. I mean, yes, I hired the current pilot, and I know the first mate, but I don't interview crewmembers. I leave that to Captain Mikos. I trust his judgment in such matters. He would know if this man served on my boat."

"I understand," replied McKay. "Perhaps this would help." He tugged at his shirt pocket, producing a picture of the dead man.

Studying it for a moment, Winthrop slowly shook his head. "No, not someone I remember, Constable. Sorry."

McKay retrieved the photo. "Well, it was worth a try. Do you think I could talk to your captain? It would he be a great help to hear from him."

Winthrop brightened. "Absolutely. Mikos would know. If you'd like, I'll call him and let him know you'd like to come by to see him."

Winthrop stood and moved to the fireplace, his hands thrust in the jacket's pockets. "The boat's in New Zion. There are just four crew on board, plus the skipper. But your timing is good. We're getting ready to take her back to Boston for the summer. Hurricane season, you know. We always like to bring her back home out of harm's way."

Returning to the armchair, Winthrop smoothly shifted the conversation. They chatted amiably for ten minutes about the cay, its families and tourism. At a certain point, something in the patrician's tone told McKay the interview was at an end. He stood, and Winthrop joined him as they crossed to the arched doorway.

"My family and I are concerned about anything that has a negative impact on this community, Constable. Anything."

Winthrop, his hand on McKay's back, urged him toward the door. "If we can do something, perhaps help this family with burial expenses, offer a reward...anything to be of assistance to you in this investigation, please call."

"That's a kind offer, Mister Winthrop, but we're still looking for his people. Other than his aunt we don't actually know who he was."

Pursing his lips, Winthrop said, "Of course. But as I said, if you ascertain who his immediate family is, and if there's a need, let Mrs. Russell know. She'll make sure we're made aware of it. Convey my offer of assistance, please."

"Thank you. I'm sure that would be welcomed by the family."

The tall wooden doors opened, and the two men moved into the entry hall where McKay replaced his hat and turned to leave. Winthrop turned the large brass handle. The door opened to reveal a tall blonde woman cradling an enormous bouquet of fresh flowers. Winthrop drew her inside and introduced his wife.

"Elizabeth, this is Constable Jeremiah McKay."

Elizabeth Winthrop reached for McKay's hand. Winthrop's wife moved gracefully. Her long blonde hair, now streaked with gray, was tied in a ponytail. She wore no makeup but needed none. China-blue eyes studied McKay and her sensuous mouth parted in a dazzling smile. Dressed in a plain, but expensive light blue blouse, and denim skirt, she handed the blossoms to her housekeeper who appeared at her side.

"Joyce, please make sure each room has some of these."

Taking the flowers, the widow retreated down the hallway.

Winthrop's wife slipped her arm through her husband's. "You're a little far afield, aren't you, Constable?" She smiled, though her question gave McKay pause.

He touched his cap's brim. "Chasing a lead, ma'am. Your husband has been most helpful."

She looked at her husband with a subtle mocking smile. "And just how did you manage to get him to do that?" Winthrop rolled his eyes in mock exasperation and the couple laughed.

"Nice to have met you, ma'am. I really must be going." McKay turned to Winthrop about the business at hand. "I appreciate your offer to call your boat. If possible, I'd like to stop by today."

Flashing his most flattering smile, Winthrop said, "Consider it done, Constable."

As if on cue, the gold cart and its robotic chauffeur appeared in the driveway. McKay climbed aboard, exchanging waves with the Winthrops. The diminutive Haitian floored the accelerator and the electric cart rolled down the big drive, past the spouting dolphins and tailored lawn, down the shaded path to the bay where McKay's boat waited.

CHAPTER 25

Burton and Martha joined the morning ferry crowd and sat forward, apart from passengers, ignoring small talk. While his son handled the run across a smooth sea, Burton dozed. When they reached New Zion, Martha nudged him awake to help unload luggage and collect fares. Six taxis lingered in the shade near the dock, waiting for fares.

Burton spoke to his son. "Jonathan, I'm going into town with Martha. Handle the return for me. We'll come back with you in the afternoon."

He patted his son on the back and motioned for Martha to join him. The two walked the length of the dock talking quietly. "I suggest we go first to Island Imports and look up this Dictionary Key. What do you think?"

"Simple enough." Taking his arm, she faced him. "Remember, this is serious business. Something's not right about this boy's death. And now here we are with this phony report from Sawyer's hired doctor, Singh."

Burton softened. "Yes, by all means let's be careful. I promise to do only what Jeremiah has asked us to do." Walking toward the taxis, he continued. "Frankly, I don't mind telling you I'm out of my depth here."

One of the taxi drivers approached the couple. Burton recognized Hollis from the previous day. "Hey, Pastor, you need a ride into town? Got no air-conditioning but we got a breeze."

Tipping his hat, the little man pulled open his taxi's door, ushering them in the back seat. He got in the driver's seat and started the engine. Immediately, the car radio crackled into life, filling the car's interior with loud gospel tunes. Hollis turned into the roadway and sped off. Glancing in his mirror, the cabby yelled over the music.

"Where to, pastor?"

Burton leaned forward. "Island Imports, Hollis."

"Island Imports," the driver parroted. "You got it."

They drove past pastel shacks crowding the waterfront and then, the marina gave way to storefronts leading into town. Morning sun broiled the roadway. Burton lowered his window, grateful for a breeze. Half-finished condos sprouted from the ground and a small gang of workers with wheelbarrows and shovels forced Hollis toward the center of the road. Waving and laughing, Hollis pumped the horn as he passed a single file of bicyclists who nodded and smiled. The cabby knew everyone.

Leaning forward, Burton gripped the seat. "Hollis, do you know Dictionary Key?"

The driver nodded and Burton posed another question. "Who exactly is he?"

Hollis tapped his head. "Smart mon. Other than you he may be the smartest fella I ever know, Pastor. He run Island Imports warehouse down by the docks, you know."

Burton rested a forearm on the seat back. "Unusual name—Dictionary."

Erupting in laughter, Hollis nodded, flashing a gold tooth in an ivory smile. "His real name Julian, but everybody knows him as Dictionary, Pastor. His family give him that name. As a child, that boy was so smart. He knew so many words, talking all the time, asking his mommy question after question. So, his uncle call him Dictionary and the name just take."

"You know him?" said Burton.

Hollis leaned forward and nodded vigorously, laughing as he answered. "Sure. Everybody knows Dictionary Key."

Martha joined the conversation. "I've never heard the name before."

Hollis smiled. "Maybe you don't know everybody, Miss. But most people in New Zion heard of Dictionary Key. You can't stump that mon, no matter what question you ask."

Hollis studied Burton's face in the mirror. He startled his passengers by pounding the horn to warn off a stray dog flirting with the idea of crossing the road. The taxi turned abruptly onto a gravel service road near the inner harbor. Looming ahead was a mammoth shed of corrugated metal surrounded by a mesh fence topped with rusting barbed wire. A huge Island Imports logo painted in turquoise, black and yellow—the colors of the Bahamian flag—was stenciled over the warehouse's yawning entry.

Key's domain was a busy place. Forklifts crabbed back and forth with loads of cement block and lumber while men in hardhats hustled rolls of fencing into vintage trucks. Two converted WWII landing craft equipped with small cranes unloaded building supplies at a wharf in the shadow of the warehouse. Choking gray dust floated everywhere. Noise from men and machinery assaulted the ear.

Just short of the yard's open gate, Hollis skidded to a stop in a shower of small stones. He leaped to open Martha's door. Burton pulled a ten-dollar bill from his wallet. Pressing the cash into the black man's hand, he made arrangements for the return trip.

"We'll be making the afternoon ferry run. We'll need you again."

Hollis interrupted. "I'll find you, Pastor. Taxi Thirty-Six always finds his fares, no problem."

Pocketing the cash, he hopped in the car. Accelerating back onto the asphalt road, Hollis honked and waved as he sped away.

Awed by the yard's bustling action, the two stood off to one side of the gate.

Bellowing to be heard, Burton jabbed a thumb at the building. "The young man I spoke with yesterday said this is where Virgil Livingston worked."

"All we're to do is find out if he was hired here. That's all," Martha cautioned.

"I told Jeremiah that's what we'd do," he said. "After we're done, we leave."

He led them toward the warehouse. Roaring, clanking machinery and moving forklifts made talking difficult, but Burton pointed out an office. They dodged a groaning pickup truck burdened with concrete blocks and reached the safety of the door.

Inside, in a small work area cleared in the midst of dusty filing cabinets, a plump brown woman wearing tortoiseshell spectacles and an ill-fitting silver wig sat behind a flyspecked counter. Digging through a stack of paperwork, she stayed seated, peering over her glasses as they approached. "Yes?"

Burton tried a smile without success. "Mister Key, please."

"And who might be wanting to see him?"

"Samuel Burton. And..." He turned to Martha, "Ms. Thomsen."

A badly painted eyebrow arched behind the glasses. "He expecting you?"

Burton smiled and shook his head. "No, actually. But if it's at all possible we'd like to see him."

Shrugging, the portly woman picked up a phone, eyeing her visitors suspiciously as she spoke rapidly in a low voice. Replacing the handset, she pointed across the room.

"Through that door and up the stairs to your right."

Burton flashed a smile and motioned to Martha. They went through a door and climbed a short flight of stairs to a landing crowded with file cabinets pushed against a wall of cheap faux paneling. Notebooks, their contents spilling from their covers, were stacked to the ceiling. A calendar with an Island Imports logo was pinned to a metal door. Burton raised eyebrows at Martha. She flashed crossed fingers. He knocked.

"Come in."

Inside a quiet, cool office, one entire wall of tinted glass overlooked the cavernous warehouse floor below. A window air conditioner's steady hum masked the bustling din. A single desk lamp glowed against dark-paneled walls and a small green vinyl couch sagged next to a wide desk piled with stuffed folders, files, and mugs jammed with pens.

A wiry black man with a shaved head and goatee, wearing a tailored khaki safari jacket, rose and extended his hand. "I'm Key. You must be Pastor Burton and Miss Thomsen, correct?"

Taken aback by Key's greeting, a surprised Burton shook Key's hand.

How does he know who we are?

Burton recovered. "Yes. We've come from Faithtown."

Key motioned to two chairs in front of the desk. Burton sat, studying the man behind the desk. Key wore a gold chain and cast sand dollar around his neck. Obsidian eyes, set behind a pair of wire spectacles, never left Burton's face.

"Now, what can I do for you and Miss Thomsen, Pastor?"

Martha forced her best neutral gaze as Burton coughed and said, "I'm looking for some information on a young man who may have worked for you."

Key shot back. "Name?"

Burton coughed again. "Ah, Virgil Livingston, I believe."

Leaning back, Key laced long ebony fingers together behind his head and stared at the ceiling. "Virgil Livingston? Can't say." Sweeping a hand toward the tinted window framing the busy warehouse, he said, "As you can see for yourself, I have a lot of local men working for me at any given moment."

Propping his elbows on the desk, Key glared at Burton. "I hire here mostly day laborers. They come. They go. Sometimes they stay for a week, sometimes longer. I pay cash. I don't ask anything but whether they can do the job or not."

Turning both palms up in resignation, Key added, "Is he a parishioner? Has the boy done something wrong? Owe you money?"

Shaking out a handkerchief, Burton mopped his neck despite the cool air. "No, it's just that I'm trying to locate him for a friend. I was told he worked here."

Flashing an indulgent smile, Key held up his left forefinger and buzzed the intercom at his right. A woman's hollow voice answered. "Yes, Mister Key?"

"Giselle, you remember a boy named Virgil Livingston working for us?"

There was a pause. Key stared at the speaker. Burton glanced at Martha, who wore a blank expression. There was a rustling of paper in the speaker. "Nothing in the files."

Shrugging, Key let go of the switch. "Sorry, no record. Your source must be mistaken."

He stood up; his part of the interview finished. "If you'll excuse me," he said, waving at his crowded desk, "I got lots of shipments to process."

"Of course," Burton said. "We understand. Thank you for your time just the same. Sorry to have bothered you."

"No problem." Key leaned against his desk; muscular arms crossed against his chest as his visitors backed toward the door. He came from behind the desk.

"Oh, Pastor."

"Yes?" Burton paused on the top step, Martha a step below him.

"Be careful crossing the yard. Always some fool running his machine too fast. You could get hurt out there if you're not careful. I shouldn't want that."

"Of course. Thank you for the warning."

Key nodded. "Pastor, Miss Thomsen."

Forcing a tight smile, Martha followed Burton down the stairs and through the front office. The receptionist, engrossed in a computer game of solitaire, ignored them.

Outside, the two faced each other. "The man is lying, Samuel."

Burton thrust his hands into his pockets and turned, smiling. "Martha, to you, everyone is lying."

She frowned. "Too many years in the Big Apple, I guess."

Pulling the crumpled picture of the dead man from a pocket, Burton gazed at the image. "I didn't think to show him this, you know."

She touched his arm. "You were right not to, it would have been a waste of time."

They walked to the front gate, Burton deep in thought. "Why won't anyone admit they know this Livingston fellow? Who is he?"

She corrected him, "Who was he?"

They crossed the yard, Burton asking questions, Martha listening.

Roaring around the corner, a forklift's steel blades caught Burton's shoulder, spinning him in the air. Martha screamed and the machine jerked to a stop in a cloud of dust. Leaping from his seat, the driver knelt beside the minister.

"I swear I never saw him! Never saw him."

Martha cradled a dazed, bloodied Burton. Two workers raced to the couple's side. Others gathered out of curiosity. Burton opened his eyes, tried to speak. Yanking a scarf from her neck, Martha quickly fashioned a compress and pressed it against the wound, slowing the bleeding.

"We'll call a doctor, ma'am," the driver said. He turned to go.

"WAIT," cried Martha. "GET A TAXI, NOW!"

Someone behind her yelled, "Flag a taxi on the road. Quick, mon."

Martha spotted Dictionary Key striding toward the growing knot of workers. The laborers parted and Key leaned over Burton. "Best he go to the doctor, Miss Thomsen."

Martha helped Burton sit upright. Pressing the cloth tightly against his cut, she turned to Key.

"I can handle this. Your man hit him deliberately."

Shaking his head in protest, the forklift driver raised both hands, proclaiming his innocence.

"I never saw him, mon! As God is my witness."

Key frowned at the couple. "I warned you to be careful. Accidents happen all the time in the yard. How bad is it?"

Though conscious, Burton's pain was obvious. Key ordered two workers to help the minister to his feet. Martha kept the compress in place. Squealing tires on pavement drew the crowd's attention.

Suddenly, their cabbie, Hollis appeared at Burton's side and reached for his arm. "Lord, what happen to the pastor?"

Martha looked past Hollis, glowering at the circle of laborers. "An accident. Help him to the car, please! We have to get him back to Faithtown immediately."

Her eyes aimed at Key. "We'll report this to the police."

Unruffled, Key volunteered, "I'll call them myself straight away. Anything the pastor needs let me know. We'll make it right."

"Not likely," Martha muttered under her breath.

Hobbling to the waiting taxi with Burton between them, Hollis and Martha helped settle Burton in the back seat. She climbed in beside him.

"Samuel," she said, "hold this bandage tight against your head. It's important to keep the pressure steady." Eyes closed, he nodded.

Hollis squeezed behind the wheel and turned to them. "We can take him quick to the doc, Miss. He fix him up right."

Scowling, Martha snarled, "If you mean Singh, I'm not taking him to some hack! Get us to the ferry," she ordered. The cabbie shrugged and raced to the marina.

CHAPTER 26

After leaving Winthrop's estate, McKay idled his boat in green swells and changed from his policeman's uniform to khaki pants and shirt. When he reached New Zion Harbor, he circled Winthrop's yacht twice, screening his reconnaissance by weaving at wake speed between sailboats anchored nearby.

The Green Turtle Two was a gleaming white ninety-four-foot Broward with classic lines dominated by a superstructure lined with tinted windows. Two domed radars and a small forest of antennae crowned the bridge.

On the top deck, a twenty-five-foot rigid inflatable was lashed next to two wave runners and sailboards. Obviously well cared for—the boat screamed serious money for any casual boater with hull envy. Tethered to a ship's ladder on the yacht's starboard side was a large runabout. The dark cabin windows gave no hint of life. Throttling back, McKay gently nosed alongside the ladder. A muscular black crewman in sunglasses, turquoise T-shirt and white shorts appeared at the rail. He waved.

"Constable McKay, come aboard. Skipper's expecting you."

The crewman came down the ladder, caught a tossed line and slipped two rubber fenders between the ladder and McKay's boat. The mate pointed topside. McKay climbed the ladder and stepped onto the polished deck. The main cabin door opened and a barrel-chested man, dressed like the crewman came forward.

"I'm Mikos," he said.

The captain fit McKay's stereotype of Greek seamen— deeply tanned, short, wiry black hair and pale green eyes. Flashing a broad, perfect white smile, Mikos thrust out a calloused hand. The greeting was polite but warm and McKay liked the man immediately.

"Good of you to come," said Mikos. "Mister Winthrop radioed me you'd be by today. He said I was to treat you as though you were family. So, how can I help you?"

McKay followed the captain to the rail and leaned against it. "Do you remember a Virgil Livingston crewing for you?"

Mikos furrowed his brow. "Livingston. Livingston. No, can't say that name means anything." The captain shrugged, then smiled again.

Tugging the dead man's picture from his windbreaker, McKay handed it to Mikos and studied his expression. A blank. Mikos held the picture for a moment.

"No, this face is not familiar to me. I select the crew, but I didn't hire this man." He handed the photo to McKay. "Is he in some kind of trouble?"

"You might say that. What about your crew? Would they have known him?"

"Not possible." The smile was still there. "There's only Jasper, my first mate, Walter, Teddy and Philip aboard today. I've hired everyone who's worked the boat for the last five years. You could ask them if you'd like."

"How long have you been with the Winthrops, Captain?"

"Eight years, actually." Mikos gazed across the harbor. "I hired on for a summer charter in the Mediterranean one year. Afterwards, they offered me a job piloting their boat between the Bahamas and the east coast. Care to see her? She's a beauty. Built in '85. Really one of a kind."

Curious, McKay agreed. He followed Mikos below into the stern section. Two massive 1,200 horsepower Detroit diesels, sharing space with an industrial-sized washer and dryer, crowded an immaculate engine room. A generator's faint hum filled the air. Crew quarters, forward of the engine room, were plain but clean. One passageway was decorated with framed pictures of trophy fish hoisted by guests and crew. McKay counted four bunks with privacy curtains. A small, fold-up mess table with bench seating sat opposite a utilitarian galley located between a water closet and storage lockers.

A separate stateroom belonging to the captain completed the crew's quarters.

Mikos led him forward to four luxurious guest staterooms, each with its own water closet.

Continuing down a short passageway to a foyer amidships, Mikos opened a door to the master suite. Mirrored bulkheads, teak dressers, soft lighting and elegant furnishings spoke of someone with rich tastes. Thick satin quilts covered a king-sized bed. The suite's water closet, with his and hers vanities, included a large tub and shower.

Mikos next led McKay up a narrow, circular stairway leading to the wheelhouse with its array of gauges, dials, throttles and wheel. A laptop computer on a chart table glowed with an image of the U.S. east coast, the screen plotted with waypoint markers. "We're preparing for the return to Boston," said the captain tapping the laptop. He reached in front of McKay and hit a key. The screen went blank.

"Everything's done by computer now, you know. Even sailing."

Behind the bridge, they passed through a spacious galley on the way to the dining room.

A crewman appeared and whispered in the captain's ear. Nodding, Mikos dismissed him and resumed the tour.

"This is the main cabin. The Winthrops entertain here."

Eight leather chairs flanked a polished mahogany table dominating the salon. Serving cabinets ran the length of both bulkheads, their crystal and porcelain contents behind etched glass doors. Two gigantic sea turtle shells hung on opposite walls.

"Those give the boat her name," said Mikos. "Oh, and I believe they were caught when it was still legal." Both men chuckled.

Beyond the dinning area, an octagonal gaming table with rows of colored chips and cards occupied one corner, a leather bar with anchored stools, the other. A plush curving sectional sofa faced a mammoth plasma TV mounted on the paneled bulkhead. Mikos gestured around the salon.

"Care to see the flying bridge and party deck topside?"

McKay declined. He had seen enough.

"Well, then, what else can I do for you? Mister Winthrop said to answer any questions you had." Motioning to the doorway, Mikos held out his hand and McKay shook it.

"Thanks for your time, Captain. Quite an impressive boat. I'll be off now."

"Back to fighting crime in Faithtown, eh?" The Greek laughed and they returned to the main deck. McKay was surprised to find Sergeant Newton waiting for them.

Jericho Island's senior policeman touched his hat's brim. "Would you excuse us, Captain?"

"Of course." Mikos nodded to a crewman coiling line out of earshot near the stern, "Call me if these gentlemen need me." He retreated to the salon.

McKay jammed hands in his pockets and waited for Newton to speak.

The sergeant stared across the anchorage, his voice even. "McKay, what are you doing here, on this boat, in my harbor, on my watch?"

"Following up leads, Sergeant."

"In my back yard, mon?" Newton huffed. "Why didn't you call me and tell me what you needed. Just what are you looking for?" Newton tucked his hat under an arm and straightened against the rail, waiting for an explanation. McKay didn't back down.

"I want to know who that young man who died was, Sergeant. Remember, he washed up on my beach, not yours."

Rebuffed, Newton tried another tack. "Okay. Listen, you find out, let me know. But you in my jurisdiction now, mon. It's professional courtesy. If we turn up anything on this young man, I'll call you. Fair enough?"

McKay forced a smile. "Absolutely, Sergeant. We done here? I need to get back to Faithtown." He moved to the ship's ladder.

Newton called after him. "You know, McKay, regulations might say you've already breached several minor violations—like being out of uniform and pursuing frivolous complaints."

Looking down at his cap and then back at McKay, Newton continued. "And you ought be careful you don't find yourself committing a major violation, too. Like insubordination or," Newton scowled, "making anonymous communications to possible witnesses. And what are you doing out of uniform anyway?"

McKay, hands on the rail, glanced down at his outfit, shrugging. "I didn't want to attract too much attention when I came calling, Sergeant."

Newton waved him off. "Well, you look like a nobody, coming round the Winthrop boat dressed like that." The New Zion cop kept his eyes on McKay as he climbed down to his boat.

Untying his line, McKay glanced up at Newton. "As long as we're reciting regulations, Sergeant, it would be good to remember Rule Number Seventeen, Major Violations."

Newton's blank stare pleased McKay. He stepped behind his console.

"Knowingly making or signing any false entry or statement or document."

Newton stiffened. McKay fired his engine and began to back away.

"Just remember who's in charge," Newton bellowed.

McKay ignored him. Smiling to himself, he felt Newton's eyes on his back as he pointed his bow toward Faithtown. *That should give you something to think about.*

Newton stood at the rail, angrily tapping his cap on the polished wood. Behind him, the main cabin's door opened and Mikos joined him on deck. Newton followed McKay's wake across the harbor. Still fuming, he faced Mikos. "What did he ask about?"

"He asked if a Virgil Livingston had ever worked *The Green Turtle Two*."

"And did the man ever work for you?"

"Not that I can remember, Sergeant."

Newton sneered, shaking his head slowly at the horizon. "He's too damn persistent, that mon."

"He's a cop. Maybe a good one." Mikos turned back to survey New Zion's harbor. "He's asking questions. Isn't that what your profession does?"

Newton sniffed. "He's out of his jurisdiction. New Zion's my district. Shouldn't stick his head where it don't belong."

CHAPTER 27

"Faithtown Police, this is Scrubs, come in."

McKay barely heard the voice. Between the radio's low volume and the engine's steady growl, he had to strain to make out the voice. Leaning over his console, he played with the volume knob. The call came again, clearer this time—Martha. *Scrubs* was her call sign when she was needed past regular clinic hours. He dropped his speed. The Yamaha purred. Her urgent voice became clearer.

"Faithtown Police, this is Scrubs. Come in, please."

McKay keyed the transmission button. "Faithtown Police."

Martha's voice came back immediately. "Meet me on One-Four."

"Going to One-Four." McKay twirled the dial and turned up the volume. At the same time, he pulled back on the throttle and slowed to let his boat drift in the swells.

"Faithtown Police, go ahead."

A rush of static crackled and then Martha's voice again—tense.

"Mac, we had an accident. Our friend is hurt. How quickly can you get here?"

McKay's stomach tightened. Calculating his distance to the shoreline, he called back. "Just passing Angel Rock. I'll be at the dock in twenty minutes."

"Hurry."

"On the way. Back to One-Six." He heard Martha key the mike in response.

McKay pushed the silver throttle forward. In response, his boat leaped from the water, engine snarling in an explosion of white water as he coaxed all the power he could from the big Yamaha.

In twenty minutes, he rounded the rocky point near Faithtown's harbor. It took all his control to appear unconcerned as he dropped to wake speed and entered the anchorage. He performed the obligatory waves to outbound boats and turned toward his dock.

No Martha in sight—just a skinny black kid straddling a rusty bike.

In one motion, McKay dropped the anchor, nosed into the dock, and killed the engine. He tossed his bowline to the child as the boat shouldered its way between two larger whalers hogging the only available ladder. He climbed the rungs and checked the mooring line.

"Thanks, Timothy. You seen Miss Martha?"

The youngster pointed toward town. "She said to tell you to go to Reverend Samuel's house soon as you got here."

He patted the child's shoulder. "Good job. Thanks."

The boy beamed and McKay hurried along the wooden dock. Grinning over his shoulder, the youngster passed him on the bicycle. McKay pushed his pace.

Lillian met him at the door with a hug, concern on her face. She led him down the hall to the study where Burton lay stretched on a couch with a fresh four-inch square bandage on his forehead.

He raised a hand when McKay entered. Martha came from the kitchen with a plastic bag of ice wrapped in a towel. She went to McKay and embraced him, sobbing softly as he held her. Lillian took the ice pack from Martha. Burton groaned and turned on his side to face the couple.

Gently prying Martha from him, McKay held her shoulders. "What happened?"

"Samuel was almost killed today," she said. She sank into an armchair. McKay knelt beside her, his hand on her arm. She said, "We had just finished talking to this Dictionary Key person and were headed back to catch a taxi when it happened."

She paused and composed herself, anger flashing in her eyes. "It was deliberate, Mac."

McKay nodded at Burton, who returned a wan smile. "Where's Jonathan?" said McKay.

"Making the last run," Lillian said. "He should be here shortly. Why?"

"Just asking, that's all. I want everyone accounted for."

Lillian cocked her head. "Are we, in some sort of danger, Jeremiah?"

"I don't really know. Accidents can happen. It could have be…"

Martha cut him off. "Coincidence? I don't think so."

Weary, McKay stood, beginning to sense he was out of his depth. He craved a drink. It would have to wait. He looked down at Martha. "How bad is he?"

She didn't answer. Instead, she rose and asked Lillian. "Would it be all right to make some tea?"

The older woman answered. "Of course. Shall I help?"

Martha waved her off. "No. I'll do it. Stay with Samuel."

She nodded at McKay and he obediently followed her into the kitchen where she filled the teapot and placed it on the stove. Arms folded, she leaned against the sink to face him.

"Jonathan made a quick trip back here between ferry runs. I had to put six stitches in Samuel's scalp," she said bitterly. "He might have a mild concussion. He should rest for the next few days."

McKay put his arm around her shoulders. "I can call him off, Martha. Just say the word. You two have done enough."

She laughed. "You might want to talk to Samuel. He's the one who put his neck on the line. Literally, it turns out." She winced at her joke. A hiss of steam prompted her to turn off the burner and empty the kettle into a porcelain teapot. She tossed in two bags and replaced the lid. While she searched cupboards for cups and saucers, McKay folded his arms, stared at the floor.

"None of this would have happened if I hadn't asked you both to do my job."

Martha set the cups on the counter. "Mac, we were just asking some questions about a dead man, that's all." She continued. "Every instinct tells me what happened to Samuel was not an accident but a warning."

She arranged the cups and saucers on a painted wooden tray and steadied herself.

"Someone is saying, 'Stay away.' You're the one to make the call about what we do next."

McKay deflated. "But I mean, what's the point? I'm not sure I think this whole thing is worth pursuing." He folded his arms. "It may be a bunch of nothing questions and nothing answers."

"Leading to what conclusion?" she said. He shrugged.

Adding a sugar bowl, spoons and a small pitcher of milk to her cargo, she ordered, "Bring some napkins." Grabbing a handful, McKay trailed her down the hall to the study where Burton was sitting upright, Lillian beside him, holding his hand. Martha set the tray on a table in front of the couch and sat next to the wounded man.

McKay hovered over the seated pair and started to speak but Burton held up his hand.

"I've been thinking, Jeremiah," he said. "Maybe Martha is right. This wasn't an accident. It was a strong warning, one hard to miss."

"Go on," said McKay.

"Well, I believe," Burton continued, "that we can turn what was meant for evil, if that's what this was, into something good."

Here it comes. The sermon, thought McKay. "Leave it to you, Samuel."

"Seriously," said Burton, "I really think The Lord used this *accident* as a way of telling us what we're up against." He managed a weak smile. "Don't you see?" Frowning at his audience's lack of understanding, Burton tried again. "The closer one gets to truth, the more one encounters opposition. It's a simple theological law. Don't you agree?"

Martha glanced at McKay, then Lillian, who was as puzzled as the pair.

Irritated, Burton said, "Look, there's a point to this. When we press for the facts in this case, we're stymied at every turn." Animated, he went on. "What seems logical to us, based on evidence, turns out to have a very different answer from what we see before us."

Burton attempted to rise. "Help me up, Jeremiah."

Steadied by McKay, he wobbled to a wall near the couch. A large white board, covered with messages scribbled in marker, hung at eye level. Wiping the easel clean with a cloth, he picked up two markers, one red, the other black, and began writing in large, bold black letters.

"First, a body is found, possible drowning." Under that, he wrote in red. "Cause of death, gunshot wounds."

Leaning unsteadily, he turned to Martha. "Am I right about that?" She nodded.

He next wrote in black. "New Zion autopsy calls it drowning, but we..."

He switched to red, "know it's a shooting, possibly murder." Back to black.

"We find a name—Virgil Livingston. Two witnesses, one is family."

Then in red, "To everyone else he's apparently an unknown."

Burton's audience followed every word, intrigued now as he scrawled in black again. "Eyewitness says he worked for Island Imports, yet..."

The red marker moved across the board. "They claim he's never worked there. Are you getting the picture?" His three listeners nodded as one. McKay pulled a stool nearer to the board.

Burton with black ink now. "Might have crewed on Winthrop yacht, yet..."

Another red scrawl. "Owner and captain say, no."

Finishing with a flourish by printing a large red question mark, Burton was triumphant. Marker in hand, he sagged on the sofa. Martha offered a cup of tea to Samuel as Lillian poured three more.

Studying the easel, McKay read the list, hands behind his back, pondering Burton's theory aloud. "I grant everything you've said. Laid out like this it's quite interesting." He paused in thought.

"But it's all circumstantial," Martha said.

McKay was surprised. "Really? You're the one who said there seemed to be some kind of conspiracy."

"I just thought all the excuses, the half-truths we were hearing, were too hard to swallow," she said. "Still, it's your call, Mac."

Lillian spoke up. "I do think there is something wrong with this picture. Everything that's happened is so...I don't know."

"Odd?" volunteered her husband.

"Yes, Samuel, odd." Lillian warmed to her idea. "We should pray about this. That's what we should do, I mean. Then we should talk to the authorities at some point."

McKay faced Lillian. "The only problem with going to the people in charge is that they may not be trustworthy, or they may not think it's serious enough to investigate."

"Despite my gut feeling, it's still pretty circumstantial," admitted Martha.

Lillian said, "Regardless, I think we need to pray about this."

A minute of awkward silence passed. McKay stared at the floor. Martha forced a smile.

"I know what you're thinking," Lillian said. "I'm not offended. But at least I want Samuel to pray about his involvement with this, this situation."

Rubbing a hand over his forehead, McKay rolled his eyes. Assuming the meeting was over, he stretched his arms, nearly touching the ceiling. "I suggest we call it a day."

Lillian stood, reaching for McKay. "I don't know any other way to decide what we should do, Jeremiah."

He smiled at her. "I know, Lillian. I don't dismiss your suggestion, but we have a set of questions and answers that don't add up, with or without God's help."

Burton's wife smiled. "I'll trust my Savior for an answer by tomorrow."

McKay shrugged. "Okay, I can wait. This case is not my first priority."

"What is, Mac?" Martha said. "Lost luggage or a missing boat?"

"That can be important to some people."

"I'm sorry," she said, instantly regretting her comment.

"No offense taken, Miss Thomsen."

Burton spoke from the couch. "Let's not turn on each other over this thing. It's important to pray, to support one another and find a solution with God's help." His comments pacified the room.

Martha settled on the couch and warned him. "Remember, Samuel. You are to rest for at least a day or two." She turned to Lillian. "Don't let him take any ferry runs for a week. Promise me?"

Burton's wife laughed. "He's stubborn, Martha. But if you ask him to stay put, he might do it."

The nurse waved her finger at the reclining figure. "Well then, I'm telling you to let your body heal for a few days."

Burton chuckled. "Would you call that laying low?"

The four laughed. After helping Lillian clear the dishes, Martha and McKay said good night and walked home.

"I was a little rough on you back there. Sorry."

He smiled. "Don't be too quick with the apology. You might be right. Maybe my priority is off center. Until you put together some of the evidence, I was content to let things slide a bit."

More silence. When they neared the center of town, she stopped to face him.

She said, "I'm still planning to make that trip to Florida with the Russells. Maybe your friend there can give us some advice."

"First things first. Let's wait until Samuel heals." He softened. "That could have been you with the cracked skull."

She smiled. "And would that have upset you, Constable?"

"I don't like to think what I would have done to those people, Martha."

"That's nice. I like that sentiment. Hold that thought, will you?"

She squeezed his hand, kissed him quickly, and then was gone.

CHAPTER 28

A rare mid-week rain filled Faithtown cisterns, delighting residents but frustrating tourists. For the rest of the week the commonplace replaced the excitement of the previous days. To McKay, seven days seemed an eternity. He pushed Virgil Livingston's death from his mind and turned to Faithtown's routine. Burton was healing. Martha visited daily to monitor his recovery. Lillian fussed over her husband while their son easily handled ferry runs during his father's absence.

Meetings between the conspirators were suspended until Burton was judged strong enough to join the discussions. Martha made final arrangements for her upcoming Jacksonville trip. McKay sent an email message to his FBI contact in Florida. With the exception of Burton's injury, Martha also felt a sense of normalcy return.

At the beginning of the second week, McKay met a charter carrying a locked satchel of cash for the Faithtown branch of Barclay's Bank. The New Zion courier's escort was Corporal Simmons. Both armed policemen met on the public dock, flanking the teller with her black valise case as she walked the narrow sidewalk to the whitewashed bank building. Once inside, with the money safe in the small vault, Simmons relaxed.

"How you doing with your investigation?" he asked, as he and McKay lounged on the bank's shaded porch.

"Which one?" McKay replied disingenuously. "I've got two stolen boats, some missing motors, and a thirsty thief helping himself to beer from Bethel's Grocery after hours."

Missing the irony, Simmons said, "I meant the boy who washed up on the beach ten days ago."

"Ah, that one. Well, I've turned it over to your department. Sergeant Newton's running the investigation now, isn't he?"

"S'pose so," said the younger man. "They buried that boy last Sunday."

That was news to McKay. He filed away the information to share later with his friends. "Huh, maybe that will be the end of it, eh?"

"I guess," answered Simmons. "Well, I got to get back."

McKay walked the corporal to the launch and waited as he climbed aboard. Once Simmons ducked into the cabin, the boat pulled away from the dock, bound for New Zion. McKay reluctantly headed to his office to face Sarah Cameron, but his luck was holding. He had fed her scraps about the progress of the case during the week. True to form, she had spread them around Faithtown, but her closed door was posted with a sign promising a return in thirty minutes. A small pile of stamped postcards protruded from under the closed door. McKay pushed them forward with his shoe so she couldn't miss them and spent the next half-hour with overdue paperwork. He called Burton's home, only to hear Lillian say her husband was resting. McKay promised to stop by that afternoon.

Later, detouring along the waterfront to avoid running into Sarah Cameron, he stopped to exchange pleasantries with a knot of visitors loitering at the gate to the Methodist church. From there, he strolled to Faithtown's clinic, rapping on the doorway as he entered.

Emerging from the back room in a white lab coat thrown over green scrubs, Martha peeled off a pair of latex gloves and tossed them in a wastebasket. She smiled at him as she rolled a chair to her desk. "Well, Officer McKay, what brings you by this morning?"

McKay removed his hat, wiped his forehead with the back of his hand, and dragged a folding chair next to her. "Just making the rounds, Martha. How are you?"

Winking, she poked a thumb over her shoulder at the side room, whispering, "Put some sutures on a nasty head wound and handed out the usual quota of pills."

She wrote something on a sheet of paper and snapped it on a clipboard.

"Who's your patient?"

She tapped his hand. "Can't say. Doctor-patient privileges, you know." She giggled softly. "Jason Sawyer. Fell off his bike on his way into town."

Raising an eyebrow, McKay made a tippling motion at his mouth. Martha pursed her lips and grinned. There was rustling sound from the side room and Sawyer, a retired boat-builder, showed, gingerly stroking a large white bandage on his pink, balding dome wreathed in wispy white hair.

"Morning, Mac."

McKay nodded to Sawyer. "Morning, Jason. Looks like you took a fall."

"Yes, and I wasn't drinking..." He paused, showing an enormous toothless grin, "for once." Both men laughed. Ignoring them, Martha signed her report with quick strokes. Sawyer shuffled past her toward the doorway and turned to bow. "Thanks, Martha. You did a fine job."

Radiating sympathy for the old man, she looked up. "Check with me in a day or two, Mister Jason. And don't forget to change that bandage tomorrow night."

He smiled, holding up a packaged dressing she had given him. Martha waved him out the door. Sawyer wheeled away on the very instrument that had landed him in the clinic.

Martha leaned over and placed her hand on McKay's arm. "Nice to see you laugh." She smiled. "Have you talked to Samuel today?"

"I called before I came over," he said. "Lillian says he's resting. I'll go by later." She told him she had also agreed to visit the Burton home after closing the clinic that afternoon.

McKay paced. "That cop from New Zion, Corporal Simmons, came over this morning."

She looked up, suspicion in her eyes. "What's he doing in Faithtown?"

McKay studied the harbor from the clinic windows. "Just the routine Barclay's Bank delivery. He said they buried Virgil Livingston."

Martha said, "How convenient, huh?" She spent the next few minutes tapping at a keyboard, entering her morning patient's visit into a health statistics file. McKay watched a large yacht negotiate the mouth of the harbor on its way to the fuel dock.

Martha joined him. "Oh, I almost forgot," she said, "there was an email from your FBI friend in Florida." She followed his gaze to the fuel barge and continued. "He said he'd meet us at the airport and give the Russells and me a ride to Mayo."

"Good. You still want to talk to him, Martha?" He searched her green eyes for reluctance but found none.

"I'm determined to do it, Mac."

They stared at the harbor, not looking at each other. She finally spoke. "Let's put it this way. After what happened to Samuel I feel that you..." She corrected herself. "We need to see just how far this whole thing goes." She stroked his arm and went back to her desk. "Maybe your Florida contact can help us. See something we can't." She leaned over her paperwork. "Remember, all that evil needs to exist is for good men to do nothing. Or something like that." She began putting away files.

He turned from the window. "I've heard that before. Who said that?"

"I did." She laughed.

McKay snatched his hat from the wall and shook it at her as he headed out the door. "All right, next week it is, Martha. I'll meet you at Samuel's later."

She batted her eyes. "I'd like it if you'd stop by and walk over with me."

CHAPTER 29

Dawn revealed a horizon streaked with thin blood-red clouds. A single brush stroke of gold light shone just above the ocean's edge. In near darkness, three figures bundled against morning's chill climbed down a ladder onto the stern of Burton's idling ferry. Once inside the cabin, the trio huddled together, suitcases at their feet. They were the only passengers as the ferry nosed from the dock and maneuvered past darkened sailboats anchored in Faithtown harbor. The lighthouse's powerful beam swept the sky as the boat cleared the harbor and knifed across a dark glassy sea.

In the distance, the low outline of Jericho Island showed signs of life. Headlights bobbed toward a larger cluster of bright lights marking New Zion. Red warning lights on twin radio towers blinked against an inky sky. The ferry raced along, its running lights winking in spray.

Inside the cabin, Martha Thomsen used her cellphone's flashlight to reassure her companions that their airline tickets were in her possession. When they were satisfied, she clicked off the light, plunging the cabin into darkness. Talking was impossible above the engines rumbling. For the next twenty minutes, the sky above the wake grew increasingly lighter. A sliver of sun peeked above the horizon as the ferry made the crossing without encountering another boat.

When the ferry slowed, Martha stood, peering from the cabin window at New Zion harbor. She heard Jonathan radio a request for a taxi to meet them at the landing near the Queen's Highway. Static mingled with a promise of a ride to the airport.

Some enterprising soul up early, she thought.

Martha went forward, put an arm around Burton's son as he studied channel markers leading to the dock, and whispered in his ear. "Tell your daddy I'll be thinking of him while I'm away."

On shore, a van pulled up, its headlights throwing long beams across the mangroves and dark water. A silhouette left the idling taxi and stepped in front of the lights. Jonathan backed the stern against the dock pilings with a soft bump. He flipped a switch, bathing dock and passengers in light.

Hefting the suitcases, young Burton moved quickly to grip the ladder at the stern with one hand while heaving the luggage up to the waiting driver. He held the boat against the dock as exhaust churned the dark coffee-colored water.

"God bless, Martha," he said as the nurse climbed to the pier.

She leaned to help Emilie Russell up the ladder. The sick woman's husband bundled his wife into the back of the taxi. Once Jonathan heard doors slam and saw the car back from the dock, he switched off the floodlight and spun the wheel to port. Easing the engines into gear, he took the ferry back into the channel between two rows of skinny white-tipped poles. With the engines opened wide, the hull skipped across slate-colored swells. Just as he gained Faithtown, the sun's orange disk broke free of the horizon.

Despite the hour Martha was glad she had insisted on the early morning start. New Zion's tiny terminal would change into typical chaos before long. At the airport, she checked the Russell's bags along with hers, got their boarding passes, and bought her first coffee of the day. Taxis filled with early birds began arriving in the parking lot across from customs.

Wrapped in two sweaters to stay warm, frail Emilie Russell squirmed in a futile attempt to get comfortable in the hard-plastic chair. Her husband Nathan, his stoic expression unchanged, sat beside her, holding her hand to calm her. After attempts at small talk sputtered and died, Martha stepped outside in morning's pink light.

On the tarmac, a single-engine plane coughed into life. The clanking sound of a baggage cart drew her attention. A burly young black man in grease-stained blue overalls hooked the yellow wagon to a battered tractor and moved slowly, stacking suitcases and coolers in an unhurried rhythm. Martha spotted her party's baggage at the bottom of the pile. A Bahamasair pilot strolled through the terminal and stopped at the airline's counter to flirt with two women on duty. The agents ignored him. Retrieving a clipboard from the desk, he flipped through the paperwork, scribbling notes as he went.

An hour passed. More taxis pulled up, disgorging tourists and luggage. There was a family of redheads, several fishing parties of portly, sunburned men with long rod cases and coolers of trophy fish.

A beautiful, self-absorbed young couple scrambled from a van, kissing and clinging to each other.

Martha nodded to several local residents, knowing the faces of those she had treated in her clinic. *Probably quarterly West Palm Beach shopping trips or family visits*, she thought.

As the sun rose higher, the morning heat made itself felt despite a welcomed breeze and the terminal began to fill. Shortly before nine, a loudspeaker crackled into life, announcing boarding for Bahamasair's first Florida flight of the day. Martha tossed her coffee cup and prodded the Russells awake. Shuffling across the concrete apron, they boarded first, struggling up the narrow metal ladder.

Martha settled into an aisle seat across from the Russells and reached for Emilie's bony hand to reassure her. When the last passenger squeezed aboard the full flight, the stocky baggage handler handed a sheaf of papers to the bored flight attendant. Glancing down the aisle, the airport worker did a head count, nodded to the crew, and backed out the door with his clipboard. The plane's starboard engine whined and fired, belching blue smoke before turning in a steady hum. As the cabin hatch locked shut, the port engine roared into life.

The plane taxied to the runway and rolled along a paved corridor among the scrawny pines to where the concrete ended. Jerking to a stop, the aircraft pivoted for takeoff, the pilot gunning the engines. Martha glanced at Emilie Russell. Deathly pale, the old woman shut her eyes, her thin lips moving in prayer. Holding hands, her husband stared out the window, expressionless.

The plane shot down the runway. Pine forest on both sides became a green blur. Lurching from the asphalt in a steep climb, the aircraft banked northeast over the sea. Martha fished in her purse for a small plastic bag. Her hand felt the outline of an index card and two Polaroid pictures. Reassured, she sat back, not hearing the flight attendant's droning instructions. Closing her eyes, she drifted into sleep for the flight's duration.

As the Bahamasair plane grew smaller against the morning sky, the muscular baggage handler drove the empty cart back to the terminal and parked. He punched keys on his cell phone, got his party and spoke rapidly.

"That's right, mon. First flight out this morning." He listened and then replied. "Yeah, mon, it was her. Had two old people with her. That's right." He nodded, smiled at what was being said, and hung up. There was more baggage to load and the New Zion terminal was filling fast.

CHAPTER 30

A whaler slipped unnoticed into Faithtown harbor. A working boat, it was piled with coils of old rope, buckets, fishing nets and scrap lumber. Shredded straw hat in place, an old man guided the battered, paint-streaked boat along the docks lining the harbor's east end. With outboard engine purring, the anonymous whaler passed towering yachts and sleek polished hulls of daysailers. Cranking the wheel left, the helmsman took his old whaler toward Burton's moored ferry.

Gliding up to the wooden pier, he killed the engine. Jonathan was wiping the water taxi's windows when he first noticed the small boat. He waited as the old man heaved himself up the ladder and looped a line over the nearest piling. The little man was uneasy, hesitant. Jonathan put down his rag.

"Can I help you?"

Touching the brim of his hat, the visitor asked, "This Reverend Burton's place?"

Jonathan squinted, shading his eyes, scrutinizing the man on the dock. "Yes," he said, "but he's not well. Can't see anyone right now. Can I help?"

A spare smile appeared on the lined ebony face. "He'll see me, I'm sure. Tell him Nathaniel Rolle come to see him." The man hooked his hands on his belt and gazed at the house in the trees.

"Very important I see him. "He was obviously going to wait.

Jonathan tossed the rag and climbed from the ferry. "I'll tell him, Mister Rolle. But he's still mending. Might not be able to talk right now."

Nodding, the man was determined. "I know. Please, tell him I'm here."

Burton's son started up the path toward the house with the visitor following a short distance behind. Beneath a spreading banyan tree, the stranger claimed a stone bench in the yard and sat in the shade. He removed his hat, slowly turning it in nervous hands.

Lillian emerged from the house, followed by her son. She walked toward the bench. The old man rose. She recognized him immediately and extended her hand, smiling, "Nathaniel, isn't it?"

They shook hands. "Yes, ma'am. I come to talk to the pastor. Important I see him."

She touched his arm. "I'll bring him to you. The air will do him good."

She started for the house and turned. "You do know that he was badly hurt in New Zion. Some sort of accident."

Rolle nodded. "Yes, I know that. Everybody knows about it."

She left them there—her son lingering at a tree, Rolle at the bench, patient and uncomplaining.

The back door opened, Burton filling its frame and Lillian behind him. He walked slowly, a small bandage on his head, and joined Rolle at the bench. They clasped hands. Burton sat beside his guest and spoke to his son keeping vigil at the tree.

"It's all right, Jonathan. Go back to the boat. You have a run to make."

The younger Burton retreated down the path to the pier. "He's been taking the ferry runs for me since this," said Burton, touching his bandaged scalp. "Don't know what I would do without him."

Rolle nodded. "Pastor, I know how you was hurt. Maybe you think it was an accident, but I tell you it wasn't like that."

Burton shook his head slowly. "Yes, I know. I think it was a warning. I asked too many questions in New Zion."

Rolle leaned forward, resting his elbows on his knees, wiry scarred forearms showing. "That's what the boys say."

Burton paused. "Who?"

"The boys working at Island Imports." The little man grew more serious. "They say you was nosing around where you don't belong."

Burton grimaced, smiled and gently touched the bandage. "They may be right. But the Lord was with me and I walked away, didn't I?"

Frowning, Rolle said, "Nobody ought to treat you like that. A pastor. It's not right to mess with God's anointed. Bible says so, right?"

Burton patted the man's arm and thanked him. The moment passed, and with it, Rolle's anger. They both smiled and the small man straightened, gripping his knees with roughened hands. His head inclined toward the pastor.

"Reason I come to see you," he said, "is they be getting ready to be doing some bad business at that place."

"Island Imports?" said Burton.

"Yes. That's right."

"Explain that for me, Brother Rolle."

"See, they building a big boathouse right near the warehouse. It sits right on the water. Big enough to bring in those fancy boats. You know the kind—forty-foot with the biggest engines you can find." Letting the image sink into Burton's mind, he continued. "Only one reason you want a place like that, Pastor Samuel."

"Drugs?"

Rolle shook his head in agreement.

"How do you know all this, Nathaniel?"

"Young man, name of Thomas McIntosh, he hire me and another brother to help him finish all the cement work. We work only around closing time. We been working to dawn these last few days."

"How long before you finish the job?"

"Tomorrow, maybe next day. We supposed to frame a deck and storehouse right on top the boathouse. When we put those doors on that place, you don't even know it's there unless you look real hard." Rolle made a sweeping motion with a thin hand. "Anybody bringing a boat in there just cruise right under the dock into the boathouse. That door come down, you don't never see them again."

"But it's not illegal to build something like that, Nathaniel. Any honest business can be turned to evil. But that doesn't mean a man doesn't have the right to build a new boathouse."

It was a thin argument and Rolle demolished it.

"You know how drugs been coming in now. Used to be bad a while back. Then it got quiet in the islands. You know that, right?"

Burton nodded. Beginning in the Seventies, drug trafficking had been wide open in the Bahamas. The Out Islands had proved too tempting for the South American cartels. Many isolated cays were sparsely populated. Rarely patrolled coastlines made perfect havens for the drug runners. When American law enforcement began helping the government turn the cays upside down, the cartels withdrew to safer havens. But today's money was easy, and Bahamians were still in the market. Burton knew Rolle was right. Circumstantial evidence. But strong enough to raise the suspicions of a simple laborer. He needed more facts. *McKay should know this*, he thought.

"Why come to me now, Brother Rolle?" Burton asked.

"We have to finish quick. Thomas said to get it all done soon. That's why we been working so hard this way." He held up a bony finger to make a point. "The concrete already set up. We going to take down the wall, let the water in, maybe tomorrow."

"And the deck and shed?" said Burton.

"Three days maybe, then we be finished, Pastor."

"And open for deliveries soon after that, I'll bet," said Burton. "Someone's gone to great lengths to make sure this is hidden from prying eyes. I assume this place will be huge when done."

"Oh, yeah. That's a pretty piece of work. You can store a big boat."

Rolle stretched out his thin arms, drawing a hull in the air. "Ain't nobody going to know what you be doing in there."

He jammed his fist into his palm. "I'm telling you, Pastor, they bringing in that bad stuff."

"I have an idea, Brother Rolle. Let me know if you'd be willing to help."

The two men talked a few minutes more, then rose from the bench, shook hands, and headed to the water's edge. Burton saw Rolle to the dock and waved as the old man stepped into his whaler and cranked the engine into life. In minutes, the little boat had disappeared in the crowded harbor.

Burton returned to his study and dialed McKay's home. No answer. He tried again. Nothing. He dialed the policeman's office. Silence. He decided against using the VHF radio. He knew he would have to act on Rolle's warning, but he hoped McKay might be the one to do it.

Where are you when I need you Jeremiah?

Lillian appeared in the doorway. "What is it, Samuel?"

Frustrated, he looked up from his desk. "I can't locate Jeremiah."

"Try the clinic," she suggested.

"No good," he replied. "Martha's gone to Florida with the Russells, remember?"

She had forgotten. "Well, could he be at the marina?"

Burton didn't hear her. He was remembering his conversation with Rolle. He stood up, suddenly determined. "Lillian, I'm going to make the afternoon New Zion run with Jonathan."

She was concerned. "Are you absolutely sure, Samuel?"

He smiled and touched his forehead, the bandage thick beneath his fingers. "Yes, it's about time. I've been cooped up here for ten days and I'm feeling much better."

Lillian put her hand against his chest, "But Martha said..."

Burton grasped her hand with both of his. "Yes, I remember what Martha said, but I'm feeling back to my old self. I think it's time to get back out on the water."

From the corner of his eye he spotted his son approaching. "Besides, Jonathan needs a break from the routine." She started to protest, but he held up his hand. The screen door opened, and their son stood in the kitchen.

"I'll be with you on the last run later today, Jonathan."

Jonathan reached into the refrigerator. "Martha said you should heal while I handled things."

His father waved a hand in dismissal. "Oh, she told me to get back into the regular runs when I felt good enough. Besides, it's been nearly ten days at least and I'm letting you do all the work."

The youngster poured himself a glass of milk. "I really don't mind."

"I know, but let's try this out today." Lillian shrugged and went into the front room, leaving her men alone to work out the details about manning the ferry shuttle.

His son emptied the glass. "All right, Daddy, if that's what you want to do."

Burton smiled. "Yes," he said. "I'll be down at the dock in ten minutes."

He tried McKay's home and office again. Still no answer. He scribbled a note, stuffed it in an envelope with the policeman's name on it and thought about running it over to him.

Too little time. Instead, he propped the envelope on his desk and told his wife to pass it to McKay should he come by. That done, he changed into khaki trousers, a blue shirt and a pair of deck shoes. He stuffed a set of old work clothes into a nylon bag and grabbed his bright green windbreaker and wide-brimmed straw hat. He called out a goodbye to Lillian and walked to the ferry dock where his son waited.

CHAPTER 31

"What's the purpose of your visit?"

Tinted sunglasses hid the uniformed immigration officer's eyes.

Nodding to the Russells behind her, Martha said, "Medical. Here to visit the Mayo Clinic."

Waving the Russells forward, the agent glanced at the passports without a trace of suspicion as he flipped the pages. "Welcome," he said, mechanically stamping the books. He wagged his finger at the line and barked, "Next."

After retrieving the Russell's passports, Martha led them to the baggage area near the Customs stalls. Baggage spilled onto the revolving rack. She snagged a cart and waited for their bags to appear. Behind Customs, a dog handler chatted with airport policemen as his leashed black Lab sat obediently at his side. The animal studied a line of people working their way through Customs, its big head barely moving. When the Russells and Martha set their bags on the metal counter a bored officer laid hands on the luggage, barely patting the leather. "Anything to declare?" he asked.

"Nothing," answered Martha.

He indicated the older couple with a nod. "You folks together?"

Martha turned to the Russells. "Yes. Appointments at Jacksonville's Mayo," she said.

Flashing a robotic smile, the officer waved them through, bags unopened. She steered the cart toward a deserted bench, the Russells shuffling behind her. After parking the couple with their baggage, she told them, "I'll arrange our ride. Wait until I get back."

Heading for the ground transportation waiting area, Martha stepped outside into thick, warm air. On her right, two courtesy vans spilled people and suitcases on the sidewalk. A trio of smokers wreathed in smoke chatted to her left. She glanced around, unsure. At that moment, a black SUV pulled into view behind the vans and stopped near a crosswalk. The driver's door opened, and a tall, casually dressed man exited. He waved to catch Martha's attention.

"Miss Thomsen." He approached, arm outstretched. "I'm Kent Bryan." She grasped his hand. "I got Mac's email," he said. "From the typing style, I take it he's a latecomer to the wired world."

Martha laughed. "Yes, he's learned to make do with minimum effort. Does his reports by stabbing his keyboard one finger at a time, you know."

The tall man smiled. "Yeah, that sounds like him."

She studied Bryan. In his early forties, tall with gray hair trimmed short, and an easy smile, the federal agent wore a loud Hawaiian shirt and jeans. There was an elegant casualness about him she found attractive.

"Where are the Russells?"

She waved toward the terminal. "Resting inside. Emilie Russell, is not well."

"Cancer, isn't it?" he said with sympathy.

"Yes. We're to see the folks at Mayo."

They walked toward the terminal. "It's kind of you to meet us, Mister Bryan."

"Kent," he corrected her.

She smiled. "All right. Kent it is. Call me Martha."

The doors hissed open and the nurse signaled to the waiting Russells.

"I'll give you a lift to Jacksonville," Bryan said. "When we get them settled, we'll talk."

She nodded. Introductions were made and Bryan pushed the baggage cart to his car at the curb. Martha and the Russells followed.

An imperious, young airport policeman approached the SUV, violation book in hand. When he stopped to speak with Bryan, Martha saw their chauffeur flash a badge at the officer. The cop nodded politely and made a quick retreat to warn lingering cars queued behind. She was impressed by Bryan's quiet air of authority.

Once bags were loaded, Bryan pulled from the curb and joined traffic headed north along the coast. They drove in silence for a few miles. In the rear-view mirror, Martha noticed both Russells had been lulled into sleep. She studied Bryan before speaking.

"May I ask, are you by any chance a Mormon, Kent?"

He laughed. "I've never been asked that question before. No, I'm not Mormon, by the way."

"Mac said you FBI types were all Mormons."

"That's an old rumor from the Hoover days. Sure, some of the guys are, but not me. As for me, I'm a backsliding Baptist, Martha. And you?"

"Raised non-denominational, then spent years as an urban agnostic."

"And now?"

"There's a small church in Faithtown. Mac's former brother-in-law is the pastor. I attend there now. Maybe I've come full circle in that respect."

He glanced at her. "Any other questions?"

"Family?"

"Divorced. Married to the Bureau now. Most of us are." He laughed.

"That's what Mac predicted you would say."

"Well, he's got a good memory. Enjoyed working with him. Quite a guy." He spoke wistfully. "Would like to team up again, under different circumstances, of course."

"Of course," she replied.

They drove in silence, the coastal highway, cars and trucks a blur around them. She directed Bryan to the Marriott near the Mayo clinic. He helped with the luggage as she registered. After a quick lunch and polite conversation, the Russells excused themselves and retired to their room. Appointments were set for the afternoon and Martha suggested Emilie nap before the endless rounds.

She rejoined Kent Bryan in the lobby. They strolled outside to a large gushing fountain. "Jeremiah said you might help, Agent Bryan."

"Kent. Remember?"

"Yes, Kent. Sorry, I forgot."

"I'll do what I can. Mac said you were on to something and needed a hand."

They found a wooden garden bench in the shade and sat. Martha took the agent back to the beginning and told every detail as she remembered it.

She faced him. "This problem is much too big for him at this point."

At the end of her conversation she pulled a manila envelope from her purse and passed it to him.

Opening the flap, he examined the contents, fingering the shotgun pellets and staring at the photos of the dead man. He held the index card with its fingerprints delicately between thumb and forefinger. "I can do this much for you," he promised. "Tell Mac we'll give the prints a run-through. We'll also pass the pictures around. I have friends at DEA. I can pull some strings. Maybe Interpol might know something."

"That's just what he wanted," she said, relieved.

The agent held up his hand. "That's what I'll try to do. Can't promise that I can deliver on everything. This is all off the books stuff." He carefully put the contents back in the envelope. "What does Mac think this is all about?"

"Drugs," she answered. "He thinks they're starting to show up again."

"They never went away." Bryan shrugged. "We've seen more action lately coming from your direction. Too bad. The Out Islands were…" He corrected himself, "Are such a nice, peaceful place." He recited his history with McKay. The two had cooperated on several investigations into drug running in the Bahamas. New Zion and Kingdom Cay had flirted with the traffic, but it had stalled there and moved north.

It pleased Martha that Bryan seemed to hold McKay in high regard. She smiled and glanced at her watch. "I have to go." They stood. She shook his hand. "We'll be here through mid-week. Call my cell phone or room if you need to reach me."

"You can reach me any time, too," he said scribbling his cell phone number on a business card. "Leave a message or a text and I'll get back to you."

As they walked back to the Marriott entrance, he made one last promise. "We'll see what this adds up to. Tell Mac for me, will you?"

"I will." They shook hands again and he got into his car. In a moment, the black SUV was gone, turning onto San Pablo Road and merging with the traffic streaming in the direction of the Inter-Coastal Highway. Martha strolled into the lobby. Her afternoon would be devoted to navigating the Russells through their Mayo appointments.

Somewhere in McKay's head a phone was ringing. He shifted in the big reclining chair, ignoring the signal. It was the second time his nap had been disturbed. He had shed his policeman's shirt and trousers, draping them over a dining room chair, his shoes placed neatly beside the uniform. Eventually, the ringing stopped.

McKay groped for a half-empty bottle near his right hand. He closed a fist around the bottle's neck and pulled it to the armrest. Raising the bottle, he drained the remaining liquor in two swallows of slow, velvety fire and then set the empty bottle on the carpet in a slow, exaggerated motion. McKay was pleasantly drunk—in a rum-soaked stupor but aware of his surroundings. Finally heaving himself from the chair, he walked unsteadily to the kitchen sink where he braced himself and splashed his face with cold water.

Afternoon shadows crept across the walls. The wind died. Soft chimes from his mariner's clock on the mantel announced the hour. McKay glanced at his watch to be sure. Five o'clock. Time to make a final appearance at his office.

Check the mail on my desk and lock up for the night, he told himself.

He paused, watching minutes tick by on the antique clock's porcelain face. With Martha gone, McKay felt slightly adrift.

Plucking his blue uniform shirt from the cane chair, he hesitated; right arm in midair, then let the fabric drift to the floor. Deciding against the office, McKay shuffled toward his unmade bed and eased himself onto his back, a folded pillow jammed under his head. A ceiling fan spun in a hypnotic circle, lulling him to sleep.

CHAPTER 32

In New Zion, Burton waited while his son unloaded the afternoon's passengers and luggage. When Jonathan backed down the ladder into the boat, Samuel put his hands on the young man's shoulders and spoke firmly. "I want you to do something for me."

He nodded at the pier behind him. "Do you see that whaler tied under the dock?"

Jonathan peered over his father's shoulder at a battered hull tethered in shadows. Recognizing Nathaniel Rolle's boat, he nodded.

"Good," said Burton smiling. "Now I'm going to get into that boat and wait here while you return to Faithtown." He continued. "When it's dark, I'm going to borrow that boat for a few hours."

Stripping off his windbreaker and straw hat, the minister handed them to his son. "Jonathan, I want you to put these on and make our usual run back home." From a small nylon bag, Burton pulled out a dark jacket and crumpled straw hat. He dressed quickly as his puzzled son stared. Burton raised his hand. "If anyone sees you wearing my jacket and hat, they'll think it's me at the helm. Right now, that's important, Jonathan. Very important."

"How will you get home? Should I come back for you?"

"No, I'll use Nathaniel's whaler to get back. We'll tow it behind us on the way over tomorrow morning." Burton reassured his son. "I'll be all right. Let Mother know."

Jonathan obediently put on the green windbreaker. The minister gently tugged the large straw hat down on the youngster's head to mimic his own style. He stepped back to approve the disguise.

"Right, then. I'm off."

Climbing from the ferry's stern onto the dock ladder's lower rung, Burton swung into the shadows under the dock and nimbly stepped along thick, tarred bracing beams. Jonathan watched his father work his way along the pilings and jump into the waiting whaler. Once the elder Burton settled in the little boat, Jonathan climbed to the landing, glanced at his watch, and began his wait for outbound passengers.

On cue, a taxi pulled up. Three passengers piled out with groceries. Jonathan walked to meet them at the end of the dock and helped carry their bags. None of the passengers noticed a man's silhouette in the small boat under the dock just yards away. The three climbed into the ferry and chatted in the cabin for the next ten minutes while Jonathan waited for stragglers.

Satisfied that these three shoppers were his only fares, Jonathan started the engine and untied the lines. As he made his way along the port gunwale, he glanced under the dock at his father's outline in the small boat. Burton gave a quick, discreet wave, which his son acknowledged with a nod.

The ferry backed into the basin and then eased forward in a slow starboard turn toward the channel. When the big diesels increased their roar, the wake widened, sending small waves sloshing against the pilings, gently rocking Burton's small boat in the gloom. Within ten minutes of the ferry's departure, two other boats tied up nearby, their owners oblivious to the whaler hidden under the pier.

With the tide dropping and dusk falling, Burton peeled off the top of a small plastic cup and daubed black grease over his face, ears and neck until his features disappeared. He tugged on the battered straw hat, buttoned his dark-blue jacket and started the outboard. Slipping the line from a huge piling, Burton maneuvered from under the timbers, passed a trio of moored boats and motored into the harbor. He kept close to the shoreline where a small boat would not attract attention. Burton made his way toward the dredged inlet serving New Zion's commercial docks.

Keeping the little whaler's outboard throttled low, Burton glided alongside rusting hulls of small inter-island freighters, listing barges and gutted hulls half-submerged near rickety docks. Stumps of old pilings from collapsed piers poked above the surface like giant rotting teeth, forcing Burton to feel his way through the obstacles. The mixed scent of sewage and diesel washed over him as he passed a row of fuel storage tanks. One hundred yards to his front, the hulking outline of Island Import's huge warehouse sat on reclaimed shoreline, its sign illuminated by a harsh quartz bulb. The adjacent storage yard where he had been ambushed was dark. A line of forklifts was backed against a high chain link fence topped with three strands of shimmering razor wire. He throttled back, coasting quietly, hugging the wharf among the tall pilings.

Ahead of Burton, a halo of lights glowed where Rolle told him his crew would be working. Burton heard voices. A saw ripped through lumber. Cutting the engine, he was carried another twenty yards in the gloom. After pushing the little boat between the hull of a cargo barge to his left and a dock on his right, Burton spotted the three-man team hard at work on the new storage shed. Perched on the roof, Rolle was wrestling a sheet of plywood into place over open rafters. Two other laborers were cutting and measuring remaining sheets for the roof.

Burton watched for a few minutes, then grabbed a long wooden staff from the floor of the whaler and silently poled his way underneath the warehouse dock. As the rod sank deep into foul muck, Burton found it difficult to propel himself through a forest of massive pilings each wearing a thick collar of barnacles. He feared the whaler's hull would scrape the crusty growth and give him away. He soon realized the hammering and sawing covered whatever sounds he might make.

Pushing closer to where Rolle said the hidden boathouse entrance would be, Burton suddenly discovered he had drifted into an opening in the pilings directly under the newly constructed boathouse. Exactly as Rolle had described, the gap in the pilings was clearly made to ease boats under the dock and into the boathouse without detection.

Burton barely made out a dark, square cavity. He reached out to steady himself against new concrete blocks, cool to his palms. He put down the pole and pushed his boat along a smooth wall, feeling damp mortar between the blocks. Slivers of light from gaps in the planks above helped Burton's eyes adjust to the rectangular, watery cavern in which he now found himself. He guessed the width of the space at forty feet by twenty feet. Above him, sawing and pounding continued.

Burton felt his heart racing. *Could they hear the echoes pounding in the darkness?*

He reached a rear wall where a loading platform had been built. To his left, a wide set of wooden steps anchored on the end of the dock rose to a metal door at the top.

It must open into the unfinished storage shed above, he thought.

In the dim light reflected from the canal, Burton made out the outline of twin metal tracks for a yet-to-be-installed overhead door rising toward a ceiling fifteen feet above. Still undetected by the workers, he guided the little whaler against the opposite wall and felt his way back to the gaping entrance. Crouching, he emerged, expecting to be discovered, but the sounds of construction continued.

When his heartbeat returned to normal, Burton retrieved his pole, propelling himself back the way he had come, keeping to the shadows under the pier. Squeezing the whaler's hull alongside a towering barge exhausted Burton.

Once on the far side of the vessel, he started his engine. He had no choice. The outboard popped into life and Burton glanced back, hoping he had not been seen as he sacrificed secrecy for speed. Hunched over the wheel, he twisted the throttle, sending the little boat down the inlet toward the harbor crowded with sailboats and yachts.

Once in the safety of open water, he turned east along a shore lined with larger homes, their lights making this part of the trip easier to navigate.

Approaching the end of the line of houses, Burton switched on a waterproof lantern and propped it against the clear spray shield where it could be easily seen by other boats. He plucked a rag from under the seat and began wiping grease from his face and neck.

Burton kept one hand on the wheel, but it was an effortless ride over a sea as smooth as ebony glass. Clearing the harbor mouth, Burton shot a quick backward glance at the lights of New Zion.

Above the engine's growl, he roared out the words of the Twenty-Third Psalm—the whaler's bow aimed directly at the Faithtown light.

CHAPTER 33

In the morning, Samuel Burton discovered his unopened note to McKay still propped against a stack of books on his desk. He turned it over in his hands. "Lillian," he bellowed, "did you forget to give this letter to Jeremiah?"

She stopped in the hallway and peered in the study. "He never came by. Was I supposed to deliver it to him, Samuel?"

"No, it's just that I thought..." He stopped, groping for a word.

She finished his sentence. "That he might come by for it?"

He smiled at his wife. "Yes."

Pointing to the telephone, she said, "Try him this morning."

"Probably drunk," he muttered under his breath.

"Samuel," she scolded.

"Sorry," he apologized halfheartedly. He sat at the desk, trying McKay's number. He let the number ring a dozen times.

No answer. Burton rose, went into the kitchen and called over the VHF radio. A voice answered, "Go to One-Four."

Acknowledging, the minister turned the dial. "This is Pastor Burton. I'm looking for McKay."

Back came Abner Russell's rasping, clipped voice. "Morning, Samuel. He's down at the dock, working on his boat."

Burton keyed the button on the mike. "Thanks, Abner, I'll find him."

"Lillian," Burton called to his wife, "I'm going down to the marina to see Jeremiah. Have Jonathan pick me up there on his way to New Zion, please."

Without waiting for an answer, he headed for the harbor after throwing on his signature green windbreaker and Panama hat.

A gentle trade wind rustled the tops of palms along his route and the sun warmed him. In Faithtown's harbor, hulls rode high on an incoming tide and gulls circled in a clear sky. By the time he reached the dock where McKay kept his boat, Burton's frustration with the policeman's absence the previous evening had disappeared. Burton was eager to share the results of the previous evening's reconnaissance.

Having removed the engine's cover, McKay was bending over his boat's big Yamaha on the stern, his open toolbox nearby. At the ladder, Burton waited, hands in pockets. Reaching for a small wrench, McKay spotted him. "Morning, Samuel."

Burton nodded, backed down the ladder onto the bow and worked his way to the stern. McKay had gutted the engine, cleaned it, and was in the process of reassembling it. "Give me a minute," he said.

Burton settled on a gunwale to watch. "Take your time."

McKay's forearms were slick with grease. Satisfied with his efforts, he reached for an oily rag and wiped machine parts before toweling his hands. "That should do it." He retrieved the engine cover from the dock. Burton helped him wrestle it into position.

"Went into New Zion last night, Jeremiah."

McKay snapped the cover shut and glared at Burton. "You did what?"

"I went into New Zion to look around last night."

McKay threw down the rag. "Are you crazy? Why?"

Burton raised a hand. "Hear me out. I called several times but couldn't raise you."

Frowning, McKay eased into the seat behind the wheel, eyes on Burton. "What time was that?"

"Late afternoon, just before the last run. Where were you?"

McKay focused on the far side of the harbor. "Busy," he said without conviction.

"I arranged for a small boat in New Zion. Jonathan covered the ferry run for me. I wanted to check on that boathouse I told you about. Remember?"

"Go on." McKay's tone was short, gruff.

Burton gestured, explaining how he had explored the docks and the hidden boathouse with its loading dock beneath the pilings.

McKay said, "How many days before this project is finished?"

Burton repeated Rolle's suspicions concerning drugs and fast boats.

"He's almost certainly right."

Burton sat back. "So now what, Jeremiah?"

McKay stood up and gripped an awning support. "I should see this for myself. Can you make the same arrangement in the next couple of days?"

"I'm sure I can. We could take the last ferry and use my friend's boat."

McKay made one change. "No, we'd go over before that and tie up near customs. There's not much traffic at that time of day. We could meet under the dock without people noticing. That way we'll be able to take my boat. And you can return your friend's boat to New Zion without arousing suspicion. We don't want to make this a habit. Then, it's back to Faithtown once we've finished our business."

Burton shrugged. "If you really think that's a better way to do it."

"I do," said McKay. "We can get back here faster after seeing what we need to."

"Do you think I made a mistake?"

"Hard to tell." McKay picked up his tool kit and moved to the bow, Burton following. At the ladder, he turned. "Promise me you won't do anything like that on your own again." Burton nodded.

Obviously, McKay wasn't going to raise the topic of his own whereabouts that had prompted Burton's solo trip to New Zion. The two men climbed to the dock and went their separate ways.

CHAPTER 34

"Jeremiah, we need to talk." Lillian Burton stood in McKay's office doorway.

He had been expecting her. Putting aside his paperwork, McKay rose and peered past Burton's wife to the post office counter. Sarah Cameron had paused sorting mail to eavesdrop. He closed his door. "Maybe we ought to take a short walk."

"Perhaps we should. It won't take long to say what's on my mind."

He sighed, grabbed his hat from the rack and opened the door to find Sarah Cameron waddling toward them. "Lillian, is anything wrong?" she asked.

"I was just talking to Jeremiah about Samuel. We're both concerned about him," Lillian replied. "He's still not fully recovered."

Her brow furrowed in sympathy, the postmistress wedged her bulk between the two and wagged a finger in McKay's face. "Tell Samuel to rest. He'll listen to you."

McKay put on his hat and took Lillian Burton's arm. "I doubt that, Sarah. I can try talking to him, but he's not likely to take my advice."

"Still, you should insist," huffed the older woman. She held Lillian's hand and spoke soothingly. "Take Jeremiah with you and have him talk some sense into the reverend."

She turned on McKay again. "Order him to stay at home until he's well."

With their confrontation with the postmistress out of the way, McKay and Lillian strolled along the harbor. They passed a cluster of schoolchildren in uniforms—white shirts, dark blue trousers for the boys, skirts for the girls—their backpacks stuffed with notebooks. He led Lillian to a bench in the shade of a wall on fire with bougainvillea. They sat and she launched into her appeal.

"Samuel told me about his excursion the other night to New Zion. Now, I find out the two of you are planning to take a second look. I told him he absolutely cannot go. Whatever you hope to find over there is far too risky. He's a preacher, not a policeman."

Her pleading eyes locked on McKay. "Can't you call in someone who handles this kind of thing? I mean, isn't there anyone higher up who can take it from here?" Her gaze shifted to the ground, pale hands twisting in her lap. "I'm afraid for both of you, and for Martha, too."

McKay rolled his hat in his hands, knowing she wasn't finished.

"What I want," she said, "is for you to tell Samuel that he has done enough and that he can't be part of this any longer." Facing McKay, she put her small hand on his. "Will you do that for me?"

McKay rubbed the back of his neck and closed his eyes, weary. "None of us know where this is going, Lillian. As God is my witness, I didn't know he was making that trip to New Zion. He did that on his own. And I certainly didn't realize how serious this was becoming. Do you believe me?"

"Yes. But now I'm asking you to put an end to Samuel's involvement, Jeremiah. The idea of him poking about on his own last night frightened me."

"I know," he said, "but he confirmed some of our suspicions. Besides, it's not that simple now." He stood, towering over her, hands clasped behind his back. "Maybe," he whispered, "this doesn't stop with just the three of us."

Puzzled, she said, "What are you saying?"

He paced. "I think we have good reason to be concerned that we—the three of us—have stumbled onto something bigger than just some kid washing up on a beach."

She remained resolute. "All the more reason to let Samuel out of this whole crazy investigation thing." She spoke slowly and deliberately. "I simply will not allow Samuel to be a part of this anymore. You must contact police authorities in Nassau and let them take over the matter."

"It's not that simple."

"Yes, it is," she shot back. "It must be done." She stood, her part in the conversation over. "When Martha returns, we should meet and put an end to this."

She turned to leave. "Will you do that for me?"

He locked eyes with her. "I'm worried about Samuel. It's important you understand that."

She softened. "I know. But I'm worried about you and Martha as well. If anything happened to either of you…" She left the words hanging.

Stepping close, he put his arms around her. "Tell Samuel I'm canceling our surveillance trip. And when Martha returns, we'll talk. You have my word."

"Good," she replied, "When Martha gets back the two of you come see him."

CHAPTER 35

A line of fishing charters, one hundred yards between each boat, headed southwest in single file toward New Zion. Four smaller craft bounced across the homebound wakes belonging to the large white sporting yachts. The afternoon ferry steered a parallel course beside the expensive boats with their towering bridges and deep-sea fishing rods lining the gunwales like rows of whips. Three-foot waves spit windy chop across their decks, but the stately boats plowed ahead without effort.

"Faithtown Ferry calling McKay, over." In the ferry's cabin, Martha braced herself as Jonathan slammed into a series of ragged troughs spawned by the wake of the last yacht. Spray hit the windshield like buckshot, forcing him to turn on the wipers. Martha called again, finally raising McKay.

"Coming in on the afternoon ferry, Mac. Meet me at the dock?"

"I'll be there," he answered. "The Russells with you?"

"No. They had to stay behind." She'd surrendered the old couple to doctors at the Mayo Clinic for Emilie Russell's initial cancer treatments.

Once the ferry reached the lee side of Kingdom Cay, winds lessened, and the water calmed. The last ten minutes of the ride turned pleasant. Sunlight broke through a towering bank of clouds. Warm afternoon light bathed the harbor mouth and its familiar lighthouse rising from a cluster of palms. A sleek daysailer, trailing a wooden dinghy, motored past the inbound ferry, its crew of family waving. Martha signaled back and shelved her sadness at having left Emilie in Jacksonville. Returning to Faithtown buoyed her spirits. In all her years in the Bahamas, the homecoming effect never changed, and she thought the little town nestled on limestone among the prettiest sights.

Her reverie was suddenly broken by a high-pitched roar from a boat passing them at the harbor mouth. Zeke Cameron, at the throttle of his smaller boat, whipped across the ferry's wake, jumping the queue into Faithtown. Zeke and his brothers routinely ignored no-wake rules. It was the only jarring note at the end of Martha's exhausting travel day. She longed for her own bed and quiet mornings. She had missed both while shepherding the Russells through Mayo's labyrinth. She also missed McKay.

True to his word, he was waiting on the town's public dock. Young Burton glided the ferry to the pier and shifted into neutral. He went to the stern to collect fares. People hauled themselves up the ladder and began sorting their bags. A grinning McKay gripped Martha's single suitcase and offered his hand. Climbing to the dock, she bussed him on both cheeks as he held up a small bag of groceries.

"Hope you don't mind, but I took the liberty of picking up a few things for dinner."

"How sweet. Are you offering to cook on my first night home?"

McKay reddened. Martha laughed. "I didn't think so. But I do love the thought of having dinner with you. Besides, I'd rather talk privately about what your friend told me. I've got a lot to tell you."

As Martha clung to McKay, she turned to Jonathan. "I'll be by to check on your father later," she reminded him. Within minutes, the ferry was headed for its home berth on the far end of the harbor with two hours of daylight remaining.

Martha linked arms with McKay. "It's so good to come home, Mac."

He smiled. "Sorry to hear Emilie Russell had to stay behind."

"She'll be well looked after at the clinic."

They walked in silence, her suitcase under his arm. When they reached Martha's house, McKay went into the kitchen and emptied the contents of the grocery bag while she disappeared in her bedroom with the suitcase.

"Your friend, Kent Bryan was very helpful," she called over her shoulder.

"I knew we could count on him, Kent's a good man."

"He certainly spoke highly of you, Constable," she said, reappearing with an envelope in hand. "He sent this to you." McKay pocketed it. "I didn't open it, if that's what you're wondering," she teased. "It might be what you're looking for. After I fix dinner, we can call Samuel and Lillian. Agreed?"

She took charge. A small casserole went into the microwave and she had McKay slice a loaf of homemade bread while she threw together a salad. When the meal was ready, they sat opposite each other. "Welcome home, Superwoman," said a grinning McKay. He hovered over his plate, ready to attack dinner. Martha shamed him by pausing to say a short grace mentioning the Russells, the Burtons and the night's meeting all in one breath. During dinner, she recited every detail of the Florida trip. As they ate dessert, McKay told her of his encounters with the Burton's.

"To begin with, Samuel did a little unauthorized sleuthing on his own in your absence."

He paused. "Apparently his mysterious friend in New Zion was on to something and thought Samuel needed to see it for himself."

Martha frowned. "You never should have let him go on his own."

McKay conceded the point. "Samuel's stubborn, always has been. You know how he can be when he makes up his mind. Had I known I might have stopped him."

"Where were you when this happened?"

McKay mumbled, "Somehow we missed each other."

She got up to serve coffee. "Promise me you won't let this happen again. I told him he needed to recover. I can imagine how Lillian felt about this little excursion of his."

"You don't know the half of it. She talked to me about his involvement in our detective work."

Martha set a coffee cup in front of him. "Go on."

He shrugged. "She's not happy about the way this is going."

Martha was sympathetic. "I share her concern, but we all need to decide where we go from here, don't you agree?"

"Completely," he said. McKay drank his coffee after drawing the FBI agent's envelope from his pocket. He scanned the pages.

"Anything new?" she asked. She got only a murmur in reply as McKay read in silence, pausing only to sip from his steaming cup. Martha began washing dinner dishes. When finished reading, McKay put away the letter and joined her at the sink to dry.

"I'll share the letter at Samuel's if that's okay with you."

Chores done, they stepped into the light of a dying sunset and headed for the Burton's home near the harbor, where Lillian greeted them both with hugs. "I'm so glad you're home, Martha."

"So am I, Lillian. Hard to leave Emilie in Florida, but it's where she needs to be."

"Go on to the parlor. Samuel's waiting for you."

McKay sent Martha ahead and lingered. Lillian, her voice in a stage whisper, said, "You know how I feel about this. But Samuel asked me to be willing to listen to what you have to say."

"I appreciate that, Lillian. It's critical I hear from all of you."

"I'm still counting on you to talk some sense into him."

"I'll give it my best." He held up Kent Bryan's letter. "There are some recent developments I'm going to share tonight."

"I thought as much after Martha called earlier." With resignation in her eyes, she ushered him to the parlor and sat down.

Burton smiled from the couch, Martha next to him. "Good to see you, Jeremiah. Martha says you have news."

Fanning the envelope, McKay said, "Evening, Samuel. There might be some answers here."

"Your FBI contact?"

"Yes. Martha had a chance to talk with him." McKay sat down, unfolded the letter and read. "First, Kent Bryan confirms that Virgil Livingston is our dead man."

Martha interrupted. "That's not news, Mac. We figured that out ourselves."

He cocked an eyebrow in irritation. "There's more. Livingston's prints and pictures both matched someone known as Junior Barnes. At least that's one of his names. He's also gone by the name of Bethel, Rolle and Risley. The Bureau knows him as Barnes. That's the name he was working under for the DEA—the Drug Enforcement Administration." He continued. "Seems he's been around. Left Parker's Inlet without finishing school; went to Nassau looking for work. Fell in with the wrong crowd. Did odd jobs. Ran out of money. Started using drugs and then selling small time."

McKay's audience exchanged knowing glances. Flipping to a second, stapled sheet with a grainy mug shot of the dead man pinned to the bottom of the page, he kept reading. "Livingston

—or Barnes, if you like—got caught in a drug bust near Key West eight months ago. You know how it goes in these cases."

"No, we don't," said Lillian. "How DO these things go?"

"Little fish give up the bigger fish," explained McKay. "Those fish give up even bigger fish. It goes right back up the line, Lillian."

"Honor among thieves," said Martha sarcastically.

"So, Livingston was working for the Americans all along?" said Burton.

"Yes. Kent's letter says that the DEA turned Virgil during the Key West bust and, at the time of his death, was using him to track something big they thought might be coming out of New Zion."

Lillian was confused. "What exactly does *turned* mean?"

Martha answered for him. "It means the feds caught the boy, turned him around by pressuring him to inform on fellow dealers in exchange for leniency."

"She's right," said McKay. "He was in a pretty precarious spot. At some point someone from his past figured out what he was doing."

"And killed him for it," said the pastor softly, twisting his hands.

"Can't your FBI friends or the DEA do something about his murder at this stage?" said Lillian.

McKay put down the letter. "My guess is that we've stumbled into the same people whom Virgil Livingston was working with. Each time we look a little further into this thing, we get deeper into something more dangerous than we imagined."

Burton took his wife's hand. Martha stared at McKay as the pastor asked the question on everyone's mind. "How do we get out of this whole ugly mess, Jeremiah?"

It was a long time before McKay answered. "I don't know, Samuel."

Excusing herself, Lillian got up from the sofa. McKay's eyes followed her into the kitchen as the parlor filled with silence.

"You've got to go to Nassau, Jeremiah," said Martha abruptly. "Find someone in the attorney general's office," she explained. "Someone involved in the anti-drug campaign. Someone you can trust."

"She's right," Burton said. "You could speak to our member of Parliament."

"You can't go to the police in New Zion," said Martha. "They all answer to Hamilton Sawyer. He may be involved for all we know."

"Be careful about innuendo, Martha," cautioned Burton.

She turned on him. "Don't be so naive, Samuel. Nothing happens on Jericho Island without Sawyer's say-so. Even if he's not involved, he'd know about it."

Back on his feet, McKay shook his head at the pair on the sofa. "I have my own suspicions about Sawyer, Martha, but Samuel's right. Without definite proof we have no case." Thrusting both hands in his pockets, McKay ambled to a window. "Besides," he said, staring at blinking lights in the harbor, "we don't have any real proof that they're even moving drugs in that warehouse."

Now it was Martha on her feet facing both men. "Oh, please. You're either in denial or even more naive than Samuel, Mac. If it looks like drugs, smells like drugs, and sounds like drugs it probably is drugs. We know," she went on, "that they likely built that place for one reason. To run dope in and out without being seen."

Lillian returned with a tray of glasses filled with lemonade. "I believe Martha's right," she said. Martha took Lillian's hand. "There probably are drugs being shipped in and out of that horrid place, that boathouse." Focusing on McKay, the older woman's voice took on an edge of iron. "Jeremiah, I've prayed about this ever since Samuel became involved. You know how worried I've been about his participation. I've prayed over this, even as late as this afternoon. As much as I hate to admit it, I feel that what Martha says is right. The Lord has shown me this, I believe."

She shifted uncomfortably in her chair. "As much as I want Samuel out of this terrible situation, I think we have to be responsible about seeing it through."

Leaning against the window frame with arms folded, McKay challenged her. "I thought you were dead set against any further involvement for him. Even tonight, you asked me to talk him out of being part of this. Why the sudden change?"

Burton looked at his wife, but her gaze was fastened on McKay. "It wasn't sudden, Jeremiah. Yes, I was against his being part of your investigation. Forgive my timidity. They're the fears of a wife for her husband. And I've thought of the risk Nathaniel Rolle took to let us know about building the boathouse. We're in danger. That's why Martha's suggestion makes sense. It's an answer to prayer."

Burton showed his surprise at his wife's change of attitude by beaming.

"If you go to Nassau," she said, "and talk to the proper authorities, you'll certainly have my blessing. You must make them see that someone is trying to bring drugs into our islands."

She reminded them of the foothold drug runners had obtained in the Out Islands in the past. They knew the history. Cartels were flooding the islands with easy money, corrupting the police, the courts and using murder as a tool.

When Lillian finished her recitation, McKay said. "I'm more than willing to go to Nassau to seek help. I'll do it because it's getting out of hand and I'm at a loss as to what I can do to end this."

"When can you go?" said Martha. The trio waited for his answer.

"This coming week, I guess. I'll need time to make some arrangements. Talk to a headquarters inspector I know." Resignation echoed in his voice.

Sensing McKay's resolve at last, Martha raised her glass. "A toast to success in Nassau."

"For Faithtown. And may the Lord's will be done," added Lillian.

McKay smiled halfheartedly and drained his glass, desperately wishing for something much stronger than lemonade.

CHAPTER 36

A false calm settled over Jericho Island and Kingdom Cay. Faithtown's ferry continued its runs with Burton sharing morning trips and his son handling afternoon runs alone. Martha kept to her usual routine with patients in Faithtown's clinic and McKay made his customary rounds to maintain the appearance of a normal schedule.

On Thursday morning, after donning civilian clothes, McKay avoided Sarah Cameron's radar and slipped unnoticed aboard the morning's outbound ferry. A load of chattering school kids making the run to secondary school in New Zion filled the seats. McKay was one of three adult passengers. Tourists, a middle-aged husband and wife, sat against the cabin bulkhead deep in animated conversation as the ferry nosed into the channel toward New Zion.

McKay, black gym bag in hand, stepped next to Burton at the helm. The clergyman eyed the luggage. "You're traveling light to Nassau."

"Just my kit and a change of clothes. I don't plan to be there long."

"I hope this puts an end to this whole wicked mess."

McKay, his expression grim, focused on the outline of Jericho Island. "So do I. Because I tell you truthfully that I am completely at wits' end right now with the whole thing. I wish that young Virgil Livingston had never washed up on Kingdom Cay."

Burton nodded in agreement. He turned the craft slightly to port to avoid a series of swells.

"What time is your flight?"

McKay glanced at his watch. "First one. Ten o'clock."

"Our prayers are with you," said Burton, placing a hand on the constable's shoulder. Ignoring the gesture, McKay stared at the sea.

At New Zion's dock, McKay was the last to leave the ferry. He pulled himself up the wooden ladder. At the end of the dock students were piling into a blue van and the tourist couple was crossing the road to a tacky souvenir stand. McKay strolled along the dock as the loaded school van, its horn blaring, nosed its way into traffic. Two taxis remained, parked on the gravel causeway, their owners lounging nearby over a game of checkers. McKay picked the closest one car.

"Airport," he said, hopping into the back seat of a station wagon.

One of the drivers took a last look at the board and forfeited to his playing partner. Ambling to the driver's door, the cabbie slid behind the wheel and glanced in the rearview mirror.

"Catching the early bird to Nassau?" he said.

"I'd like to," replied McKay.

"You just about there, mon," promised the driver. Spitting gravel, the car leaped onto the main road's crowded blacktop. "When you coming back, mon?"

McKay locked on the driver's questioning face in the mirror. "Not sure."

The driver offered a crisp white card. "Here's my number, mister."

McKay read aloud, "Taxi Thirty-Six, Twenty-Four Seven."

Tucking the card into his breast pocket, he smiled at the hustle. After squealing through a roundabout, the car turned north on the airport road with the driver repeatedly tapping his horn as he passed a string of slow-moving bicyclists. A blur of faded pastel homes with threadbare lawns and scrubby bushes rushed past the window. Skinny black children in threadbare shorts played on barren lots behind an unbroken mile of chain link fencing. Trash trapped at the base of the fence along the route dampened McKay's mood.

How many of these kids will end up battling drugs, he thought. *Life is so unfair at times.*

The station wagon glided beneath the carport of the New Zion terminal. McKay grabbed his bag from the seat. He handed the driver a folded ten. "Thanks."

"All right, mister," said the driver bobbing and grinning. "Don't forget. Call me when you need a ride back. Just ask for Hollis, mon." After a quick wave over his shoulder, McKay joined a noisy queue in the terminal.

The line slowly shuffled forward. McKay paid for his ticket and claimed a seat against the far wall. He scanned the crowded waiting room. According to the schedule his flight was on time, but the reality of domestic flights was sometimes at odds with the posted times. The constant drone of incoming flights and whining props did not prove a relaxing wait. At last, Nassau-bound passengers were called.

McKay took his place behind an aged couple poised at the gate. After giving his ticket to a sleepy agent busy stamping anything put in front of her, McKay walked briskly across the tarmac in the rising heat, passing the old couple. The Bahamasair plane was a Short—an aircraft with high gull-like wings bolted onto a box-shaped fuselage. The plane had a well-earned reputation as a dependable commuter workhorse between the islands.

Taking a window seat on the forward right side of the aircraft, McKay hoped the adjacent one would remain vacant. Three stragglers scurried aboard. The older pair who he had passed earlier painfully climbed the narrow stairway and, once aboard, took forever to find their seats.

A thin black man wearing an expensive suit that hung on his frame like a burial shroud followed them. He settled across from McKay and smiled graciously as the cabin attendant stowed his briefcase in the overhead compartment. After shutting the hatch and locking it, the attendant recited safety instructions in a bored monotone.

Both turboprops coughed into life. McKay buried his nose in a travel magazine as the aircraft taxied. The plane made a tight, jerking turn at the end of the runway and then surged forward. In sixty seconds, they were airborne, Jericho Island's skeletal pine forests and tidal flats dropping beneath the wings. The plane dipped northwest toward Nassau.

CHAPTER 37

"Make sure that your seat belts are securely fastened as we begin our descent into Nassau. Please stow any carry-on items you may have been using in preparation for landing." The flight attendant, a young ebony-skinned woman barely out of her teens, strolled the aisle, nodding at her charges.

McKay flexed his legs and gazed out the cabin window. Nassau floated into view. Anchored on a strip of mottled green and sand, the capital city was a scrambled collection of hotels, government buildings and houses stacked like shiny blocks. In the harbor, four cruise ships towered over wharves like bloated white whales, disgorging hundreds of tiny colored dots from holes in their sides. Working boats carved the dull green water with wide wakes. The plane's tires screeched on the scarred runway as the Short braked. Both engines whined in the heat rising from concrete as they taxied toward the terminal and shuddered to a stop behind three smaller eight-passenger craft.

McKay rose with the other passengers and grabbed his small overnight bag from the overhead, then joined the queue at the forward hatch, emerging into blinding sunlight.

Heading for the domestic traffic gate, he weaved through the terminal crowd to a bank of phones. He sat down; bag pinned between his feet. The black man in the ill-fitting suit from McKay's flight passed, heading for the taxi stand.

Clamping a hand against his ear to muffle the terminal's cacophony McKay dialed, and spoke into the receiver. "Good morning. This is Constable Jeremiah McKay calling. I'd like to speak to Inspector Ethan Bethel."

"Please wait while I transfer your call."

A soft, feline voice answered. "Inspector Bethel's office. May I help you?"

"Yes, this is Constable Jeremiah McKay, from Kingdom Cay. The inspector told me to call."

"Please hold." As he waited, McKay scanned the bustling terminal and its mob of incoming passengers rapidly filling every available space. Drivers held large placards aloft in the midst of a relentless flood of people surging around them. Confusion reigned.

McKay recognized the voice in his ear. "Mac? Ethan. Where are you?"

"Just got in. You available for lunch?"

"Of course. I cleared my schedule for you. We can break bread and talk."

"Meet me in the car park at the top of the Queen's Steps," said McKay. "We'll go from there."

"Why not just take a taxi to my office," he suggested.

"I'd rather not," McKay said. "I'll explain later."

"Sounds mysterious, but it's your call. Want to shop with the tourists?"

McKay smiled. "You could say that. There's safety in numbers."

"Okay, I have some paperwork to finish up here. The district commander is off this week. I'm swamped. How's one o'clock at the top of the Queen's Steps. Good enough?"

McKay laughed. "Better than meeting at the bottom."

"And don't forget, Mac, you're to stay overnight at our place. Lanette wouldn't have it any other way. She and the girls will be glad to see you."

"I accept. And I look forward to seeing them. One o'clock then, thanks."

McKay replaced the receiver, picked up his bag and went hunting for a ride.

It took the taxi thirty minutes to run the ten miles into Nassau. Traffic was knotted throughout the city. McKay got out near a milling crowd at Fort Fincastle, near the top of the Queen's Steps. He peeled off thirty dollars for the fare and made his way through the throng. Arriving fifteen minutes early for his rendezvous, he stood to one side, observing the unending stream of tourists and street hustlers.

The Queen's Steps, sixty-six stone stairs chiseled by nameless slave masons, dropped almost vertically from the Eighteenth Century battlements above the city. The fort's commanding view of Nassau was worth the climb, but McKay was content to watch others make the trek. A group of sausage-shaped Germans stood at the top, apprehensively eying the challenging descent. Three chattering Japanese couples posed for pictures by a shaded pool at the bottom of the stairs. The Asians began a spirited ascent, dodging other visitors timidly descending to ground level.

A pair of policemen in crisp blue uniform shirts, their eyes hidden behind mirrored sunglasses, strolled past the landmark, ignoring the swirl of tourists. McKay followed the two as they swam upstream against the surging crowd. He spotted Ethan Bethel, a lithe ebony figure, confidently marching towards him. His uniformed friend waved, and McKay did likewise. The two men clasped hands.

"Mac, it's great to see you."

"You too, Ethan." McKay smiled back.

"Why are you out of uniform?" said Bethel. "Isn't this police business?"

"Unofficially, yes," said McKay. "I'll tell you what I'm here for over lunch. I have to admit, you look like the perfect picture of a man on the rise."

"Don't let the rank scare you. I'm just an inspector," Bethel corrected him. He gestured to his uniform. "Actually, this should be my day off, but with the boss gone and you coming by I thought I'd dress to impress."

"Well, consider me impressed, Ethan. Now, how about lunch? I'm starving."

"I know a quiet place not far from here," said Bethel. "It'll have a few tourists, but most of them don't frequent the place. C'mon, we'll take my car."

They climbed into an older Land Rover with a pristine interior.

"Hard to tell you have kids, Ethan," quipped McKay, slipping into the car.

Bethel fished for his keys and started the engine. "All Lanette's doing, Mac. She's a real tidy person. Tidy car, tidy house and a tidy mind." He laughed. "But I love her anyway."

He steered through the flow of people in the parking lot and in minutes, they had driven to one of Bethel's favorite haunts. A hostess ushered them through a quaint pub's front room and out onto a small, bricked patio shaded by huge potted palms. One dozen tables lined the walled veranda. Bethel asked for one away from the few remaining diners. He ordered for them and then eyed his guest.

"Did you want something to drink?"

Saying he was on duty, McKay asked for water, which prompted a laugh from Bethel. "Not the Jeremiah McKay I know."

"I can live up to your memory of my old habits later," McKay responded.

"We'll both be off duty by..." Bethel looked at his watch. "Four. We can pass the bottle after dinner tonight."

The two talked quietly about family, Nassau politics, and earlier days as newly minted constables before their careers had taken opposite turns. After their lunch arrived and the server had discreetly retreated, McKay laid out his problems on Kingdom Cay.

A willing listener, the Nassau policeman only interrupted twice to ask questions.

Lunch lasted two hours. Bethel paid the bill over McKay's protests and suggested they return to his office. "I need to make a few more calls for you, Mac. Put you in touch with some people who might be able to help. Won't be much we can do today other than confirm tomorrow's appointments."

McKay, grateful, sensed progress.

At headquarters, Bethel worked the phones for two hours, scribbling notes which he passed to his guest. Most of the names were unknown to McKay but titles that went with them read like a government roster. After one final call to someone with the Royal Bahamas Defense Force, Bethel was finished. He stood, grabbed his saucer cap from his chair and slapped McKay's back as they left. On the way out, Bethel dropped a pile of paperwork on his secretary's desk and led McKay down the stairs to his car.

"One advantage of having your boss away is using his parking space."

Pounding the horn, Ethan maneuvered through Nassau traffic, unnerving McKay until the city thinned, yielding to scruffy packed neighborhoods, then progressively nicer homes. After several turns on a series of shaded streets, McKay, hopelessly lost, began noticing yards and architecture improving. They pulled into a packed gravel drive and parked at a stuccoed bungalow fenced by a chain link barrier disguised with vines. They crossed a wide, well-kept lawn defined by clusters of palms and fruit trees.

Inside the front door, both daughters engulfed Bethel. His wife hailed the two men from a kitchen pungent with spices. "Hello, Mac. Welcome to Nassau."

Lanette Bethel, luxurious long black hair held in place with a tortoise shell comb, her mahogany face breaking into a wide smile, came from behind the counter and embraced the Faithtown constable who towered over her. "And you too, Inspector Bethel," she bantered, kissing her husband.

Ethan knelt by his girls. "Say hello to Officer McKay."

The oldest, Kennedy, her light brown face framed by brightly beaded braids, stepped forward and shook the big pale hand offered to her. Her younger sister, Avery, shyly clung to her father's leg.

"Hello, ladies," said McKay. "You're so tall. I'd forgotten how pretty you were."

Giggling, the girls scampered back to a pile of books in a corner of the living room. Ethan led McKay down a hallway to a guest room with an adjoining bathroom.

McKay tossed his bag on the bed. "Beautiful home, Ethan. You've done well."

"We've only been here three years since promotion. Make yourself at home, Mac. Come to the kitchen when you're ready."

For the first time in a long while, McKay found himself part of a family. He relaxed during dinner, joining in the laughter over stories of Bay Street politics, Nassau's weather, and girlish school tales. After the meal, Ethan dismissed his daughters and helped his wife in the kitchen while McKay made his way to an outdoor garden.

At nightfall, Lanette marched her daughters into the garden to say good night. Tomorrow, she reminded McKay, was a school day. The little ones each rewarded McKay with a hug. Alerted before dinner that their visitor was there to talk about police business, Lanette begged off further conversation. She got McKay to promise a greeting to Martha when he returned to Faithtown. With that, she and the girls left.

Bethel produced a bottle of dark rum and two tumblers and settled comfortably into a large rattan chair. McKay quickly downed one glass and Bethel obligingly refilled it each time he emptied it.

They talked late into the night.

CHAPTER 38

"Daddy, that man gave me this for you." Jonathan leaned across the ferry's gunwale and handed his father a scrap of paper. His father took the note.

"What man was that, son?"

"Same old man who came by last Sunday to see you, remember him?"

Burton nodded. *Nathaniel Rolle.* He stood on the dock reading as his son finished his chores aboard the boat.

"Jonathan, tell Mother I need to drop by Martha's house for just a few minutes, will you? I won't be late for supper."

Jonathan turned to answer but his father was already striding toward the garden gate. Ten minutes later, Burton settled in the swing on Martha's porch. Brow furrowed, she read the note, then gave it back to Burton. Her feet pushed against the porch boards, the swing barely moving.

"Shouldn't we wait for Mac?" she said.

"Martha, this may be just the break we need. If we can establish for certain that there are drugs being moved in and out of that boathouse."

"How good is this information?"

"My friend's been right about everything he's told me so far."

"We'd have to be so careful. Not do anything other than watch."

Burton nodded. "Of course."

"Maybe we should ask someone else to come with us."

"Who else can we trust, Martha?"

"I don't know. What will Lillian say? She'll never let you go, Samuel."

"Leave Lillian to me," he said reassuringly. "She'll see the logic in this."

Martha surrendered with an impish smile. "Mac will be furious with us when he gets back. You know that, don't you?"

"Yes, but if he were here, he'd agree with us."

She gripped the chain, halting the swing's slow arc. "Well, we might as well try. But I'll need to change. Something dark."

Burton rose from the swing. "God will watch over us. Trust that we're doing the right thing."

Taking his hand, Martha stared into his eyes. "God, let alone Lillian, would never forgive me if I let you do this alone."

"I'm not worried about what the Lord wants me to do." Burton chuckled. "It's Lillian who needs convincing."

Within the hour, Burton was at the wheel of his small boat headed for the harbor mouth, Martha beside him. Both had dressed in dark clothes. A skeptical Lillian had not been completely convinced. Only a promise that they would watch from a distance had won her permission. That, and the fact that Martha would accompany her husband made Lillian yield.

Crossing the channel in the last half-hour of sunset, they slipped into New Zion's upper harbor where Burton and Martha found Nathaniel Rolle's battered whaler tied beneath the pier as promised. Martha boarded the little craft. Burton moved his larger boat under the wharf and tied it to a horizontal support beam. Out of sight near the shuttered customs building, his boat was to be their escape.

Once Burton was satisfied no one was about, he worked his way among the pilings and scaled the stone steps to the pier above. Making his way back to where Martha waited, he descended a ladder to join her in the whaler. Thirty agonizing minutes crept by before darkness settled over New Zion.

With Burton at the controls, they cast off, nosing their small craft toward the Island Imports warehouse. By hugging the shoreline and leaving almost no wake, they were able to motor up the inlet undetected.

Fifty yards from their goal, Burton killed the motor. They poled the remaining distance to the hidden boathouse. Clumps of turtle grass, discarded foam cups and sewage ebbed about the tar-covered pilings. They changed positions. Burton crouched in the bow, poling quietly between massive black beams beneath the Island Imports wharf.

In the stern, Martha, pushed a long wooden rod into the muck and tried to remain calm. Squinting in the gloom, she saw Burton's right hand shoot up, signaling a halt.

He knelt to steady the small boat against the current. The musky stench beneath the dock made Martha gag. Burton shot her a warning glance. She nodded, breathing through her mouth. Bracing his hand against a huge piling, Burton pulled the boat forward by inches.

Martha's eyes strained against the inky darkness. Just ahead of them a wall of aluminum panels dropped beneath the murky surface.

"I thought you said the door wasn't finished," Martha whispered.

Muted sounds of things being moved came from behind the barrier. The small whaler began moving again. Martha's heart hammered in her chest. She grasped her pole for balance as Burton took them closer to the boathouse. Boldly crossing in front of the metal door, they ended up in the shadows on the opposite side. Signaling a halt, Burton stepped lightly onto a crossbeam. He looped the whaler's line around a piling the size of a man. Putting a finger to his lips, he pointed to the shed above them.

Martha cautiously pulled her pole from the mud. Waving her disapproval, she shook her head.

Burton ignored her. Flashing a mischievous grin, he gingerly worked his way to a gap between the wharf and shore and, seconds later, was gone. Martha, angry at being put in danger, mouthed a silent prayer and thought of Lillian's warning. She peered into the gloom; certain they were about to be discovered. Noises behind the boathouse doors increased. To her, it sounded like a boat being unloaded.

On the bank above, Burton squeezed behind a stack of lumber. Keeping to deep shadows alongside the new boathouse, he felt his way in the darkness to a door and froze. Ten feet away, a parked pickup sat with its tailgate open. A tiny red glow from a cigarette startled him. Reggae pumped from the truck's radio. In the cab, a dreadlocked silhouette behind the wheel bobbed to the music.

A lookout, Burton thought, *but not a very alert one.*

Part of him wanted to retreat. *Get thee back to the boat,* he told himself. *Get out now.*

He squelched the thought. Breathing slowly, his hand on the doorknob, he pushed. No light spilled from the frame. Instinctively, he drew a breath and slipped inside, easing the door shut behind him. Standing in the dark, Burton leaned against the door, expecting someone to come crashing through behind him. Seconds passed. No response from the sentry in the truck.

Below him was movement. Lowering himself to the floor, Burton pressed his face to narrow gaps in the boards. Beneath him, two men dragged large bags from the interior of a long, knife-shaped cruiser. The loaders wrestled burlap sacks onto pallets at the bottom of the stairs. Fascinated, Burton counted twenty bulging bags.

He never heard the door open behind him; never sensed another person.

Suddenly, he felt steel jammed against his neck. "What you doing, mon?"

The voice threatened. Burton tried to turn but the metal pushed into his flesh.

"Don't say nothing, or I finish you right here."

Sweat poured from Burton's face. He tried to twist to face his captor but heard a hammer click. "Move again, you dead, mon! You hear me?"

"I hear you," Burton rasped. "Don't do anything foolish. I won't move."

"What you mean foolish? You the one done something stupid."

Footsteps drummed on the loading dock below.

"Hey, mon!" barked Burton's captor. "Got somebody here."

Movement below froze, followed by angry voices. "That you, Connie?"

"Yeah, mon, we got ourselves a visitor."

"Watch him," came the command from beneath the floorboards.

The voice above roared, "Doing just that, mon."

Boathouse doors suddenly began rising from the dark water below the pier. An aluminum door rattled in its tracks. A powerful inboard motor growled into life. Gas fumes and voices drifted upwards.

Helpless, Burton silently begged God's forgiveness for his bravado. He prayed his life would be spared. *Was Martha lying helpless, caught as he was?*

Burton heard the boat beneath him gun its powerful engine and tried to rise on his elbows. The heavy barrel pushed him down. He knew he was going to die.

THUMP! The man above Burton collapsed on top of him. Pushing from under his captor's body, Burton rolled to one side and rose into a crouching position, fists in front of him.

Martha's outline filled the doorway, a heavy timber in her hand.

Signaling Burton, she dropped the club beside the fallen figure and kicked a black handgun across the floor. They bolted from the shed. Tumbling down a steep slope behind the pilings in a shower of limestone fill, they came to a tangled stop under the wharf. Martha led Burton across support beams to their tethered whaler.

At that same moment, a cruiser shot from the boathouse, roaring past them, its hull carving a deep wake in the inlet, the boat's pilot unaware of the fleeing pair under the pier.

Martha steadied Burton as they stepped into their small boat bobbing in the cruiser's wash. Untying the line, she joined Burton in frantically poling the whaler from the dock. Behind them, the boathouse doors clanked down into the water. Those unloading the boat would soon discover the unconscious guard and come looking for them. When they reached the end of a line of timbers, Burton threw his pole aside and tore at the engine's starter rope. Once. Twice.

Finally, the balky Yamaha snarled to life. Burton opened the throttle wide, sending Martha sprawling in the bottom of the open boat. Behind them, loud angry cries erupted.

Powerful spotlights mounted on the warehouse roof suddenly switched on, bathing the scene in blinding light. The powerboat's flight up the inlet had left a wide wake and Burton followed it toward the harbor. Martha raised herself on her elbows in the bow, pointing. Burton risked a backward glance.

The sentinel's pickup truck had roared into life and was moving along a parallel service road running the length of the canal. The harbor's safety beckoned, but the pickup was gaining speed.

The whaler neared the inlet's mouth.

If they reached the harbor first, Burton and Martha would be safe.

"God help us now!" Burton yelled.

They reached the end of the inlet. The pickup ground to a halt in a cloud of dust.

"GET DOWN!" screamed Burton.

Martha dropped to the bottom of the whaler. For a split second the truck's headlights caught the fugitive craft in its high beams—Burton clearly visible as the hull skimmed the water. Figures leaped from the truck. Two sharp cracks rang out.

Burton instinctively ducked.

Both shots passed harmlessly overhead.

Burton and Martha continued into New Zion's harbor, weaving among anchored boats. When he was sure they were not being pursued, Burton cut their speed. He decided to risk returning Rolle's boat to its original hiding place. Martha tied the whaler under the pier and waited nervously as

Burton climbed the ladder and jogged to retrieve his moored runabout at the Customs dock.

A lifetime passed before Burton reappeared in his larger boat. Martha leaped aboard as he came alongside. Collapsing at his feet, she trembled in exhaustion, sobbing in relief. Burton opened the throttle wide, battling chop in the dark channel.

They risked running without lights for twenty tense minutes.

Finally entering Faithtown's quiet harbor, they motored to Burton's dock without attracting attention. An alert dog barked, but most of the village was in bed. The familiar lighthouse beam swept the harbor as the shaken fugitives climbed from the boat.

Martha steadied Burton when his rubbery legs failed him on the dock. Supporting each other along the concrete path, the two hobbled toward Burton's house. Halfway there, Martha dropped to her knees, retching in the grass.

The final steps across the yard were agony for both.

Again, Burton's knees buckled, sending him to the pavement.

Despite apologies for his inability to move under his own power, Martha reassured him that she understood completely.

CHAPTER 39

As Martha and Burton recovered from their nighttime ordeal, a hastily called meeting prompted by the pair's aborted reconnaissance was underway on Jericho Island. In a back room of a darkened office, two figures faced each other across a wide mahogany table. A small table lamp provided minimum light. An air conditioner hummed in the room's single window, more to cover conversation than to cool the air.

Dominating the conference room, the corpulent Hamilton Sawyer took up one side of the table, his massive arms folded on its polished surface, his floral print shirt open at the collar. Even in the cold room, Sawyer's shirt was soaked with great spreading crescents of sweat. Opposite the attorney, Dictionary Key sat passively, fingers laced in front of him, his gold spectacles reflecting the lamplight.

The discussion had turned edgy.

Sawyer in particular, was furious. "We knew we might have to deal with something like this when we started our new project." He slapped a fat hand on the table to underscore his frustration. Dictionary Key nodded, saying nothing for a moment. He leaned back, both palms pressed down as if to rise from the table. In a clipped, authoritative manner he said, "I think we must move deliberately and decisively at this point in the game. My boys say it was the pastor from Faithtown in the boat that got away."

"You believe them?" snorted Sawyer.

"Of course," replied Key with a hint of indignation. "They recognized him just before he disappeared in the harbor."

"And they let him go," Sawyer retorted. "Like they did when he had the accident in your yard." Both men stared at each other, circling each other mentally.

"They did their best, Counselor," snapped Key. "Someone got the drop on them. The pastor had somebody with him."

Sawyer leaned forward. "Your boys said he was alone in the whaler when he made the break. Isn't that what you told me?"

Key nodded. "Yeah, mon, but Connie says it was definitely the pastor he caught in the shed. It was dark, but he told me he had him face down on the deck when someone took him out from behind. That means two people involved, mon."

"Brilliant deduction on Connie's part." Key let Sawyer's insult pass. "Probably that nurse from Faithtown," brooded the lawyer. "They're friends, you know. What's her name?"

"Martha Thomsen," volunteered Key. "American. From New York. She was with Burton when we clipped him in the yard."

Sawyer blotted his forehead with a silk handkerchief. "Yeah, mon," he said. "That's the one. She and the others been making so many problems for us."

"Maybe not a woman," said Key. "Connie's too big to be taken by a girl."

Sawyer studied his hands. "Coulda been the pastor's son. They pilot the ferry together. Never seen those two apart. Yeah, the son."

Key leaned forward. "Possibly. Burton wouldn't try this alone."

"Well then," sniffed Sawyer, "don't tell Connie he got hit by a kid."

Key let the second insult pass as well. "Don't matter. We got to stop Burton and his friends before they go for help."

"Maybe they already have." Sawyer fanned himself with his handkerchief. "You forget the policeman went to Nassau?"

It was a detail Key had missed. "Then we don't have much time, do we?"

Sawyer shifted in his chair, his shoulders hunched forward, face blank.

Key spoke with confidence. "You think somebody will come looking if the pastor says he knows something? Won't happen. And I'll tell you why, mon. Up until now it didn't matter what they knew. Even after tonight, they won't really know what to do." He sat back, satisfied with his explanation.

"You mean, like us?" suggested Sawyer, not following Key's reasoning. His statement hung there in the air unchallenged, another criticism.

Key got up to pace, hands clasped behind his back. "Look, that's why the cop went to Nassau. Trying to find some help. Say he gets someone there to listen to him. Maybe even agree to come take a look. So what? You know how long it will be before they actually investigate?"

Key laughed, "We'll be cleaned out and have the place piled high with coffee, flour, concrete or whatever else we want to put in there."

Sawyer studied Key. "Your boys move everything?"

"Yes, Counselor. It's completely clean right now."

"No traces?"

"Affirmative. You could eat off the floor now. Won't be used again until we're sure it's safe."

Sawyer forced a thin smile. "And when might that be?"

Shrugging, Key removed his glasses to clean them, deferring to the big man.

Sawyer spoke. "Okay, mon, here's what we do for now. You don't risk more shipments until we can put an end to this interruption. We got a lot invested up to this point and we don't move more product until it's completely clear."

"We may not have that luxury," warned Key. "This interruption as you call it, has already put us behind. Our associates will insist that we keep to our schedule regardless of our problems here. You know they will." Sawyer did not like what he was hearing. Out came the silk handkerchief. "The money up front was their investment," continued Key. "They have their own schedules to keep and they are not used to being disappointed."

Reviewing construction costs of the new boathouse, the two men debated the need to continue operations. In the end, it was Key who proposed a solution to their dilemma. "I'll talk to our mutual friend and get him to eliminate our problem."

"How can you be so sure he'd risk making a problem like this disappear?" said Sawyer. "I never thought of him as one willing to pull his share of the load." He underlined his concern. "I am also of the opinion that he may not have the backbone necessary for sterner measures. Won't want to dirty his hands, mon."

"I think you misjudge our man," replied Key. "At this point in the mix he has too much of an investment to let amateur sleuths throw it all away. And don't forget, he also has partners who don't accept half-measures where their money is concerned. We're talking some very big money."

"Whatever you decide, I mustn't be told," warned Sawyer.

"I understand," said the younger man in a flat voice.

Sawyer's eyes turned hard. "All right, we're done here. As usual, we never had this conversation." The large man smiled but Dictionary Key's expression never changed.

CHAPTER 40

Tuesday's dawn carried humidity hinting at a front heading toward Nassau. Ethan Bethel kissed his sleeping wife and made his way to the kitchen where he found McKay sitting at the table, his hands around a mug of pre-dawn coffee. He had risen early. An empty rum bottle sat on the counter as a silent witness to the previous evening. The rum had slowed McKay but he was dressed and ready for the day.

Bethel poured himself coffee. "We've got our first conference set for eight. Remind me, what time is your return flight?"

"Five o'clock. Last one to New Zion."

"All right, we've got about seven hours of productive time to set your problem straight. Let's get started." Bethel slipped into a pressed blue uniform blouse and grabbed his hat from the front hall table. After giving his shoes a final buff, he and McKay jumped into the Land Rover and headed to Nassau. In fifteen minutes, they had negotiated early morning traffic and arrived at police headquarters.

McKay, in civilian clothes, followed Bethel up a flight of stairs and through a maze of cubicles. A sleepy secretary in no mood to flirt directed them to a narrow conference room crowded with plain wooden chairs and a long, tired-looking table. The secretary poked her head in the door and offered tea or coffee, but the pair declined.

A pair of tall windows filtered early morning sun against pale yellow walls. Foam cups and two beakers of ice water on a plastic tray were the only signs of welcome. An easel holding a large white marker board covered with graffiti from a previous meeting occupied a corner at the far end of the room.

Bethel and McKay took two chairs and waited.

Bethel said, "First up this morning you'll get your chance to tell your story to a couple of detectives from the Drug Enforcement Unit. I know one of them, a younger chap named Lyman. He's sharp, a good man. I don't know his partner."

Flipping open his notebook, Bethel scanned a scribbled page. "Then, if we're lucky, and if he's in town, we'll catch a fellow I know who's with the American DEA. First rate. Works with your Coast Guard and our defense forces."

McKay forced a smile and Bethel sensed his nervousness.

"You'll have to sell this, Mac. There's so much of this stuff going on now that it'll take something really important to make these gentlemen sit up and take notice. If what you've told me so far holds up, they may be interested."

Glancing at his watch, Bethel leaned back. The detectives were late. He busied himself with his notebook. "Our last appointment is with the honorable Lionel Parker, former MP now with the Attorney General's office." He turned serious. "He's high in the food chain, Mac. He'll clear the way for you if he likes what he hears."

McKay was about to share his opinion of politicians when the door to the room opened. Two black men entered. Bethel and McKay rose. The lead man, heavy and balding with a deeply carved scowl behind a thick mustache, wore an expensive tailored suit. He took his time working his way to the head of the table. Once there, he busied himself arranging a legal pad and a line of pens in front of him without glancing at McKay and Bethel. He pulled up a chair and waved for everyone to sit.

The second man, the younger of the two, wore an ill-fitting tan linen sports jacket and dark baggy slacks. His hair was clipped high along the sides, leaving a remnant of what once must have been a pompadour. He managed a tight smile, his light-skinned face breaking into a wrinkled map. He sat opposite Bethel and McKay.

"Good morning, gentlemen," said the older cop. "I am Detective Pindling from DEU and my associate..." he motioned to his slouching colleague, "is Detective Lyman."

Leaning across the table, the younger man shook hands with the others. Pindling, seated, did not offer his hand, opting instead for a perfunctory nod. Bethel introduced himself and McKay. Focusing his attention on McKay, Pindling said, "Inspector Bethel seems to think you have information that may be of highest national interest, Constable. Right off, I must tell you I'm extremely wary of why you think it's necessary to jump the chain of command to be here this morning."

Forewarned, McKay began a careful recitation. During his story both policemen scribbled notes. Neither asked questions until the presentation was finished. Speaking in deep tones, Pindling dominated the room. To McKay's irritation, the detective seemed more interested in police protocol than reasons for his suspicions about the New Zion police. Playing good cop, Lyman was the more sympathetic of the two. McKay laid out his reasons for distrusting local authorities.

In the end Pindling summed up the situation as he saw it, promising only that the DEU would do discreet background checks on Sawyer and Key's business associates. He added a vague promise of further investigation. Extracting a promise of confidentiality on McKay's behalf, Bethel volunteered to act as liaison for the Kingdom Cay policeman if needed. Pindling ended the interview by noisily rising to his feet and stuffing his notes into a large manila folder. This time, he shook McKay's and Bethel's hands. Detective Lyman did likewise and followed his senior partner from the conference room.

Shrugging, Bethel tried to reassure McKay. "They may not act interested, but I'm sure they'll start digging through their files at once."

McKay frowned. "I'm not as optimistic as you, Ethan. In fact, I'd say they seemed bored. Maybe it's old news here, but in Faithtown we think it's a life or death situation."

Bethel patted him on the back. "Nassau moves a bit too slow for most of us Mac, but don't write them off yet. You might be right about Pindling, but put your money on Lyman. He's got a good reputation. He's a driver. He'll shake something loose."

"I hope so," lamented McKay. "I don't think we've got much time to wrap this up before something drastic happens. I've put my friends' lives in jeopardy, you know."

Bethel tried to smile. "I know, Mac. You've done the right thing, though. Coming here gives you the best chance to open this thing up before you lose Kingdom Cay."

"What about Jericho Island and New Zion?" McKay said.

"You could be seeing the rebirth of the drug trade there," Bethel said. "With the way the economy is right now, the nation is fighting a war. And the reconstruction after the last hurricane sucked up a lot of money. People are hurting. We both know it. And the cartels know it. Hate to say it, but if it were not for American help on the drug scene, we wouldn't have a chance."

"It's a battle both countries have to win," said McKay.

They exited the room in grim silence.

Back in Bethel's office, the two readied themselves for the next meeting. The inspector rifled through his mail, returned some calls, and then dialed his contact in the DEA office.

"We're on, Mac. We'll meet them at the harbor in twenty minutes."

McKay sat forward in his chair. "Them? I thought this was one contact."

Bethel waved away McKay's concerns. "Don't give it any thought. My man in the DEA is the genuine article." Bethel hunched over the desk, lowering his voice.

"Besides, this potentially puts you in touch with people in the U.S. Coast Guard. If your friends at Island Imports are running drug boats, you'll need something bigger and faster to take them out. It makes perfect sense, doesn't it?"

McKay knew the connection was strategic, but he was concerned. "I don't like spreading this all over the place," he said. "You know how it is. People talk. It could find its way to the wrong crowd."

"It's a risk, I know, but even a little sunshine can work wonders in a dark corner. Trust me on this, okay?"

McKay slumped in his chair. "Do I have a choice?"

"Sure," said Bethel. "You could turn tail and run back to Faithtown."

"Not doing that. They're depending on me to get the government's attention."

CHAPTER 41

"Are you sure the fuel line's been severed?" Burton sat in his study weighing his options after hearing the disturbing news. His son's answer cut through a rush of static on the VHF radio in Burton's hand, reaffirming his discovery aboard the ferry.

Burton did not doubt what Jonathan had told him, but his response to the unnerving information was automatic. The eight o'clock ferry was scheduled to leave its mooring in one hour, but its departure now seemed doubtful.

Through a window, Burton focused on his son standing on the dock fifty yards away. With one foot propped against the ferry's hull and radio cradled in his hand, Jonathan waited for his father's reply.

Lillian paused in the doorway. "Anything wrong, Samuel?"

He smiled reassuringly at his wife. "Some mechanical problem with the engine. I'll have to give Jonathan a hand."

She retreated down the hallway without reading his worried expression. Burton pushed back from his desk, leaving his big study Bible open to the Book of Psalms. He snagged his straw hat and windbreaker on the way out the back door.

On the ferry's stern, blue, waterproof carpet had been peeled away to reveal an open hatch. Lowering himself into the cavity, Burton knelt to study a surgical cut in the fuel line. Diesel had pooled beneath the cut, soaking rags that Jonathan had piled to contain the spill. It was obvious the tubing had been deliberately severed. Standing in the hatch, Burton pondered their options and made a decision.

"There's just enough play in the line for us to pull these ends together for a temporary fix. We'll put a slightly larger sleeve of pipe over one end and run the other one into it, then clamp it tight. That should get us through the day."

Gripping his son's outstretched arm, he pulled himself on deck.

Burton retraced his path to his home and rummaged through a tool shed attached to the back of the house. Returning with tools, rolls of tape and short lengths of different-sized pipe, Burton squeezed himself into the hold again. Squatting alongside the engine, he rigged a repair to his satisfaction in ten minutes. Any permanent fix would have to wait until evening when the entire line could be safely drained and replaced. Crawling back on deck, he wiped his hands on an oily rag.

"Try the engines," he ordered. The improvised seal held.

"I'll keep a better watch from now on," apologized his son. "I promise."

"Not your fault," said Burton, putting his arm around his son's shoulders. "This was done by someone who wanted to make trouble for us. But they failed, didn't they?"

Suddenly feeling defenseless, he scanned the harbor. *A warning?*

To sever the fuel line, someone had probably come at night. *Maybe the same pair from the Island Imports encounter,* he thought. *After all, they had taken a shot at him the other night. Whether or not they had meant to hit him was unclear.* Burton realized the tampering with the ferry was a message. *If they know it was me, they could also hurt my family.*

Bowing his head, he silently prayed for God's protection. But the feeling of vulnerability would not leave him. In all his years in Faithtown, Burton had never been aware of a single act of vandalism other than youthful pranks causing no lasting harm.

He quickly cobbled together a plan. "Would you mind taking the runs today, Jonathan? I think I should stay here and watch things."

Not sensing the larger drama, his son readily agreed. Burton pretended calm.

"Oh, and on your way out, stop by the marina and tell Abner we'll need that line replaced. Get one of his boys to go along with you on the runs, just to keep an eye on things, you know."

Jonathan agreed and began readying the boat for the first trip.

"One more thing," Burton cautioned. "I want you to stand by the radio and check in with me on the way over and the way home. Agreed?"

Jonathan nodded. With his son making the ferry trips Burton could stay close to Lillian. He would not share his suspicions about the sabotage.

I upset her enough last night with my little escapade. No need to make it worse, he decided.

Burton found himself wishing McKay was back on the cay.

In Nassau, clouds obscured the sun and the sea changed to the color of slate. A line of squalls driven by stiff northeastern breezes threatened another perfect day. Palm trees swayed in the increasing wind. Beneath the toll bridge leading to Paradise Island, angry whitecaps pushed moored rental boats against their docks. Radio broadcasts repeated small craft warnings. As a precaution, hotel staffs collapsed umbrellas ringing the pools. Thatched-roofed resort bars began to fill with chattering guests in swimsuits who crowded two deep under shelter. They drank and laughed, waiting for the sun to reappear. A teasing sun burst through the low ceiling, bathing Nassau in light, then hid behind scudding clouds. The visitors took the hint and retreated indoors to wait out the storm.

With its white hull marked with the telltale diagonal orange stripe and crest, a U.S. Coast Guard boat strained at its lines in the restless chop. Uniformed crewmen were busy in the wheelhouse. On the bow, a pair of sailors worked under an officer's watchful eye, covering a .50 caliber deck gun with a tarp. Bethel and McKay hurried toward the cutter along the quay.

They were halted by a guardsman carrying an M16 and sidearm.

After showing their ID's, the two were directed to the officer on the cutter's bow.

"Good afternoon," yelled Bethel.

The officer on deck turned, bracing himself against the railing. Spotting the policeman's uniform, the American pointed to the gangway amidships and headed aft to meet them. Bethel and McKay waited at the bottom of the gangplank. The officer, tall, with close-cropped blonde hair and light gray eyes set deep in a tanned face, joined them on the quay.

"I'm Commander Neil. You must be Deputy Inspector Bethel," he said shaking hands. Bethel in turn, introduced McKay.

"The others are already here," said the officer, pointing to an oversized trailer on blocks. As they walked, the commander explained he had arranged for the DEA man to meet them in his modest headquarters ashore. An armed, pacing sentinel halted and saluted the officer as the trio mounted the prefabricated building's wooden steps.

Inside, two men sat hunched over a chart of the Bahamas and the Florida Keys. One of the duo, a wiry black man in his early thirties with large hands, muscular forearms, and short hair, wore a dark blue T-shirt with yellow DEA lettering on the back. Blue jeans and a nine-millimeter Sig-Sauer holstered on his right thigh completed his uniform. Putting the maps aside, the man shook hands with Bethel.

"Good to see you, Brother," he said.

"You too, Jacob," answered Bethel. "I'd like you to meet Constable Jeremiah McKay from Faithtown, out on Kingdom Cay. Mac, this is Jacob Speare, the DEA contact I told you about."

Shaking McKay's hand, Speare looked him over carefully. Behind them, Commander Neil poured himself a cup of steaming coffee at a kitchen counter nestled between metal lockers. At the map table, a fifth man—stocky, white, in his forties and wearing khakis, plaid shirt and loafers without socks, remained seated. His shaved head, clipped mustache and heavy eyebrows gave him a brooding no-nonsense look.

Speare gestured. "This fine fellow is known only as Bud." The silent man nodded at the introduction. "No one's really sure who he works for. At least, he's not willing to say who he works for. Right, Bud?"

Remaining silent, the man in the plaid shirt showed a wry smile at Speare's description and threw up his hands in mock resignation.

"All I can say," added Speare, "is that he has friends in high places and can move around wherever he wants to."

Commander Neil locked the trailer's door and set folding chairs in a semi-circle facing a wall papered with maritime charts. In one corner of the bulletin board a dozen scowling mug shots from FBI, DEA and Interpol glowered from the wall.

Speare took command. "It's thirteen-hundred hours," he said, glancing at his watch. "We have exactly six-zero minutes to get an update from our guest, gentlemen. I'd love to give you more time, Constable, but we've got a mission to run. We have to clear the harbor no later than fifteen-hundred hours if we're going to beat this front."

Speare sat, nodding to McKay. "The floor is yours."

For forty uninterrupted minutes, McKay ran through his tale. Like the Bahamian detectives earlier, his listeners constantly took notes, barely glancing up as he spoke. When finished, McKay sat down, expecting questions. There were none. After a minute of silence, Speare, the DEA man rose to address the quartet.

"Gentlemen, Constable McKay has obviously stumbled onto something major. I can also confirm the dead youth's role as an informer for us. For some time, we've been aware that Jericho Island was being used as a possible drug depot. Until today, my shop and the FBI were still in the dark about the main actors."

Speare nodded at McKay. "Thanks to your efforts we're not flying completely blind at this point. When we're done here, I'll get in touch with my superiors and immediately push for commitments to follow up your discovery."

Hands on hips, Speare wrapped up the meeting. "You can count on my command to give you as much support as we can. However, I have to remind everyone here that Commander Neil and I are under orders to work directly with the Nassau government. We can only interdict these drug boats if direct orders are given by Bahamian authorities. Remember, we have to carry members of the Royal Bahamas Defense Force on board to give us legal cover for searches in island waters. Without that kind of approval, we can't get involved from the naval angle."

"Too often, prior approval means leaks," added a caustic Speare.

The commander shrugged. "No one said life was fair, Jacob."

Wry chuckles filled the air and the Coast Guard officer yielded to Bethel.

"I think I can confidently predict the kind of high-level authorization we need," he said. "This afternoon, Constable McKay and I will meet with someone from the attorney general's office. I see this as the final step in the process we started this morning." With that statement, the meeting ended.

CHAPTER 42

Northeast of New Providence Island, Faithtown was feeling the effects of the approaching front. While Nassau was being lashed with rain, turquoise waves capped with foam were turning Jericho Island's channel into an unruly sea. As Burton's son returned from his morning run, clouds blotted out the sun. Passage between the cays was rapidly changing to what locals called a *rage sea*.

In his study, Burton monitored the VHF radio on his desk as he outlined his Sunday sermon notes. Standing guard near the parlor window, Lillian anxiously watched for the ferry. Emerging from a wall of rain shrouding the channel, Burton's white-hulled boat hove into sight. Once inside the safety of the anchorage, the ferry easily bested the tide and swung into position at the end of the public dock for the afternoon's return trip.

"Thank the Lord, he's back," Lillian said.

Her husband did not look up from his writing. "Oh, he's seen worse seas, Lillian. This will probably pass over us within the hour. He'll have clear sailing for the two o'clock run." Disappearing into the kitchen, his wife put on water for tea.

At the wharf, rain drummed on the wide weathered planks. Jonathan collected fares from three passengers who emerged during a break in the deluge. Packages tucked in their arms, the trio hurried off the pier and Jonathan drew a tarp over the open deck. After checking his mooring lines, he walked home through the downpour, pulling his father's green windbreaker about him and holding tightly to the familiar straw hat.

In the capital, heavier rain arrived, lashing palms, and driving diehard tourists from Parliament Square, the Straw Market and other landmarks. Tardy from long lunches, government workers crossed the pavement in front of the Post Office Building, soggy newspapers shielding them from the shower.

Inside the colonial-era building, Bethel and McKay stood at a window, amused by the street ballet below their second-story perch. They waited in a comfortable meeting room set with a dozen high-backed leather chairs flanking a massive polished wooden table.

The same obsequious bureaucrat who had received them in an outer office reappeared, announcing, "The honorable Lionel Parker."

On cue, the former MP dramatically burst through the door, aides in tow. The politician was tall, his thick eyebrows knitted together above eyes set in a long ebony face. Flashing his smile, Parker swept around the table, shaking the policemen's hands. He wore a gray Savile Row suit and a pale silk tie.

Discreetly shadowing the former parliamentarian, an aide jockeyed the tallest chair in place for his boss. Without a cautionary backward glance, Parker sat as one who was accustomed to having doors opened and chairs held for him. As his staff arranged pens and a red leather folder in front of him, Parker impatiently drummed manicured fingers. He dismissed all but a single clerk who obediently took a seat behind Parker and opened a notebook to record the meeting.

With the door finally closed, Parker smoothed his pomaded hair and broke into his wide politician's grin. "How's the family, Ethan?" he asked.

Bethel warmed immediately. "Fine, sir. Thanks for asking."

"Your wife still as pretty as the last time I saw her? That ministry of tourism affair, right?"

"Yes sir, we were there. Wonderful event."

Parker wagged a finger. "Make sure to remember me to her, Ethan."

"I will, sir. Thank you." Bethel gestured to McKay. "Might I outline the..."

Parker held up a hand to silence the officer. The former MP opened the folder in front of him and spoke without looking at his guests. "Yes, the problems in New Zion and Faithtown. It's all here, thank you, Ethan."

Glancing across the table at McKay, Parker scanned a single sheet summarizing the situation. He flashed a robotic smile. "I see you've already interviewed with two of our finest detectives from the DEU. And, you've met our American friends from the DEA and Coast Guard. So, what exactly is it that you wish me to do for you, Constable?"

McKay said, "With your backing, sir, the government might possibly move more quickly to investigate what's happening on Jericho Island. The situation is beyond my means and I'm afraid that others there may be in danger even now."

Swiveling in his chair, Parker laced his long fingers together beneath his chin. "Do I understand that you feel you cannot enlist the help of the New Zion police to deal with this situation?"

"That is correct, sir."

"Hmm, most unusual, McKay, to keep fellow officers uninformed about your investigation."

"I've explained my reasons, sir. They should be in your report."

Parker nodded. "Oh, they are." Tapping the open folder before him, Parker launched into a mild scolding. "You say..." He corrected himself. "You allege, that Hamilton Sawyer is somehow involved in all this. Is that correct? Am I to assume that your investigation has actually tied him to this drug business?"

McKay answered cautiously. "I believe that if there is a drug operation happening in New Zion, sir, then Mister Sawyer may have knowledge of it."

Cradling his chin in his left hand, Parker leaned back in a studied regal pose.

"Hamilton Sawyer is well known to many members of Parliament, Officer. He's been a generous contributor to the prime minister's party. The fact that one is successful in business does not automatically mean that one would be involved in, or even know of, nefarious deeds of this sort."

Palms down, McKay leaned across the polished table. "But that's precisely why I thought it necessary to come to Nassau, sir. I have simply run out of options within my scope of resources. Friends convinced me to come here and speak with those in authority; to alert the government that we are on the edge of something big, something evil that could have an impact on our country."

Parker attempted to draw McKay into his camp. "We share your concern, Officer. And we appreciate your courage in trying to battle this scourge on your own. If anyone is behind a resurgence of the drug trade in our islands, you can rest assured the prime minister will back extreme measures to put an end to it at once."

McKay sat back. "I appreciate that, sir."

Parker spent ten minutes listing the governing party's devotion to stamping out the flow of drugs into the Bahamas. "I might remind you, Officer McKay, that as a member of Parliament it was I who strongly pushed for the involvement of the Americans in this fight."

There were nods of agreement across the table.

Pushing back his chair, Parker stepped to the window to study rain dribbling down the panes. He thundered, his voice echoing off the glass. "If your allegations about Mister Sawyer prove correct..." His voice trailed off. "Then we shall hold him accountable as well." He turned to the two men.

"I hope I make myself very clear on that point, gentlemen."

It was the answer McKay had hoped to hear.

Whirling on his assistant, Parker stabbed a finger in the air. "Lucius, I want you to draft a memo to the attorney general— copy to the commissioner of police—whatever resources are needed to flush this Jericho Island thing out in the open are hereby recommended by our office. Add the usual language and get it distributed by the end of the day."

Scribbling furiously, the aide bent over his notes as the tall man paced behind the table. It was Nassau political theater, but it was still impressive.

Pivoting back to the two policemen, Parker asked, "Is that what you needed to hear, Officer McKay, Inspector Bethel?"

Knowing their audience was over, the policemen rose. "Thank you."

McKay offered his hand. The former MP took it and then pumped Bethel's hand.

"Return home, Constable McKay, and remain alert as your government begins to work. Lucius, please show these fine officers out."

Parker's assistant put away his notes and leaped to his feet to usher the men into the hall. After closing the door behind them, he escorted the two policemen down a flight of stairs to the lobby.

Alone in the upstairs conference room, Parker sat at the long, polished table. He put away his paperwork and shut the red leather binder. A door to his left opened and a thin, well-dressed black man slipped into the room. He sat across from Parker.

"Did you get all that?" asked the politician.

The newcomer frowned. "Yes. Most troubling, Lionel. Most troubling."

"This Sawyer business is disturbing, wouldn't you agree?" asked Parker.

Nodding, the visitor pursed his lips. "Yes. It's my personal opinion that circumstances in New Zion are moving rapidly to some sort of conclusion. I fear it may not be pretty, nor tidy."

Parker rose, the leather folder held behind his back. "I do hope Hamilton doesn't do anything stupid at this most delicate stage. Can you assure me of that?"

His guest shrugged. "Well, you know Hamilton."

"Yes, that's what worries me," said Parker. "How much time do you need?"

Twirling a pen, the seated man gazed at the ceiling, calculating. "I should think at least one week. Can you guarantee that?"

Parker nodded. "A week will be no problem. Two if need be." Chuckling, he added, "You know how slowly the wheels of government can work."

"The slower the better. We appreciate whatever you can do for us, Lionel."

Parker paused. "Appreciation can be expensive these days, mon."

Drawing a tiny slip of paper from his suit's breast pocket, the visitor slid it across the shiny surface to Parker who quickly pocketed it.

"The account number is the same, Lionel. Don't you want to note the sum?"

Parker headed for the double doors. "Don't need to, I trust you, mon." He paused. "You'll let yourself out as usual, won't you?"

"Of course. Always a pleasure to see you, Lionel. We're grateful for your alerting us to your meeting with McKay."

As Parker shut the tall doors behind him, Hamilton Sawyer's law partner rose from the table. He straightened his tie, his mind now set on returning to his hotel for a late lunch at Sawyer's expense. The thought made him smile. After lunch— a taxi to the airport for his five o'clock flight to New Zion.

"Looks like you'll be spending the night with us again, Mac. Bahamasair has canceled all late afternoon flights to the Out Islands." Bethel put down the phone in his office and nodded at the darkening clouds outside his window.

McKay stared at the foul weather. "I ought to be home," he said.

Bethel shrugged and returned to sorting through police reports on his desk. The sound of phones ringing, hallway conversations and keyboards being worked hard drifted into the office. McKay slumped in his chair.

"Try calling them, Mac. See if they're all right. Use the office next door." McKay spent fifteen minutes trying to connect with Kingdom Cay without success. He returned, concern on his face.

"Can't raise them. No cellphone reception, either."

"Your friends are smart. They'll know what to do until you get back."

McKay leaned against a window framing a darkening sky. Rain washed the glass and pooled on the stone sills.

"Look at the bright side, Mac. If we had put you in a cab for the airport, you would have gone out there only to be told the flight was canceled. At least this way you'll be assured of a hot meal and a bed for the night."

Forcing a smile, McKay resumed his vigil at the window.

At the Graycliff Hotel, Isaiah Russell lingered over a steaming cup of tea laced with milk and sugar as restaurant staff cleared away late luncheon dishes. During a leisurely meal the New Zion lawyer summoned his waiter to ask the front desk about arranging an airport taxi. Russell finished reading the *Nassau Guardian*, sipped tea and occasionally glanced at the worsening weather. The sky was deteriorating by the minute. As if reading the attorney's thoughts, his server approached to tell him of his flight's cancellation.

"Regrettably sir, Bahamasair will not be flying to New Zion this afternoon," the waiter informed him. "They say perhaps tomorrow."

Russell thanked the server for the notice, feeling somewhat upbeat despite the unexpected delay. He tipped the man generously and arranged for his luggage to be retrieved from the bell captain's possession and immediately deposited in one of the hotel's available rooms. Russell smiled again, amused to think of Hamilton Sawyer paying for his prolonged stay in Nassau.

CHAPTER 43

Faithtown's ferry made the day's final trip by plowing through punishing waves that fought the boat the entire trip across New Zion's channel. Passengers retreated from the fantail's spray and crowded together in the cabin. The hull bucked and shuddered its way into Kingdom Cay's harbor.

Slashing rain broke long enough to give those waiting on the public dock a brief respite as they met family members. The marina owner's son, his escort duty with Jonathan done, was the last to leave the ferry. Jonathan folded cash from his fares into a thick roll and stuffed it into a small black zippered bag. He nosed the ferry past the pier and motored up an inlet to the Harbour Lodge dock with a box of produce that had missed his morning run. With that accomplished, he returned to his own mooring. As he was preparing to shut down for the night, his radio crackled into life.

"Faithtown Ferry, Taxi Ninety-Six, come in."

The call was repeated, and Jonathan responded. "Faithtown Ferry, go to channel Nine." He waited for the call as the hull chafed against the pilings.

"Taxi Ninety-Six here. Got a party of six needing a charter to the Harbour Lodge."

Jonathan paused, not pleased with the idea of battling his way back to New Zion. Clouds had taken on a darker, menacing look. The gray-green seas were growing more chaotic. It was not Jonathan's nature to strand visitors in New Zion overnight, but the worsening seas gave him pause.

A charter of six, however, would fatten a day's fees made scarce because of the weather.

A scratchy voice cut through the static. "Faithtown Ferry, did you copy?"

"Yes, I copy," Jonathan stammered. "Stand by."

He switched channels and called his father, who he knew was monitoring the radio in his study. The father-son exchange was terse.

"Ferry to base. I've got a charter of six in New Zion who want to get to the lodge. Should I take it?" He peeked from the stern at his father's silhouette in the study's lighted window.

"Is Abner's son still with you?

"No, I let him off with the others."

Burton hesitated. "What's it like out there?"

"Ugly. Getting rougher the longer we talk this over."

"Are you good on fuel?"

"I can get over and back, if that's what you mean."

"I don't know, Jonathan. I'm worried about the channel."

"If I leave now, I can turn around and be back before it shuts down completely. I can handle it."

Burton gave in. "I don't doubt that. Hate to leave those people out there on a night like this. Okay, go ahead, make the run. But call Abner and get his boy to go over with you. After that, you're done, agreed? And stay in touch both ways."

Jonathan keyed the mike twice to signal agreement and waved to the figure framed in the lighted window at the top of the slope. Burton returned the signal and Jonathan went forward to let go of his lines. Hugging the cabin roof, he stepped carefully along the narrow gunwale and swung into the cabin. He revved the idling diesels and let the current carry the hull from his dock. After tapping the throttle forward to begin his return to Jericho Island, he kept one hand on the wheel and plucked the microphone from the radio set mounted overhead.

"Taxi Ninety-Six, Faithtown Ferry."

"Taxi Ninety-Six, go ahead."

"Inbound to New Zion. Half an hour with this sea."

"Copy. Party's name is Jensen. They'll be at the dock shelter for pickup."

"Copy. Faithtown Ferry back to Sixteen."

In his home, Burton eavesdropped and made a note of the time. He had been wrong about the weather. The front was stronger than predicted and he knew his son would have to return in the dark, fighting a raging sea between the islands.

Jonathan is earning his pay tonight, he thought.

Burton used the VHF to call Martha. "Scrubs, this is Ferry Base, come in."

In her kitchen, Martha heard the call sign and picked up. "Scrubs here, go to Twelve." She waited on the channel for Burton.

"Martha, it's Samuel. You there?"

"Go ahead, Samuel."

"I think you ought to stay with us until Jeremiah returns."

"I'm not sure that's necessary," she answered. "I'm buttoned up tight here."

Burton tried not to alarm her. "We had some problems with the ferry this morning and it made me think."

"What's the connection?" she asked, puzzled.

"Well, maybe we could talk about this over supper. Can you come by?"

"Supper, I can do."

"Good. Come now if you can. And pack an overnight bag just in case."

"If you insist. On my way in ten minutes."

"We'll be watching for you." Burton left the squelch button on to kill the irritating static but turned up the volume to follow radio calls.

Outside his window, the wind bent palms and hurled dead fronds like javelins. In the harbor, sailboats fought their mooring buoys. Wind-driven rain plastered the town's sidewalks red with blossoms stripped from bougainvillea hedges. Lights across town dimmed, flickered, then failed, plunging Faithtown into howling darkness.

CHAPTER 44

Content to wait out the growing storm under a thick mangrove canopy, the Haitian sat on his inflatable boat's single wooden seat. Oblivious to the drenching rain, he hunched under a glistening poncho. His expressionless cast-iron face, barely visible under the brim of a sodden straw hat, turned into the wind. Heavy-lidded, jaundiced eyes remained focused on a dock just beyond the mangrove roots. Every few minutes, he fingered a small, carved-bone talisman on the leather cord around his neck. As ordered, he had dressed in dark clothing. He and his craft were nearly invisible among the roots lining the inlet.

Sporadic flashes of lightning revealed Faithtown's rain-slicked roofs across the narrow waterway. Most of the town had been swallowed by darkness but lights glimmered at the Harbor Lodge. The hotel's powerful generator was providing emergency electricity, but few homes were similarly prepared. Only a dozen lights showed in households that had planned ahead for nights like this. Interruptions in electrical power were not unknown on the cay. Most residents routinely resorted to oil lamps, candles or flashlights to dispel the darkness.

Arriving with the growing storm, the Haitian had slipped into the harbor without attracting attention. A small outboard motor mounted at his boat's stern was tilted out of the water. Under his poncho, protected from the rain and wrapped in an oily cloth, the heavy blade of a razor-sharp machete rested on his knees. His instructions were simple: wait in the mangroves until the right moment. Pulling the poncho tighter, the little man shifted on the rubber boat's single seat, patiently peering into the rain.

In New Zion, Jonathan's ferry labored toward the public dock near the harbor's turning basin. He was alone. Abner Russell's sons had not responded to his radio calls. As the boat's bow bumped against the ladder, Jonathan strained to locate his charter's passengers. Flipping a switch, he swept a spotlight over the vacant ferry shelter. Throwing the throttle into neutral, he looped two lines around the ladder and climbed onto the landing in driving rain. A cone of light from the boat's lantern pierced the rain, illuminating the abandoned shelter. Beyond the empty shed, the flooded access road was deserted, no taxis in sight. High on a pole, a streetlight worked itself loose and pitched wickedly, casting wild shadows everywhere. Zipping the green windbreaker tighter, Jonathan fought the wind to the gravel road and looked in both directions. There were no signs of life.

Hurrying through the rain to his moored boat to use the radio, he called, "Taxi Ninety-Six, Faithtown Ferry, come in." No reply. He repeated his call twice more but got no answer.

"Any taxi, Faithtown Ferry, come in."

In this weather, most drivers would be home with their families. There would be no one seeking rides until morning. Still, the charter call had come, and he had arrived to take the Jensen party to Faithtown. Jonathan raised his father, shouting above the wind and static to be heard.

"Base, I'm here at the dock but no one's here."

His father radioed back. "Can you raise the taxi?"

From the shelter of the ferry's cabin, Jonathan strained his eyes toward shore.

"No answer! I checked to see if they were waiting! No taxis in sight."

"Try several more times to raise them. If they don't respond, come home."

Jonathan's final call was greeted by silence. In a sense, he was relieved not to have to jockey passengers and luggage on such a violent night. Even so, he regretted using precious fuel for no-shows.

"Ferry to base."

A rush of static, followed by, "Base. Go ahead."

"They must have gone to a hotel in town. I'm heading home."

"We'll be watching for you."

After casting off, he fought the current to the harbor, the ferry drifting sideways, uncomfortably close to tall channel markers topped with winking lights. Once past the poles, he opened up the engines, opting to skim oncoming wave troughs in a punishing ride, trading speed for time. In the distance, Kingdom Cay disappeared in a deluge of rain. Only the lighthouse beam broke through curtains of spray exploding off the ferry's bow. Jonathan aimed for the beacon.

Reaching the harbor mouth, the water taxi shot through the narrow cut and dropped its speed. Flashlights bobbed in the anchorage where worried sailboat crews were checking lines to their mooring buoys. Jonathan lined up his bow with the Harbor Lodge's entrance ablaze with light.

Save for a warm, familiar glow in the kitchen window, the Burton home was dark. Jonathan imagined his parents at the table bathed in a brass oil lamp's light. He turned the hull to port to angle the ferry's bow toward the harbor. Once moored, with extra lines and fenders in place, Jonathan battled the wind to fasten a large tarp over the exposed stern. With the boat finally secure for the night, Jonathan headed along the concrete path toward home.

Oblivious to the small shape pressing into the bushes ahead of him, he held the straw hat tight against the rain. Leaning into the wind, the younger Burton moved wearily up the walkway.

Drawing a shiny oiled machete from under his poncho, the killer stepped from his ambush site.

In a single powerful stroke, the heavy blade crashed down on the unsuspecting youth's neck, cleaving flesh and muscles.

With a startled cry, Jonathan collapsed. Blood sprayed the crouching assassin.

Hovering over his victim, the killer delivered a second strike.

An animal-like whimper, followed by a moan, escaped from the dying youth. A sudden burst of rain washed the crumpled form. Rivulets of blood streamed the length of the concrete path to the pier.

No stranger to killing with a machete, the Haitian knew his first blow had been mortal. The second strike had been delivered to seal his prey's fate. The man's eyes darted to the house. With the storm's cover, he had not been seen. Machete in hand, he ran quickly to his waiting boat. Tumbling into the rubber craft, he washed his weapon in the water then wrapped the machete in the oily rag.

Casting loose from a twisted mangrove root, he paddled in steady strokes until carried past the dock where the ferry strained against its lines. Once beyond the pier, the Haitian lowered the prop into the water and fired the small engine. He raced through a flotilla of bucking sailboats moored in the anchorage.

In deep water outside the harbor mouth, the killer grasped the bloodstained wooden handle, shook the big knife free of the rag and heaved the murder weapon into the rainy night without looking back. He heard the machete splash in his wake just as a curtain of rain swallowed the rubber boat.

CHAPTER 45

Nassau Airport finally cleared McKay's delayed Bahamasair flight for the return trip for New Zion. With the exception of the thin, well-dressed black man who had flown in with him two days earlier, none of the outgoing passengers were from the original flight. Airline traffic was backed up and they left thirty minutes late. McKay fidgeted in his seat, willing the plane into the air. For him, the forty-minute flight seemed like two hours.

Eventually, Jericho Island's familiar shape appeared beneath the wings but the sight only increased McKay's anxiety. He longed to be back on Kingdom Cay, sharing his news about the Nassau meetings. The last weeks had drawn the conspirators closer. Even McKay's past differences with Burton had faded in light of their shared experience. The rescheduled flight meant McKay would be marooned in New Zion hours ahead of the afternoon ferry. He thought about calling Martha and coaxing her into using his boat to pick him up. Once on the ground, McKay lifted his carry-on bag from the overhead and joined the exiting queue.

Crossing the taxi apron toward the terminal, McKay spotted Sergeant Newton and Corporal Simmons standing at the terminal doors. Newton hailed him with a wave.

Not a good sign, McKay thought.

He broke from the file of passengers entering the terminal. He braced for fallout about his Nassau trip and a lecture about using the chain of command.

"We need to talk," said Newton, quietly.

"How'd you know I'd be arriving this morning?" McKay asked.

Newton shrugged. "Hard to keep secrets in New Zion."

"Well, I'm flattered that you're here to meet me," said McKay sarcastically, "but I'm not really interested in another scolding about police protocol."

"I'm not here for that. I have bad news, I'm afraid."

McKay's stomach tightened. "Bad news? I'd better not hear that something has happened to one of my friends in my absence."

Simmons averted his eyes, grateful not to have to answer. Drawing a deep breath, Newton spoke in a flat voice. "It's Samuel Burton's son. He was killed last night. Murdered."

"Someone cut the boy down last night with a machete." The officers stared at the ground.

McKay winced. "Any witnesses to what happened?"

Newton said, "No one saw or heard a thing. Power went out last night when the storm first hit."

Both New Zion officers looked away. The trio stood on the tarmac, oblivious to the chaos of new arrivals.

"Who found him?"

"The pastor went to look for him when he saw the ferry but couldn't raise him on the radio."

I should be with him, McKay thought. *I never should have left them.*

"I assume you want to get to Faithtown as soon as possible," said Newton.

McKay nodded.

"Corporal, bring the car around," barked Newton.

Within minutes, Simmons reappeared with the department's station wagon. A numbed McKay followed Newton to the car and slipped into the backseat. Simmons headed for the marina; the car filled with awkward silence. At the ferry wharf, Simmons leaped from behind the wheel to open the passenger door. McKay retrieved his bag.

"Would you radio a charter for me, Sergeant?"

"Already done," said Newton pointing to the pier.

The Faithtown ferry was tethered at the end of the dock. Abner Russell's two sons perched atop the cabin roof, waiting. The white hull floated peacefully in translucent green water. For the briefest of moments McKay thought if he didn't board the ferry the news about Jonathan's murder would not be true. He hesitated.

Newton said, "With you in Nassau, I had to conduct the initial investigation. I'll be over tomorrow to share my conclusions with you and the boy's parents."

McKay's chin sagged against his chest. Simmons and Newton watched their stunned colleague walk slowly down the jetty toward the waiting ferry. Abner Russell's sons climbed down from the cabin's roof and took their posts in silence. The youngest stood by the bow while his older brother assumed the pilot's post, cranking the diesels into life.

Not a word was exchanged as McKay climbed down the wooden ladder.

The younger boy cast off the line, freeing the stern. At his brother's signal, he tossed the nylon lanyard onto the deck and pushed the hull from the pilings. The boat reversed in a graceful funereal turn. When the ferry cleared the rock breakwater and picked up speed, McKay took his customary seat on the stern, his back against the bulkhead, away from prying eyes. The Russell brothers huddled at the wheel, stealing shy glances at their lone passenger.

McKay stared at the receding outline of Jericho Island as the ferry cut a foaming wake in the turquoise. *How many times*, he thought, *have I taken this ride with Jonathan at the helm?*

Only then did he allow the tears to come.

CHAPTER 46

Shifting uncomfortably on a hard, wooden pew in the second row, McKay tugged at his tie. The confinement of a seldom-worn dark blue suit annoyed him. The green silk tie that Martha had picked for him pinched his neck. Crowded by other mourners, Martha sat close to him. Despite the occasion, the small church had never looked lovelier. The morning sky was scrubbed clean of clouds and the sun seemed particularly brilliant.

A simple white casket, its top smothered in blossoms, lay perpendicular to the altar. Two Styrofoam crosses, covered in lilies, were propped on either side, their wire legs wrapped in white silk ribbons embroidered with scripture.

A thin woman with a pale face painted with freckles, her long red hair tied back with small white flowers, sat at the organ in a blue dress; playing soft depressing organ music. People continued to climb the church's broad coral steps, swelling the numbers. Sweating latecomers were forced to stand in the open door or mill about the lawn under the sun. At the front, an empty front pew awaited Samuel and Lillian Burton.

McKay's eyes brimmed with tears he willed not to fall. Martha's ineffable sadness somehow gave her a beautiful aura. Her auburn hair was tucked under a wide brimmed straw hat. She had chosen a simple elegant black dress. McKay's thoughts drifted back to his wife's funeral in this same church. The sky, the gentle breeze, the open beams of the whitewashed interior and the bowing palms outside mirrored the day Felicity had been buried. He remained silent, his emotions in check. Martha gently squeezed his hand, but he dared not glance at her. He tried to smile but failed, his mind replaying the previous day when he had gone directly to the Burton home after arriving from Nassau.

That day, Lillian had remained secluded upstairs with Martha and two close friends. Burton had planted himself in his study, pain etched into every line of his handsome face. He had few words in response to McKay's offered sympathy. Two ancient cousins of Burton's had hurried from Cherokee Sound in the Abacos to share his grief. The gnarled men in shiny, ill-fitting black suits had greeted McKay and then discreetly filed out when he began speaking to their cousin.

"Samuel, I'm deeply sorry for what has happened," McKay began. "I wish to God that it had been me instead of dear, sweet Jonathan. Lillian was right," he continued. "She worried someone was going to be hurt. I wish I had listened to her."

McKay had stared at the floor.

Burton had spoken slowly, measuring each word. "The greater guilt lies with me, Jeremiah. He was wearing my jacket and hat. I had convinced him to do that the first time I poked around that boathouse. You warned me not to do that again. With you in Nassau, Martha and I thought we were doing the right thing by going back to New Zion that night. We should have waited for your return."

"You did what you thought was right, Samuel. I can't fault you for that. I might have done the same thing had I been in your place."

"Don't patronize me, Jeremiah. I had promised you I wouldn't go back there. I broke my word."

McKay listened to Burton unburden himself. "Whoever killed Jonathan thought it was me. Oh, God, how I wish it had been me." He stared out the window at the harbor, his hands twisting behind his back.

"The men who shot at Martha and me that night have something to do with this. Did I tell you someone had cut the fuel line of the ferry on Wednesday?"

McKay had not remembered. Burton continued. "They were trying to frighten me. I never should have let him go back for the charter that night. What a fool I was."

"How were you to know, Samuel?"

Burton wept. He let a deep sigh escape. "I have to trust God, Jeremiah."

"You have no other choice, Samuel."

For once, Burton smiled faintly. "How odd to hear you say that."

McKay shook his head sheepishly. "I know that sounds strange coming from me, Samuel, but you've said that to me and others so many times."

"Used to say it to you," admonished Burton.

"Right. Used to say it to me." said McKay, his eyes filled with tears.

"Do you wonder if I believe it now?" said Burton.

Embarrassed, McKay lifted his gaze. "I have no right to ask you that."

"Well," said Burton gazing again at the harbor, "I do believe it. But right now, I'm struggling, to be honest with you."

"I would imagine so." McKay didn't know what else to say.

Burton smiled wanly. "How like God to bring me round like this to his word. Do you remember the passage in Romans, chapter eight, Jeremiah?"

McKay didn't respond. Burton recited. "All things work together for good, for those who love God." McKay looked at the minister, waited. "You're probably thinking how this can work together for good, aren't you?" said Burton.

"I'm not sure what to think right now, Samuel."

"I'll need your help in the weeks ahead."

"Anything you need, or want, Samuel. Just ask."

Burton reached for McKay's hand. "I may need your help in keeping my faith, Jeremiah." McKay was speechless. "Remind me on days when I seem like I'm sinking that God is still there."

McKay drew back. "Samuel, you know that I don't have that kind of faith. I mean, I believe of course, in some sort of larger way, but I'm still working through my own struggle."

"You're still family, my brother-in-law, Jeremiah. Really, you're all Lillian and I have left now."

To end the conversation, the two men had awkwardly embraced, and McKay was struck by his inadequacies in the face of the tragedy.

Music faded. The Burtons entered from a side door and quickly took their places in the front.

An elder from district headquarters, one of Samuel's early mentors, took the pulpit to open the service. After acknowledging the family, the wizened, stooped evangelist recited Jonathan's life and read Scripture about the resurrection. The effort seemed to exhaust the old man and he sat down as the crowd's voice rose in a hymn. Fans slowly turned, helping a gentle sea breeze cool the packed chapel.

From a sister congregation in New Zion, a beautiful young soloist with long blonde hair tied in black velvet bows, sang two selections in a clear plaintive voice. As her notes died, Burton willed his leaden legs to move and he mounted the platform to address the congregation. With remarkable courage mustered only for the moment, Burton spoke from a wounded heart, drawing on the Bible for the lesson about Abraham yielding his son to God. Soft weeping was heard as the handwritten pages fluttered on the podium. Martha sagged against McKay. He took her small hand in both of his. A dignified, somber hymn, with everyone standing, closed the service. Pallbearers carried the white casket from the church into blinding sunlight.

Although some in the crowd dispersed, the majority made their way along the shaded path to Faithtown's cemetery. There, on a high cleared ridge behind the town, mourners clustered around a fresh grave. Jonathan's final resting place, like most of the surrounding above ground graves, was a low wall of concrete holding sandy soil in place. McKay and Martha stood beside the Burtons as final blessings were said. Pallbearers lowered the pine casket. A prayer was recited, and the crowd filed away in twos and threes after offering condolences to the bereaved parents.

"Excuse me, Constable."

McKay and Martha turned to face Spencer Winthrop and his wife.

"Sorry to meet again under such terrible circumstances," said the American sympathetically. He gestured to his wife. "You remember Elizabeth?"

Winthrop's wife extended her gloved hand to McKay who introduced the couple to Martha. After a few pleasantries, the well-dressed pair politely excused themselves and moved on to offer their respects to the Burtons.

"You know, Mac," whispered Martha, glancing at the couple, "in all the years I've lived here, I've never met the Winthrops. Never laid eyes on them until now."

McKay smiled. "Don't feel slighted," he whispered, "I'd never met them either until this whole rotten business started."

He and Martha waited quietly as the Winthrops consoled the Burtons.

"We're so sorry for your loss," said Elizabeth Winthrop. "I...we can't begin to imagine the pain you both must be enduring at this moment."

The tall Bostonian took Burton's hand. "Elizabeth and I want you to know how deeply saddened we are at this occurrence. We pray God's justice will be done in your son's case. I've spoken with friends in the government and I am personally offering a very sizable reward to find those responsible. This tragedy must not be allowed to stand."

The two couples held hands for several minutes—Lillian embraced by Elizabeth Winthrop, while her somber husband gripped the minister's hand. As quickly as they had appeared, the reclusive couple moved on, exiting the cemetery with the last mourners.

McKay and Martha stepped back to allow the Burtons privacy at the gravesite. At the entrance to the burial ground, Sergeant Newton stood in the shade of a huge banyan tree, waving to McKay.

"Excuse me, Martha, I won't be but a minute."

He strolled to the waiting officer and the two talked for several minutes.

"What was that all about?" said Martha, when he returned.

McKay drew her aside, his voice dropping, taking on an edge. "Newton says Taxi Ninety-Six does not exist. He also told me the Harbor Lodge confirms there was no party named Jensen scheduled for arrival that night. Jonathan was set up."

She nodded in shock at the news. "Are you going to tell Samuel?"

McKay shook his head, whispering, "Not a good time."

He approached the mound of flowers. "Samuel, we'll see to visitors. Take your time."

Martha hugged the Burtons and rejoined McKay on the sidewalk. They linked arms and walked toward the shade, leaving the parents bereft and alone at the grave of their only child.

CHAPTER 47

That night, a twenty-foot whaler came alongside *The Green Turtle Two*, bumping against the big boat's hull as she lay anchored in New Zion's harbor. Three shapes stepped from the boat, secured a line to the ship's ladder and climbed to the yacht's deck.

The trio was met by a crewman at the railing. In silence, he guided the three toward the stern, their path illuminated by soft lights embedded in the teak. The men were ushered into the yacht's salon where Spencer Winthrop waited. Gesturing for his guests to seat themselves in leather chairs arranged around a low glass table, the American sealed the door leading to the bridge.

"Anyone see you come aboard?" he said.

"No, we waited until dark as requested," answered Hamilton Sawyer.

Winthrop opened the meeting. "Gentlemen," he said, "we have a lot on our table."

Before he could continue, Sawyer blurted, "I'll start by saying that I am most distressed by these events." Flanked by law partner Isaiah Russell and Dictionary Key, the porcine lawyer glared at the American opposite them.

"Understandable, Hamilton. None of us is happy with what occurred."

"What exactly did you tell your man?" Sawyer said.

The men knew the Haitian killer had been Winthrop's employee. The yacht owner leaned forward, grasping his knees. "I remind you, Hamilton, that you're the one who told Key something had to be done about Burton because he knew too much."

"I never should have listened to you," said Sawyer. "Cutting a fuel line is one thing, but you never should have turned your man loose that night."

Winthrop bristled. "Don't be a such a damn fool, Hamilton. Burton had to be stopped and you know it. With McKay in Nassau, it was time to hit back. Besides, my man thought it was the pastor. How was he to know the kid would be wearing his father's clothes." Waving away their concerns, Winthrop added, "Anyway, the storm was a blessing. Any evidence was probably washed away."

"Never should have gone along with you," whined Hamilton, perspiring despite the salon's cool air. He tugged a handkerchief from his breast pocket and began blotting his forehead. Winthrop rose and went to the bar to pour a drink. He offered the bottle to his guests, but the others declined.

Sawyer shifted his bulk on the sofa. "This absolutely must not be tied back to us," he declared.

"You'd better hope not, Hamilton," said Winthrop as he dropped ice in his tumbler. "Because if it recoils on my head, it takes the three of you with it."

"Best not to panic in this situation," soothed Dictionary Key.

"Well, we've bought ourselves at least a week or more before anything happens on the government's end," said Russell.

Turning to the cadaverous lawyer, Winthrop said, "You don't get it either do you, Isaiah? This killing changes everything for us. It might even end up putting some backbone in your esteemed law partner."

A malevolent silence filled the cabin. "I can't believe we could be this stupid," hissed Sawyer.

"Where's your man now?" Key asked Winthrop.

"At my estate, with orders to stay out of sight."

"Can he be trusted?"

"He's a loyal soldier," replied Winthrop, "he'd never say a word."

"Can we get him out of the country? Maybe back to Haiti?" asked Russell.

Winthrop settled in his chair, his right hand twirling a glass. "He can't go back. He's wanted. *Ton Ton Macoute*. Plus, he has no ties. His entire family was killed in the earthquake." He casually offered a solution. "We could put him to work on one of Island Import's freighters, Hamilton. You know, out of sight for a while until things cool down. Maybe Key here can arrange for him to fall overboard at night. The Gulf Stream can take care of a lot of problems."

"You said he'd keep quiet," countered the bulky lawyer.

"Hamilton, maybe Spencer's right," said Russell. "Why not eliminate him?"

"You should listen to Isaiah, Counselor," said Winthrop. "We're talking about one Haitian, an invisible man. He became expendable the moment I sent him into Faithtown. Believe me, no one will miss him."

Winthrop eyed Sawyer. "I don't recall your objecting to getting rid of Virgil Livingston." He took a long swallow of his drink and stared at the perspiring lawyer. "Then again, you don't seem to have much of a problem letting others decide to do some of the more indelicate things, do you?"

Cornered, Sawyer brooded, lost in the group's predicament.

"Better think of something, mon," counseled Russell, "because this place is going to be crawling with Nassau police soon enough."

"Do it, Hamilton," ordered Winthrop. "Show us what you're made of. Besides, what's one more at this point?" Rising to refill his drink, the yacht owner stretched his long legs and addressed Dictionary Key from the salon's bar.

"You have weekly freight going to the Abacos every morning, right? I'll have my man at Island Imports by seven o'clock tomorrow. Find a berth on board for him, Key. You can certainly do that."

Sawyer shook his head, knowing they were signing yet another man's death warrant. His forte was finances, politics and drugs, not murder. Virgil Livingston's killing had been an aberration he wanted to avoid repeating.

"You need to be hard, Hamilton, much harder," sneered Winthrop. "It amazes me that you've survived as long as you have in this game. You've got to move fast. Young

Burton's death was high profile and people will demand something be done."

Sitting back, Sawyer pouted. He was not used to being addressed this way.

"Here's what you need to do, Hamilton," continued Winthrop. "Tomorrow as planned, your boys are going to load my boat with that big order, courtesy of our friends." Winthrop sat down, reached out, and slapped the man's plump knee. "It'll work out perfectly. Just don't screw up and lose your nerve. We'll load up after dark as usual. Mikos knows the score. His entire crew can be trusted."

Warming to his plan, Winthrop grinned at his associates. "I fly to Boston tomorrow at noon. I'll wait for the shipment's arrival. Our associates will be there to take delivery. Anything else to discuss?"

"Do you think your showing up at the funeral was wise?" said Sawyer.

"No, no, it was quite appropriate, Hamilton," Russell said, sensing the logic.

"Isaiah's right. It would have looked odd if he had not been there," explained Key. "It was a major event for Faithtown. People would never have forgiven him if he hadn't been there to console the grieving parents. It was wise not to skip it."

"Well, I didn't feel a need to go," said Sawyer.

"You wouldn't have been welcome," snorted Winthrop.

Changing the subject, Sawyer asked, "What about your wife?"

"She'll follow in a week or two, as usual," Winthrop answered. "She always stays behind to help our housekeeper close the place. Everything must appear normal. See, Hamilton," smiled Winthrop, "one can be hard if one needs to be." He swept his hand around the salon. "By the way, this is a celebration of sorts for our partnership. This is it, gentlemen. I'm done. This last shipment is it. I'm out of this for good after this run."

The others didn't appear surprised.

"We can all quit the game after this shipment," purred Winthrop. "This will be our biggest score yet. It should make us all very happy. Can't be too greedy for too long," warned the American. "You should smile, Hamilton," he teased. "This gets you what you want."

"And what's that?" said Sawyer.

"The big score! It's time for you to get back that seed money you've been investing. Every year we've increased our cargoes," said Winthrop, "but it's been leading up to this final payload."

He painted a money picture for his partners. "We should pull in twenty million dollars tax free and clean as a whistle."

Russell spoke from the couch. "I'm sure brother Sawyer and I will be quite comfortable with our own modest profit. We don't require much to be content. Brother Key here feels the same."

Contentment would mean at least five million American dollars laundered in Nassau through a series of dummy corporations.

"Then I think we're done," declared the yachtsman, grinning.

"Yes," agreed Sawyer, struggling to his feet and avoiding the American's hand. Winthrop registered the slight but refused to let it dampen his spirit.

"Bon voyage," said Russell, thrusting his bony hand at Winthrop.

Key gripped Winthrop's offered hand and followed the others out on deck. As the Bahamians moved to the ladder, Key reminded Winthrop, "Have your man at Island Imports at seven sharp."

"He'll be there. Just make sure he doesn't come back."

Winthrop stayed at the rail to watch his reluctant business partners pull away in their whaler. He went back to the salon, dimmed the lights and sipped his drink. He raised Captain Mikos on the intercom and asked to meet on the bridge to plan the loading of their special cargo and Thursday's sailing.

CHAPTER 48

The day after the funeral, Martha busied herself helping church women serve a second large meal in as many days to remaining family and guests who had stayed for Sunday's service. Following a lengthy evening worship led by the visiting evangelist, the faithful trooped to several candlelit pavilions erected on the church lawn where tables covered in ivory linen groaned under the weight of food. White folding chairs magically appeared, and a line of chattering village residents moved down both sides of the serving tables, helping themselves to the bounty. A soothing trade wind cooled the packed crowd.

Most of Faithtown passed through the tents. With so many visitors it was easy for McKay to slip away unnoticed. He went home, changed into jeans, a khaki shirt, and dark cap. He walked unnoticed to his office and once inside, shut the door behind him, flipped on the overhead light, and opened the safe.

McKay felt for his holstered Smith & Wesson automatic. He slapped a loaded magazine in the nine-millimeter handgun, jacked a round into the chamber and flipped on the safety. After locking the safe, he tucked the loaded pistol under his loose-fitting shirt. Grabbing a VHF radio from his desk, McKay stepped into the archway and locked the door behind him. The sun had begun its drop to the horizon by the time he reached the dock and stepped into his boat.

A glassy sea with little wind made for good time to New Zion. Unaware he was being watched; McKay began a slow trip up the inlet toward Island Imports.

At the wheel of Taxi Thirty-Six, Hollis spotted McKay's approach. From his vantage point in the parking lot of a marina laundry, the cabbie knew the policeman was headed for Sawyer's warehouse. Normally congested with the sailing crowd, tonight the dockside facility was deserted save for a single patron, a voluptuous brown-skinned woman stuffing a load of soiled clothes into three machines.

Hollis had been finishing a carton of conch chowder when McKay slowly cruised past the laundry. Suspicious, the taxi driver flipped open his cell phone and punched in a number. Glancing around, he spoke warily.

"It's Hollis. Better do something quick, mon. McKay just came by in his boat. He don't look happy and he's headed your way."

McKay's boat disappeared behind a set of pilings. To take his mind off the policeman, Hollis continued his surveillance of the laundry's lone customer who had stripped off her T-shirt to stand unashamed in bra and panties. She picked up a magazine to read while the load ran. Laughing, Hollis turned on his radio to troll for fares.

At a low building adjacent to Island Imports, McKay killed his Yamaha and let the boat's momentum carry him toward the pier. Tying alongside a pair of half-sunken boats, he left the key in the ignition and climbed the ladder, his attention focused on the deserted warehouse and its yard.

A security light high on a corner of the warehouse buzzed into life as evening deepened, forcing McKay into the building's shadows. He was out of the line of sight for anyone using the gravel access road running along the docks.

In his warehouse office, Dictionary Key eyed a reclining Zeke Cameron on the office couch. The blonde youth was twirling a short-curved knife in his right hand.

"McKay's here," barked Key as he replaced the phone in its cradle. Ignoring the warning, Zeke continued playing with the blade.

Key punched in a phone number and spoke rapidly into the receiver. "Ah, Doctor Singh, you'd best get over here. We're about to have an unwelcome visitor. I'll need your particular skills shortly."

The voice on the other end argued about the summons and Key changed his tone. "I'm not asking, Singh, I'm telling you. Get over here now. Use the back way." He slammed down the receiver.

Key leaned over, unlocked a bottom drawer and grabbed a green box, which he set before him on the desk. Snapping open the lid, he placed a black plastic handgun in front of him and hefted the weapon.

Sheathing his knife, Zeke sat up, curious. "You gonna use that on McKay?"

Key smiled. "Yes, the good constable's going to be sorry he stopped by tonight. It's a Taser gun. Anyone hit with this will be instantly disabled." He pointed it playfully at Cameron, who flinched.

"Hey, don't mess around with that thing."

Key stood, turned on a small radio and set the music level loud enough to be heard downstairs. He turned off the overhead fluorescent lights. Weapon in hand, Key moved quickly to the stairs.

"All right, let's go welcome our guest."

Zeke picked up a wooden baseball bat and followed Key to the landing outside the office. Key held the Taser gun high against his chest. Leaving the door half-open behind them, Key shut off the hall lights and led the way downstairs, creeping cat-like onto the warehouse floor.

"You're the bait," he whispered. Key ordered Zeke to take up an exposed position near the bottom of the steps. Stepping into deep shadows fifteen feet away from the doorway he knew McKay would have to use, Key leveled his weapon and waited.

For the next ten minutes, Zeke played his part to perfection. "Hello, Zeke."

Cameron spun, his groin catching the full force of McKay's foot. Screaming, the blonde youth folded into a clump of denim, his wooden bat clattering harmlessly across the concrete. McKay twisted Cameron's right arm behind his back and patted him down. He pulled the wicked looking knife from Zeke's belted sheath. "What exactly were you planning to do with this? You're a troublemaker, always have been."

McKay slipped plastic ties around Zeke's thin wrists and tightened them. With the young man disarmed and bound, McKay surveyed the darkened steps and the partially opened office door at the top of the stairs. Drawing the nine-millimeter from under his shirt, McKay hauled his prisoner into a seated position on the step.

Zeke, trying to regain his breath, gulped air as McKay pushed him upright.

"I think you were involved in Jonathan's murder," he said. "Where's Key?"

No answer. "Who else is here?" The decoy whined.

Hidden in the shadows, Key aimed the Taser at McKay's back and fired.

Two tiny darts slammed into McKay's trunk, their trailing wires instantly shooting 50,000 volts of electricity through the big man's body. Writhing in excruciating pain—unlike anything he had ever experienced—the policeman dropped to the cement floor, his frame arching out of control. McKay's muscles twitched in spasms, burning from within. He passed out; his handgun useless.

Key kicked McKay's handgun aside and stepped around the prone officer. He picked up the knife and moved behind Zeke Cameron to cut the plastic restraints.

"Did it kill him?" the young man wheezed.

"No, but it probably felt like it."

"Good," he said, limping to the doorway.

"Tie him up," said Key, handing Zeke a roll of duct tape. The two wrapped McKay's ankles and knees, binding his arms behind his back, securing his hands as well.

McKay groaned in agony.

"He musta been expecting some serious trouble," whistled Zeke. He picked up the weapon and fondled it. Key, suddenly worried about Cameron's carelessness, demanded the handgun. As the sullen youth surrendered it, the building was suddenly bathed in headlights.

Key stepped into the courtyard and yelled, "Put out your lights, idiot!"

The headlights went dark. Key unlocked the chain link gate to let the vehicle enter. The car rolled to a stop and Singh stepped from the sedan with a black bag.

"You're just in time, doctor," grunted Key. The two entered the warehouse where McKay lay trussed and immobile on the floor.

Singh asked, "Is he…"

"Dead? No. He's harmless for now. I used this," said Key, waving the Taser triumphantly.

"I want you to knock him out for a few more hours."

Singh hesitated. "What's to be done with him?"

"Not your worry, Doctor."

Placing his bag on the steps, Singh shakily withdrew a large syringe and small vial. After filling the needle's reservoir, he looked at Key.

"This is phenobarbital. Two hundred milligrams. It'll take effect in five minutes."

"Go ahead, work your magic, Doctor."

Singh knelt and plunged the needle into the unconscious man's left bicep.

"How much time will that give us?" said Key.

"He'll be out for a good two hours."

"Perfect. Let's get him in the inflatable," ordered Key.

Singh did not move. Key said, "Give Zeke a hand, Doctor."

Reluctantly, the physician and a limping Zeke manhandled the unconscious McKay down the stairs leading to the concealed boathouse. At Key's direction, they loaded their bound prisoner in a twenty-five-foot Zodiac. Key hit a button, raising the hidden doors giving him access to the inlet. Leaping into the black rubber craft, he cranked the twin motors into life and donned a dark jacket.

Key yelled over the roar. "Singh, help find McKay's boat. After that you can be on your way."

"Remember, Zeke," warned Key, "we've got a job to do! You know where to meet me."

With that, the big inflatable roared from under the docks and turned into the inlet as the boathouse doors reversed direction and clanked down into place.

Zeke and Singh walked along the docks near Island Imports, searching with flashlights until they found McKay's boat. Zeke scrambled aboard and started the engine. Singh tossed the rope in the bow and stayed until the younger man departed for his rendezvous with Key.

"Samuel, have you seen Mac?"

Burton did not respond. Martha repeated her question. "Do you know where Mac is?" she asked.

Burton shook his head, fatigue and grief etched across his face. Stragglers from the church meal filed through the sanctuary to share a last word with the Burtons. Martha patrolled the tents among the dwindling guests, bagging trash and collecting coffee cups. In the small kitchen at the back of the church, Faithtown's postmistress and a cousin laid out borrowed silverware to dry on a large towel.

Depositing a stack of china cups, Martha asked, "Sarah, have you seen Mac?"

Spreading a handful of wet forks across the linen, the plump woman spoke without taking her eyes from her duties. "Not since they started serving, Martha."

On the lawn, a team of men dismantled tents and folded chairs. Martha made one last sweep around the grounds and then walked to McKay's house. Her insistent knocking at the front door went unanswered. She let herself in. In the darkened parlor, she found McKay's uniform shirt and trousers draped over an armchair but no sign of him. She went out back, hoping for once he was sprawled in a drunken stupor. His hammock was empty. A quick check of the marina revealed a telltale gap in the moored boats.

Her panic mounted. Out of options, she went to the Burtons. In the parlor, Lillian and Samuel sat with the few remaining well-wishers, chatting quietly.

Martha hid her anxiety from the Burtons and wandered to the screened porch.

In the distance, New Zion's lights beckoned.

Where are you, Mac?

CHAPTER 49

At the southwest tip of Kingdom Cay, two small craft entered Charity Bay. In the lead, Dictionary Key piloted a sleek, black, twenty-five-foot Zodiac, its blunt snout sending up geysers of spray on either side of its glistening hull. Thirty yards astern, Zeke followed in McKay's runabout. Key dropped his speed and approached the private pier below the Winthrop estate.

Zeke pulled in behind and cut his engine. Their arrival, observed from the hilltop home, immediately sent a golf cart weaving its way toward the moored boats.

Wrestling McKay's trussed body onto the pier, Key yelled, "Give me a hand, Zeke, before our unhappy host shows up."

Each man shouldered one end of the burden and climbed chiseled steps to a cavern carved into the limestone bluff. Inside a large hollowed-out room, they dropped McKay on the damp floor.

Key flipped on a diving light, set it next to their prisoner and tossed the bat to Zeke. "Watch him," he growled. "If he so much as blinks, use this."

The young man hovered over the unconscious McKay, club at the ready, hoping for the slightest movement. Voices on the bluff above made the men pause. Footsteps echoed on the steps.

Two figures filled a limestone arch, blinding Key and Zeke with powerful flashlights. Shielding his eyes, Key signaled to the newcomers to lower their beams.

"What the hell is this, Key?" raged an angry Spencer Winthrop.

"An insurance package," shot back Key, gesturing at the comatose McKay. "He came calling at the warehouse. I had no choice."

"Are you out of your mind?" yelled Winthrop. "This is completely idiotic."

Key didn't yield. "He was going to ruin everything. He had to be taken out. We had to take action."

Winthrop threw up his hands. "I'm flying to Boston tomorrow! Did you forget that?" He walked over to look at McKay. "What happened to him?"

"I had Singh give him something to knock him out," said Key.

"Now what?" said Winthrop exasperated. "You can't leave him here! Did you think about that?"

Key looked at his prisoner and then back at Winthrop. "That's where you come in. We need your help to get rid of him."

"Do you have some brilliant plan?" said Winthrop. Key didn't answer.

"I didn't think so," the American sneered. "You don't think that far ahead do you?"

Nostrils flaring, Key stood his ground. "You said Sawyer's problem was not being hard enough. Well, here's your chance to lead by example."

Fuming, Winthrop stepped back from the unconscious McKay and spoke rapid Creole to the Haitian holding a flashlight. The little man hurried up the rock steps and took the cart back to the house.

When Winthrop's man returned, he carried a wicker basket down the stairs to the cavern and set it down. Nodding at McKay, Winthrop snapped, "Prop him up." Key and Cameron pushed the limp form against a wall. McKay groaned. "Is he regaining consciousness?" said a worried Winthrop.

"Calm down, he's in no condition to resist," said Key.

From the basket, Winthrop took a large metal funnel and twisted the end into a length of soft, half-inch rubber hose. Handing the assembled contraption to Key, he ordered, "Push the tube down his throat as far as you can."

Key took the hose and pried McKay's jaws open.

"Hold the funnel over his mouth," said Winthrop. Despite the sedation, McKay shook instinctively, struggling to reject the tube. Rum splashed Winthrop.

"Hold his head steady," he commanded.

Winthrop poured one bottle into the funnel. His servant handed him another bottle. He washed down a third, and final, bottle down the tube. Before Winthrop quit, he pulled the hose from McKay's mouth, letting him sag against the wall.

"Keep him upright for now." McKay gagged, his chest heaving spontaneously, drawing in air.

It dawned on Key what the American was doing. "Sawyer should see this, mon," he said smiling.

Winthrop told them to cut loose McKay's bindings. Like a rag doll, the policeman's limbs and head flopped awkwardly. Consciousness did not fully return. McKay's brain registered only colorless blurs of movement. His eyes were unable to focus. His captors dragged him outside.

Winthrop pointed to misshapen coral blocks scattered outside the cavern's entrance. "Use those," he directed Zeke. "Break his arms and legs."

Picking up a ragged hunk of rock, Zeke looked at Key, who shrugged. Raising the stone over the helpless lawman, the youth dropped the fragment on McKay's upper right arm. The rock smashed down, snapping the humerus between shoulder and elbow.

"Now the other one," snapped Winthrop.

The second rock, heavier than the first, caused McKay additional silent agony. His body flexed in response to the stone's impact. The only sound between dull thuds was ocean surf crashing against the rocky beach below. Zeke sought revenge a hundredfold with blows to McKay's remaining limbs.

The gruesome task complete, Winthrop directed Key and Zeke to dump McKay into the policeman's boat. After wiping the rum bottles, Winthrop jammed the empties under the seats and waterproof storage cabinet by the wheel in McKay's boat. He read his watch and glanced at McKay's pain-wracked frame sprawled in the bottom of the twenty-footer.

An occasional spasmodic twitching and heaving of the chest were the only signs of life.

Winthrop turned back to Key. "High tide in half an hour," he said casually as if discussing an upcoming picnic. "Take your inflatable to West Point. Zeke, you follow in McKay's boat. Take him and run him onto the reef in his own boat. Everyone knows McKay's a drunk," said Winthrop derisively.

"Obviously, he was under the influence, lost control. Couldn't swim. Couldn't save himself."

Coral ledges along Kingdom Cay's West Point resembled sharpened spikes of wrought iron. Any hull caught against the razor-sharp shelf would be systematically shredded by the waves action.

A human body would be even more vulnerable.

Zeke pursed his lips, glancing for direction from Key who stood with arms crossed.

"Let's do it," said the black man. They stepped into the boats. Engines roared to life and the tall American tossed the inflatable's line to Key.

"You coming with us?" asked Key.

Winthrop shook his head. "Not really my style. I trust you to handle it."

Scowling at Winthrop's cowardice, Key didn't argue. He hit the throttle and the shiny rubber boat jumped from the dock. Zeke followed in McKay's boat, the policeman slumped beside him. Both craft cleared the bay and vanished in the night. Winthrop scanned the interior of the cavern. Satisfied nothing incriminating remained, he and his servant climbed the stone stairway to the parked golf cart. Purring quietly, the little vehicle followed the winding path between hedges of sea grape, up the hill to the lighted mansion.

CHAPTER 50

Key, listening to the sounds of crashing surf to his front, jockeyed his throttle to avoid the reef. His flashlight caught flashes of foam marking the edge of the coral. Alongside, in McKay's boat, Zeke shifted the unconscious policeman behind the wheel of the rocking hull, its engine's throttle in neutral.

"READY?" bellowed Key.

The younger man gave thumbs up and both craft roared toward the reef. As the boats drew parallel to each other, Zeke straddled the two rocking hulls, one hand on the throttle of McKay's boat, the other gripping a rope handle on the rubber boat to his right.

"NOW," yelled Key.

Zeke shoved the smaller boat's throttle forward and nimbly leaped behind Key.

McKay's boat shot toward the surf. Zeke tumbled aboard the inflatable and Key cut sharply, racing away from the deadly coral in a tight turn that stood the Zodiac on its starboard rail. He risked a backward glance. McKay's twenty-foot runabout went airborne over the back of a large wave and crashed on the coral in an explosion of whitewater.

Wrenched loose from the stern, the big Yamaha cartwheeled across ragged rock in a shower of sparks, its prop spinning as the engine smashed into an anvil-shaped coral head. Another large wave twisted the hull sideways and dragged it along the ledge.

Mesmerized by the crash, Zeke fell back against the rubber hull, giggling. Key planed the waves, opening the distance between his boat and the reef.

Spilled by the impact, McKay, covered with shards of fiberglass, temporarily came to rest against remnants of an upholstered seat. Cold water and salt air shocked him awake but he was only dimly aware of his surroundings. His heavy lids would not focus.

Dazed, drunken, unable to recall why, he was suddenly aware of pain seizing his body. He tried to raise himself from the battered wreckage. His arms would not function nor would his legs respond. Nothing worked.

The boat came to rest at an odd angle, sending him into a section of shattered control panel. Another explosion of foam submerged the hull. He fainted, and then awoke when another wall of water jolted the wreckage. By turning his trunk, he was able to worm his way higher.

Must...have...had...accident, his blurred mind reasoned. *Have to...get out. Where am I?*

More waves surged across the shelf, choking him. The water briefly receded. McKay's mouth and nostrils burned with salt. Retching in spasms of agony, he emptied his stomach's contents. The transom broke apart as another powerful wave hit what was left of the stern.

I'm going to die!

"Oh, God, HELP ME," McKay cried.

Seas swept over the reef, dragging the boat's shattered shell back and forth across the coral, chopping the debris into smaller pieces. McKay cursed, then pleaded with God, then cursed again as he was washed out of the wreckage and deposited at the edge of a tide pool. He rolled, trying to avoid the next wave but the entire reef shelf was disappearing beneath a rising tide.

A powerful surge raked McKay across the shards of coral. Screaming in pain, he rolled again, hoping to escape more punishment on the deadly rocks. Helpless as a wall of white water tossed him about, he sobbed in agony.

McKay felt his body being dragged across the coral. Blood poured from wounds on his back and face. His mouth filled with the taste of copper and salt.

Resigning himself to death, McKay gave up. His body relaxed. Bright lights came closer, filling his world. Foaming seawater rushed over him. McKay drifted, no longer wracked with suffering.

Surrendering, he felt himself gently lifted by his arms into the lights, beyond the pain.

CHAPTER 51

Two hundred miles north, *The Green Turtle Two* knifed through four-foot seas at its normal cruising speed of eighteen knots. On the bridge, Captain Mikos inhaled the strong aroma of fresh coffee from a thick porcelain mug. The big Broward had reached its first plotted waypoint an hour ago and was now on a heading of three hundred and ten degrees. His crew of four was down in the mess finishing their evening meal. Two big Detroit diesels hummed perfectly, each engine turning the screws with its twelve-hundred horsepower. The lights of Great Abaco Island faded off to port.

Knowing he was piloting a twenty-million-dollar cargo, Mikos would not relax until the cocaine hidden in the hull below the waterline was safely delivered. It was the largest cargo he had shepherded from Jericho Island to New England. Though he shunned drugs himself, Mikos felt conveniently amoral about transporting them.

A bearded face appeared at the bottom of the spiral staircase. "Skipper, you want some dessert?"

"No thanks," Mikos replied. Coffee was enough after an earlier solitary supper.

The previous night's loading in New Zion harbor had gone smoothly. Dictionary Key's team had done their job well. Two tons of pure Colombian cocaine, molded into kilo blocks sealed in plastic, had been secreted in watertight spaces in the bilges. Once the cargo was hidden, steel plates had been welded in place.

After supper, his crew would grind down the weld lines and prime the surface. In the early morning, while nearing Georgia's coast, two coats of new paint would be applied. When the paint dried the hiding places would be invisible. Eventually, they would approach New England and report to U.S. Customs. No one would be the wiser about the payload sealed in the hull. Besides, Mikos knew East coast authorities were familiar with *The Green Turtle Two's* routine summer return to Boston.

Six years ago, the two had begun experimenting with small shipments. Each succeeding year emboldened them to increase the haul and the payout had increased proportionally. But they had pushed the odds long enough. Mikos was relieved to hear this trip would be Winthrop's last.

Unknown to his employer, Mikos also planned this voyage to be his final one.

He yearned to retire to the island of Skopelos in the Aegean Sea and had been secretly saving for years. He was about to realize his dream. Smiling at the thought of his own arrangements, he checked the yacht's progress on the laptop's glowing screen.

Everything was progressing as planned.

At ten that night, Mikos turned over the watch to Jasper, the first mate. The five-day weather report promised no changes. A low-pressure system forming over the Azores was days from causing any concern. East coast seaboard predictions were the same. Mikos went out on deck and studied the night sky before returning to the pilothouse and bidding the mate good night. He went below to his cabin and read two chapters in a mystery paperback before turning off his light.

Awakened an hour before dawn, Mikos shaved and dressed in a thick wool sweater and dark slacks. He went aft to check the diesels, then emerged topside to inspect the deck in the faint pink glow of a new day. Stepping into the pilothouse, Mikos relieved the crewman at the wheel, sending him below after checking their course.

As the horizon split apart in streaks of gold and orange, the cook ascended the spiral stairway with breakfast. He set the tray on the chart table and climbed back down to the crew's galley. Mikos took a sip of strong coffee, the first of many cups that morning, and wolfed down a fresh roll.

Aware of the powdered gold below decks, each of the crew was as anxious as their skipper to deliver the cargo intact.

The morning delivered a glorious beginning. Breaking free of its ocean tether, the sun floated above a cobalt sea. The yacht's graceful white hull cut the water effortlessly.

Captain Mikos relaxed and drank his coffee.

That evening they would pass the Carolinas. There, he would run close to shore for an unscheduled rendezvous of his own. Mikos would handle the helm for the detour, taking *The Green Turtle Two* perilously close to Cape Fear.

A separate pallet of four, bright yellow, fifty-five-gallon barrels, each packed with sealed packages of Colombian cocaine, was lashed to the diving equipment locker.

The drums were Mikos' retirement.

CHAPTER 52

McKay focused on a vaulted sky filled with gauzy scraps of cloud. On the horizon, the sea's ultramarine horizon changed to shades of aqua closer to shore. Great purple coral heads floated in the turquoise shallows and small waves washed the white, sugary shore. Graceful palms leaned over him, casting cool shadows. McKay looked at a wide, endless beach running as far as he could see in either direction.

To the left, a figure slowly approached. He waited. A woman was waving to him. He tried to wave back but was unable. The woman came closer—Martha.

She drew near but he could not rise to meet her. Distraught, he watched her smile seductively and pass, casting a green-eyed gaze over a tanned shoulder as she strolled by without stopping. His body lay anchored in the soft sand, incapable of rising.

Am I dead? he wondered. *Is this heaven? Something like it?*

Turning to look longingly at the sea again, he heard someone behind him call his name. Faint at first, the voice became more insistent. He concentrated on the horizon.

"Jeremiah. Jeremiah McKay."

The sea slowly dissolved, and a face emerged, inches from his. He opened his eyes.

"Mac, it's Martha. Can you hear me?" He squinted, trying to focus. No good.

"Do you know me?"

An echo. He tried to speak but no sound came.

"Don't try to talk. You've had a rough time. It's all right now."

He felt comforted somehow, though dull waves of pain began working their way up and down his body. He wanted to speak. Something touched the fingers of his right hand and he recoiled in response. The disconnected face above him floated to one side and smiled. He sensed what he thought was a smile on his face, but even that felt odd. Drifting sideways into unconsciousness again, he stayed down, then surfaced.

Welding scars marking the steel plates hiding the cocaine had been ground down to smooth perfection and primed. The crew had vacuumed the metallic dust and were now painting the surface with its second coat. The captain stood behind three men, watching.

The first mate called down from the bridge. "Skipper, approaching Cape Fear in forty minutes."

Mikos patted the nearest painter on the shoulder. "Excellent job. It's looking good. Make sure you feather the coat to blend in with the rest of the bulkhead, understand?"

They grunted in unison. "It has to be perfect," he reminded them.

"I'm coming up, Jasper."

On the bridge, the first mate was busy with the computer. Peering at the screen, he tapped a key and the maritime chart leaped to twice its size on the flat display. Depth markings for the waters off Cape Fear were plotted across the graphic. Leaning over the table, Mikos scrutinized the plots.

"Come to two-eight-zero," he said. The mate rotated the ship's wheel to port and looked down at the compass floating in the glass dome. Green light from two radar screens cast a dull glow on his face.

"Right. Two-eight-zero it is, Skipper," he replied.

"Keep this heading for three-zero minutes, Jasper. I'm going below."

Winding his way down the spiral staircase to his cabin, Mikos shut the door and packed his belongings in a waterproof bag. From under his bunk, he drew three manila envelopes, checked the money inside each and sealed them. From his overhead locker, Mikos retrieved a thick white envelope with *Jasper* written in marker. He grabbed his bag and the envelopes and went topside to the salon. After placing the three manila envelopes in a pile on the table, Mikos tucked the thick white envelope inside his jacket and went below to check on the painting. The men had finished. Their brush strokes were invisible. "Perfect," he said. "Clean your gear and give it plenty of time to dry."

They smiled at his compliments. "Mind you don't move the lockers or spare parts before it's dry," he warned pointing at the fresh paint.

The tallest of the three insolently saluted with his brush. Mikos grinned at the juvenile gesture and stepped on the spiral staircase. "When you've cleaned up come topside to the salon. I have something for you." He climbed to the bridge.

"It's about three-zero minutes, Skipper," said Jasper glancing at his watch.

Mikos eyed the ship's clock, turned the laptop towards him and gave a new heading. "Come to three-zero-zero and drop her down to twelve knots."

"Aye, Skipper." Jasper repeated the commands. The yacht slowed, both diesels humming flawlessly. Ten minutes passed.

"Got a contact, Skipper," said Jasper.

Glancing at the radar screen, Mikos read a tiny blip off their port bow.

"All right. Drop to eight knots. Steady on course."

The other three crew emerged from below. Mikos gestured for them to go into the main cabin. "Let me know when the contact is almost on us, Jasper."

Stepping into the main salon, the captain motioned for the men to sit. Having never been guests in the Winthrop's private world, they grinned like schoolboys.

"Gentlemen, I make you a proposal."

Mikos spread the thick manila envelopes on the table. Their eyes fastened on the packages.

"Inside each of these is twenty-five thousand dollars."

Their eyebrows rose. The cook let out a low whistle.

"But here's what I expect for this kind of money," Mikos said, sliding the envelopes toward them across the polished wood. "I expect you to take *The Green Turtle Two* into Boston Harbor as scheduled." Leaning back, he draped one arm across his chair. "Once moored and through customs, I want you to stay with the boat until you're relieved by a new crew. It's all arranged. They'll take over for you and will deliver your cargo at the appropriate time."

The three looked at each other, expecting something more. "That's it?" said the cook, the oldest of the trio.

"That's it," said Mikos. "Once the new crew shows, you're free to go. Job done."

The men stretched in the plush chairs, grinning at their luck. Gathering up the envelopes, they stuffed them in their jackets. "What about you, Captain?" the cook asked.

"I won't be there, gentlemen. I'm taking a detour at Cape Fear."

Jasper's voice rang from the bridge. "Visual, Skipper! Looks like a trawler."

"Drop down to three knots," said Mikos.

Leaping to their feet, the men exchanged high-fives in the salon as Mikos returned to the bridge. *The Green Turtle Two* slowed from eight knots. An ugly, blunt-nosed trawler passed them to port and made a tight turn astern of the yacht. Charging ahead in a wreath of diesel smoke, the boat pulled alongside. A small, hand-held searchlight played across *The Green Turtle Two's* decks. Leaning from the hatchway, Mikos hailed a seaman on the other vessel and sent his three, suddenly rich crewmen to hang fenders over the yacht's port side. That done, he ordered them to line up the plastic barrels stored in the stern diving locker. The trawler muscled closer, both vessels now in tandem on the evening's glassy sea. Mikos ducked back inside the bridge.

"Jasper, I've got a package for you." Mikos plunked down a thick white envelope on the controls console. "One-hundred thousand," he whispered.

Hands still fixed on the ship's wheel, Jasper eyed the white envelope.

"I've already paid the others," said Mikos. "They're each richer by twenty-five thousand. They're very happy right now. Let's keep them that way."

Jasper nodded. "Not taking *The Green Turtle Two* into Boston, are you?"

"Correct," replied Mikos. "I'm taking a little bite and sending you ahead."

Eyeing the trawler plowing the sea alongside the yacht, Jasper asked, "Friends of yours?"

Glancing at the squat boat, Mikos said, "Hardly friends. More like business acquaintances. That's all you need to know."

On the stern, the crew was ready with the yellow barrels.

"Take her into Boston," said Mikos. "Go through the routine at the marina. As I told them, another crew will relieve you. At that point, walk away. Find a girl. Get drunk. Open a bar. Invest," he said, nodding at the envelope. "It's a once-in-a-lifetime chance."

"What do I tell Winthrop?"

"Winthrop and I have an arrangement," lied Mikos.

Jasper shrugged. Unbuttoning his jacket, he stuck the envelope inside.

"Keep her steady until we've loaded," said Mikos. He lifted his bag and went out on deck to oversee the transfer of the yellow barrels. Maneuvering next to the cruiser's fantail, the trawler's crane, a heavy cargo net attached to its boom, reached over the yacht's stern.

Beauty and the Beast, thought Mikos.

He supervised his crew's loading of the four barrels into the netting. Once the load was secured and the crane's arm lifted, Mikos threw his bag into the sling, grasped the net's lines, and rode the precious freight across the water to the other boat. The bulging net settled on the trawler's deck. Mikos leaped from the ropes, recovered his bag and climbed the ship's ladder, disappearing into the wheelhouse. The trawler's crew wrestled the cargo net over an open hold forward of the pilothouse and lowered the treasure into a new hiding place. They secured the hatch cover and stowed the net. Oily black billows belched from the stack as the smaller boat turned toward North Carolina's coast twenty miles west.

On the bridge of *The Green Turtle Two*, the first mate was joined by his jubilant crew.

"How much did he give you?" queried the cook.

"Equal shares for the equal risk," drawled, Jasper. "Twenty-five thousand big ones."

"Pretty good chunk of change for a little heavy lifting, don't you think?" giggled the youngest.

"Yeah, but a word to the wise—Let's make sure we get to spend it," cautioned Jasper. "Better get below and put those lockers and engine parts back into place. We don't want nothing looking out of place when we get to Boston."

Grumbling good naturedly, his crewmates descended the spiral staircase and began the job of camouflaging their handiwork. Jasper set the yacht's throttles to resume their original cruising speed of eighteen knots and flipped open the laptop computer to restore their plotted course. Both diesels responded to the call for increased power and sent the big white hull slashing north through coastal waters.

CHAPTER 53

"Martha, where am I?"

McKay heard his own words. His mind worked but he had to form his questions slowly.

"I'm right here, Mac." Martha's face was poised above him.

"What happened, Martha? How long have I been here? And, where am I?"

"You're in a hospital in West Palm Beach, Mac. You've been here three days."

She began to cry. He tried to reach out to her, but his arms would not cooperate. "You're a wreck, Jeremiah McKay." She laughed through tears.

"I feel awful," he mumbled through swollen lips. "How do I look?"

She smiled. "You've looked better."

He grimaced in response. Other voices. A nurse and doctor entered the room and joined Martha bedside. "Officer McKay, I'm Doctor Dirks. We almost wrote you off, but Miss Thomsen here insisted that you were needed back home."

He scribbled on a chart and passed it to his nurse. "You're a pretty tough character, given what you've been through." He smiled. "Consider me impressed. We're all impressed."

"How bad is it?" said McKay.

"Bad. You had fractures of both arms, both legs and multiple lacerations over your body from coral. We've cleaned those and stitched where we needed to. You lost quite a few units of blood. We did some minor skin grafts to patch some of the worst spots. They look good. But you're going to be pretty sore for quite a while. We'll keep splints on your broken bones until the swelling goes down. From the X-rays I'd say you'll be able to avoid surgery. You'll get some casts soon. That should allow you some mobility in the coming weeks." The doctor paused.

"There are law enforcement folks who want to talk to you when you're up to it. I told them maybe tomorrow. We'll have to see. I'll stop by to check on you then. Things are looking much better than they were."

The physician left the room and Martha reappeared. "You went to New Zion after the funeral, didn't you?"

He nodded.

"I knew that's where you had gone, but I didn't know what you were going to do."

"Went to Island Imports to find Key. Zeke was there. That's the last thing I remember."

"Nobody knows where Zeke is, Mac."

"Probably dead," mumbled McKay.

"Dead? Yeah, I'd guess," she said. "These people play for keeps."

"What about Key?" he said.

"Behind bars for now. It took some doing, but Samuel finally got hold of the authorities. Your friend Ethan Bethel went through the roof when he heard what had happened to you. He sent a team to New Zion to pick Key up for questioning. Key's sitting in Nassau but he's not talking. Oh, yes, Sergeant Newton's been temporarily relived. Bethel thinks he may know something about the connection between Sawyer and Key. Before I forget, Mac. The DEA man in Nassau wants to talk to you. And I called Kent Bryan, your FBI friend. I wanted to let him know about your close call and how you were doing."

McKay began to drift. Martha continued talking. A nurse came by to check IVs and vital signs.

"Anyway, your Nassau contacts want a piece of you too," said Martha. She leaned over him, but McKay did not hear her. He was asleep. Martha kissed him on the forehead.

Dawn ushered *The Green Turtle Two* into Boston Harbor. Following a well practiced protocol there would be no cell phone calls to Winthrop to announce their arrival. As a precaution, once the boat left Bahamian waters, the yacht owner had strictly forbidden any contact with his home or office. Jasper had no way of letting Winthrop know that Captain Mikos had left the yacht off Cape Fear. Instead, he concentrated on their final approach.

Early morning flights from Boston's Logan International Airport screamed over the harbor, spoiling the serenity of the yacht's progress. The three deck hands covered their ears as successive aircraft headed out to sea, climbing steeply in the early morning. Lights from the city's skyline shimmered on the water. Jasper backed off the throttle, slowing to wake speed. A City Water Taxi, its white hull marked in the familiar checkerboard pattern, emerged from the Boston Shipyard and Marina and headed for the Commonwealth Pier, passing its twin going in the opposite direction.

Trailing the yacht unseen, a twenty-seven-foot Boston Police Department whaler moved into position astern of the *The Green Turtle Two*. Jasper used the radio to alert the marina staff to his progress. Off to port, in the historic heart of Boston where new skyscrapers stood next to elegant older buildings, offices came to life in a thousand lighted windows. Traffic flowed through the city's arteries as Jasper began a slight turn to starboard.

The police boat in *The Green Turtle Two's* wake closed to within fifty yards. The yacht's first mate and crew were unaware, their attention focused on the Kremer Marina and Dockyard dead ahead, where Winthrop berthed his yacht for the summer. From his reserved slip, he sometimes cruised north to Marblehead for weekend regattas and social events among peers.

The Kremer Marina and Dockyard, a commercial operation converted to private yacht services provided 150 slips, and proximity to Winthrop's home and office. It was the company of fellow owners of large yachts that attracted Winthrop. Knowing that *The Green Turtle Two* aroused covetous hull envy delighted him.

Jasper spoke into a hand-held VHF radio, ordering his deck crew to drape four huge white fenders over the port side. A golf cart, with attached trailer, moved along the long arm of the pier toward morning's first arrival. The little vehicle parked, and two figures got out, positioning themselves to catch the cruiser's mooring lines. A pair of unmarked delivery vans pulled up at the larger wharf and parked. *The Green Turtle Two* eased within six feet of the pier. Jasper dropped to neutral as the big yacht's momentum carried it to the dock. Bow and stern lines were thrown to the marina workers who looped them through heavy hawsers fore and aft. With a final gentle bump, the cruiser settled flawlessly against her mooring. *The Green Turtle Two* was home.

Across town in a converted office in the dignified brownstones of gilded Boston, Spencer Winthrop's day had already begun with coffee at an antique desk in a well-appointed office overlooking the harbor skyline. His family investment firm did business from a building listed on the National Historical Registry.

The first floor's entry was a locked door set in a carved marble arch. Once inside, guests found themselves in a large tastefully decorated lobby guarded by a receptionist's desk. Behind her were an associate's office, a conference room, plush bathrooms and a small galley kitchen and dining room. On the second floor, reached by either a small elevator or spiral staircase of hand-forged iron railings and marble steps, Winthrop had installed an executive secretary and another office suite with private lavatory. He alone occupied the top floor with its Persian carpets, private bathroom and high ceilings. Here, special clients would be treated to the former politician's considerable charm.

This morning, after a light breakfast, he read the *New York Times* online before skimming foreign markets and double-checking his day planner. Winthrop paced, fighting his urge to rush down to the harbor to watch *The Green Turtle Two* finish the last leg of her long voyage.

An antique China Tea clock on the carved marble mantel above his gas fireplace prompted him to compare the heirloom's time with his heavy gold Rolex. Winthrop willed himself not to call the marina and ask whether his yacht had docked.

Mikos should be calling within the hour, perhaps sooner, he thought.

He returned to some correspondence that needed his signature and was startled by his secretary's voice on the intercom. "Ken Wolf from Kremer Marina on your line, sir."

At last. Winthrop picked up the phone. "Morning, Ken. How are you?"

"Fine, thank you, Mr. Winthrop. I just came in and…"

Winthrop interrupted. "That's great, Ken. I was wondering when she'd put in. Everything all right?" He leaned back, pleased at the news.

"Not exactly, sir. Thought I'd better call you right away and let you know what's going on here."

Winthrop sat up. "What are you saying, Ken?"

"There are cops all over the boat, sir. DEA and Coast Guard, too. They've cordoned off that part of our pier. Mister Winthrop, I don't know what's going on."

Winthrop paled but covered his surprise. "Your guess is as good as mine, Ken. Damn, I hope nothing has happened to the crew. Do you know anything? Where's Captain Mikos?"

Winthrop's caller had no further details but promised to relay any news when he became aware of what was happening on his watch. Winthrop rang off and waited, his heart racing.

Best to stay away from the marina, he told himself.

As a precaution, he surveyed the pavement below his window—a woman walking her dog, a single car negotiating the boulevard, and a couple crossing at the corner. His street was quiet. Winthrop settled back into his chair.

When McKay regained consciousness, he was not alone. Martha moved to his bedside. "Afternoon, Mac. You've got visitors." She stepped back, replaced by FBI Agent Kent Bryan and a vaguely familiar face.

"You really took a beating," said Bryan. McKay responded with a lopsided smile.

"Our office is interested in what you uncovered," said Bryan. "We think it has implications stateside. I'll bring you up to speed about what's happened since you ended up here." The FBI agent gently touched McKay's shoulder. "DEA picked up Winthrop's crew when they got to Boston. Captain Mikos was not on board. He apparently stopped somewhere en route and off-loaded some of the cocaine we think they were carrying. The first mate still isn't talking but we think he'll cooperate eventually. The others are all small fish." The FBI agent was confident. "Right now we've got teams going over the yacht with a fine-toothed comb."

McKay's other visitor, a stocky man with a mustache, heavy eyebrows and shaved head, stepped closer to the hospital bed. "Bud Noble, DEA," he announced.

McKay placed him as the silent note taker at his Nassau meeting with the Coast Guard and the DEA's Jacob Speare. "We thought you might like to see this."

Noble lifted a manila envelope and pulled out an eight-by-ten glossy photo. He held it for McKay's inspection. There on a pier, with *The Green Turtle Two* in the background, Winthrop and a knot of people beamed beside a huge suspended sailfish.

"What's this all about?" McKay asked.

The DEA man grinned. "Look at who Winthrop has his arm around."

A second glance made McKay rise from the pillow. "Martha, it's Virgil Livingston." The two agents parted to let her approach the bed.

"I know," she smiled. "See the man on Winthrop's left? You never got a chance to meet him, but Samuel and I did. It's Dictionary Key."

The photo in McKay's hands implicated the American politician. She laughed. "So much for Winthrop saying the kid never crewed on his yacht, huh."

McKay handed back the picture. "Where did you get this?"

Bryan smiled at McKay. "It came to your office, the same day you went to New Zion. Sarah Cameron found it stuck in your door. She gave it to Martha, who brought it back with her on her last trip to West Palm Beach."

Doctor Dirks entered the room behind the trio. Conversation ceased as he checked on his patient. "How much more time do you need?" he asked, annoyed.

"We can come back tomorrow if need be," volunteered Bryan.

"Good." The doctor pointed at McKay. "I'll stop in again at the end of my rounds."

He left the room. Bryan and Speare promised a return visit and gathered their belongings. After they left, Martha drew her chair closer to the bed. McKay turned to her. Conversation exhausted him but he wanted to talk. "You haven't told me how I ended up here."

"We had to evacuate you by plane, Mac," she explained. "You would have died if we hadn't brought you here."

"But I don't remember anything after going to the warehouse."

"Joyce Russell, the Winthrop's caretaker, and one of their Haitian workers saved your life."

He was confused. She said, "This worker—Louis—apparently witnessed the whole thing. He said you were drugged when Key brought you to Winthrop's estate, *West Wind*. Winthrop wasn't very happy about it. He came up with a plan to kill you and make it to look like an accident."

He sank back on the pillow, suddenly feeling the story's weight. She said, "Louis told us they filled you with rum and then..." Martha faltered. "Zeke broke your arms and legs with rocks."

"Winthrop? Zeke? I don't remember any of that."

"How could you? Anyway, after that, Winthrop ordered Key and Zeke to run your boat onto West Point reef. It was supposed to look like an accident. Like you were drunk. God only knows how you survived, Mac."

He barely smiled. "You said I was drunk, right?"

Martha wiped away tears after telling the details. She leaned closer, trying to race his fatigue to close her story. "When the Haitian got back to the house, he panicked and told Mrs. Russell what had happened. He says it was his friend, Paul, who was sent to murder Jonathan. He hasn't seen him since. He didn't like being part of the plan to bump you off as well. Thought he'd be next, I guess."

McKay grinned. "I can't believe I got that drunk and didn't enjoy it."

She frowned. "Anyway, he persuaded Mrs. Russell to help him find you. They used one of Winthrop's inflatables to get you off the reef."

She stroked his head. "The two of them nearly drowned rescuing you. You were such a mess when they brought you to the clinic. I didn't think you'd survive the night."

"Winthrop know any of this?" he asked groggily.

"I'm not sure. Samuel and I brought you to New Zion on the ferry. He got a pilot friend out of bed to fly you to Florida." She paused and her tears began again. "You were unconscious the entire time. We had to get you out of the Bahamas, Mac."

"I know, I know," he said softly. He reached for her hand. "Thanks, Martha. But who sent me that picture of Winthrop with Virgil Livingston and Key?"

She shrugged. McKay's doctor reappeared at the foot of the bed. "That's it for the day," he solemnly declared. Martha kissed McKay's forehead and left.

Surrendering to weariness, McKay slipped into welcome sleep.

CHAPTER 54

"Bingo, people," announced a uniformed officer. A drug-sniffing German Shepherd stood obediently below a polished turtle shell in *The Green Turtle Two's* salon. Poking a pocket-sized light into the shell's interior, the dog's handler yelled. "Got something here, Lieutenant."

A balding figure in shirtsleeves came down a ladder from the flying bridge where his team had been tearing storage lockers apart. "Whadaya got, Burns?"

The dog stiffened, emitting short nervous whines as Lieutenant Sam Halloran approached. Ignoring the animal, the detective peered into the shell. He spoke into a cell phone and in minutes, a crime lab technician appeared.

"Check it out," commanded Halloran, nodding at the mounted shell.

Probing the shell with latex gloved hands, the tech withdrew a gray block wrapped in plastic. He carried it carefully to the salon's table and set it on a white cloth.

"Check the other shell, too," ordered Halloran to the dog's master. Instantly, the German Shepherd became excited, straining at its leash. Same result. Another wrapped bundle was extracted from the matching carapace and placed on the table.

"Gotcha," Halloran exulted. He slapped the canine officer on the back. "Good job, Burns. Excellent work." He smiled at the dog. "You too, Jetta. Good job."

The animal panted, mouth curled in a toothy grin.

Halloran said, "Get our photographer in here. I'm going topside to call this in. Maybe this will prompt the crew to talk."

When the find was relayed to the FBI office it produced immediate results.

Whoever talks to us first, interrogators told their prisoners, has the best chance of cutting a deal. Within the hour DEA had welders on board, cutting ugly incisions in locations revealed by the crew. The first mate, Jasper, maintained his silence and was informed that he might have forfeited a chance for leniency. In quick succession he traded Captain Mikos, then Winthrop, for future consideration. The U.S. Attorney, though promising nothing, said he would take his cooperation into consideration.

By one o'clock that afternoon, the cruiser was still swarming with FBI, DEA, Coast Guard, and Boston Police. In the waters at the marina, the same twenty-seven-foot police whaler that had tailed *The Green Turtle Two* into the harbor circled the gleaming white hull, providing security from the curious. As word spread, news helicopters buzzed the waterfront.

In a federal judge's chambers, in addition to search warrants for Winthrop's office and home, paperwork for seizing his yacht was begun under the provisions of RICO, the Racketeer Influenced and Corrupt Organizations Act.

The escalating news came as a shock to Winthrop as he took calls in turn from the marina dock master, his lawyers, and Boston media concerning his recently arrived yacht and its hidden cargo of cocaine.

Unaware of the crew's capitulation, Winthrop told his lawyers to release a statement about his being betrayed by employees who had used his yacht for criminal purposes.

High-ranking members of Boston's mob family watched the early afternoon breaking news with increasing anxiety. Video of a growing pile of wrapped bricks of cocaine being triumphantly stacked on the marina pier was being repeated on the half hour. Talking heads on CNN picked up the story and recycled new details every half hour. City papers worked their crime beat reporters' overtime.

None of this was what the crime bosses wanted to see. They would go to ground and sort out the details later. Their sources inside the police department told them the yacht's crew was talking.

That the process would work its way up the ladder and possibly put Winthrop and them in the spotlight increased their discomfort. For the time being the crime bosses were keeping their own counsel.

CHAPTER 55

Spencer Preston Winthrop's normal routine was coming apart by the minute. He told his two harried, bewildered secretaries to hold all calls except those of his senior lawyer and retreated to his spacious office. The view of Boston Harbor from his aerie was a commanding one, but providentially the marina was beyond his direct line of sight. He was spared the ongoing violation of *The Green Turtle Two*.

Pouring himself a generous scotch in a heavy crystal tumbler, Winthrop sank into his high-backed leather chair. In shock, he gazed at Boston's skyline.

The yacht's cargo was supposed to have been the answer to his mounting financial problems with the brokerage firm. The towering mountain of shaky investments in real estate development had depended on this final payout. His years of robbing Peter to pay Paul were finally due, and his scheming was collapsing despite his careful planning.

A numbing paralysis slowly took hold of Winthrop. Bereft of ideas, he waited, nursing his second scotch. His intercom broke the silence.

His secretary's voice was stressed and shrill. "Lyle Epperson on line one, sir."

"Thank you, Lois." He punched a button on his speakerphone.

Winthrop's lawyer, the senior partner at one of Boston's most prestigious firms was boiling.

"Spencer, it's Lyle. I just got off the phone with the U.S. District Attorney and he is intimating that you have a very serious problem."

Winthrop swallowed some scotch and pushed down his panic. "Well, Lyle, what exactly could O'Brien say to rattle one of Boston's finest legal minds?"

"He wasn't specific. You know his style."

Winthrop nodded and poured himself another whiskey. "Hmm, yeah, he's long on intrigue and short on substance, as usual, but it plays well on the evening news. What about my boat? What the devil is going on over there?"

"You tell me. He's talking about a RICO seizure, Spencer. It's much too premature to threaten you with something like that, but he claims there's cause. From what I've been told, the police have uncovered a staggering cache of drugs that was hidden on board."

The patrician exploded in profanity. "I told you that this came as a complete surprise, Lyle."

"Yes, I know that's what you told me when this first happened, but..."

Winthrop interrupted. "But what, Lyle? I wasn't even on the boat. I trusted those people completely."

"Did you know your pilot wasn't on board when she came in?"

Winthrop was stunned. "Captain Mikos? Not on board?"

"That's what the DA told me. Seems he abandoned ship along the coast somewhere. That's all O'Brien would say."

The revelation knocked the wind from Winthrop.

His lawyer rattled on. "According to the news, the FBI or DEA found cocaine hidden in the sea turtle shells on the walls of your main cabin. Did you hear that?"

A weight pinned the politician to his leather chair.

Who would have planted cocaine in the open like that?

He camouflaged his alarm. "They're not walls, they're bulkheads, Lyle. And NO, I haven't listened to the news," lied Winthrop.

His lawyer prodded him. "Well, maybe you should."

"What about the crew?" Winthrop asked, his voice suddenly hollow.

"They're in custody and rumored to be talking."

Winthrop pictured Jasper, the first mate. *Good, solid man. Tough. Probably wouldn't crack. Not sure of the others. This was turning horribly wrong very quickly.*

He began to unravel, then caught himself. "I suppose the police will need to talk to me about this nasty business."

His lawyer agreed but warned him, "Don't say a word without me present."

"Of course," agreed Winthrop. "Do me a favor and call Elizabeth for me Lyle, will you? Give her a heads up on this situation."

"She really should hear it from you, Spencer. And you might want to think about retaining a good criminal lawyer for the long run."

What am I paying you for? fumed Winthrop.

He tried to ignore the suggestion. "You think it's that serious?"

"Yes, Spencer, I do. You're in a very tight spot."

"All right. Call me back with some names then. Goodbye, Lyle."

He rang off, emptied his glass and poured another. He stood, stretched, and wandered to the wide window. Local news crews had arrived and were crowding the sidewalk in front, hoping for a statement. A Boston cop was holding the curious at bay.

As Winthrop watched, two plain sedans pulled up and parked. Dark-suited men got out of the first car and scanned the brownstone. A pair of grim looking men in blue jackets with large "FBI" letters stenciled on the back joined the suits.

Winthrop froze, then abruptly backed from the glass, craning his neck to see where the men had gone. But only the camera crews remained.

On the ground floor, the bell rang and the middle-aged woman manning the firm's receptionist's desk admitted four unsmiling gentlemen. The quartet shouldered their way through an unruly crowd of television crews, which had scrambled up the steps behind them. The cop pushed the cameras back.

The first man through the door flashed a leather holder with a gold badge.

"Agent Giles, FBI, Ma'am. We need to speak with Mister Winthrop."

Momentarily hypnotized by the waved badge, the woman stammered. "Yes, of course. Whom shall I say is calling, please?"

"Giles, FBI," repeated the man politely.

She buzzed the second-floor office. "Lois, a Mister Giles from the FBI is here with three other gentlemen to see Mister Winthrop." She nodded, replaced the phone and indicated the gilded door behind her. "Second floor, gentlemen. You may use the elevator if you wish."

Giles rattled off orders to two of his companions. "Bill, call the Boston PD and tell them to get another uniform out here to handle the press. Tyler, take the stairs. Theo, we'll ride." Sweeping past the front desk, the men made their way to the second floor.

The FBI man who had taken the stairs waited as the ancient lift reached the office with the other pair. "Try the stairs next time," he quipped, grinning.

Lois Winstead, executive secretary to Winthrop for half her life, stood by her desk.

She said, "You're here to see Mister Winthrop?"

"Yes Ma'am, is he in?" said Giles.

"Of course. I'll ring him for you." She turned to her desk and punched a button.

Winthrop's voice boomed through her intercom. "Yes, what is it, Lois?"

"Some gentlemen from the FBI are here to see you, sir."

"All right. I'm finishing up a call with Lyle Epperson, my lawyer. Give me two minutes and then send them up."

She turned to the agents and Giles nodded. His team wandered about the room.

In his office, Winthrop gulped the rest of his drink and shakily lowered the glass.

Less than two minutes to act.

He sat down and unlocked a top drawer on the right-hand side of his desk. Jerking open the drawer, he reached toward the back, probing beneath some papers and a small leather notebook.

Less than a minute now. They'll be coming for me. How could this all end so fast?

In the office below, instinct took over and Giles leaned over the secretary's desk to eye her phone bank. Winthrop's call button was dark.

Giles whirled, pistol in hand. "We're going up," he barked, running for the stairs.

Winthrop withdrew his right hand from the drawer, a small silver automatic in his grip. As he released the safety, he heard hurried footsteps on the stairs.

He took one deep breath, put the barrel in his mouth and squeezed the trigger.

CHAPTER 56

After three months in a West Palm Beach rehabilitation center, Constable Jeremiah McKay was anxious to go home. His care had been excellent. He had learned basic conversational Spanish from his health aides. A fawning CNN profile of his role in cracking the *Jericho Island Connection* as reporters dubbed it, had given him something of a celebrity status. Roaming the rehab center's halls, he encouraged fellow patients—the less mobile *inmates* as he called them.

The staff came to love their Bahamian visitor.

McKay's deep coral cuts faded to tender pink stripes—in a year they would toughen in seawater and sun. His arms worked well, the result of twice-daily therapy. His legs still caused him trouble, though they would eventually heal. He would learn to live with minor pain as a constant reminder.

Martha Thomsen had been at McKay's side continuously in the hospital, visiting every other weekend while he worked his way back into shape. He lost forty pounds and looked better for it. Each day, he walked longer tours of the grounds and encouraged others in similar therapy. The FBI and the DEA gave him courtesy briefings as the case unfolded. The Bahamian government talked of a promotion and hero's welcome when he returned to Kingdom Cay. Finally, McKay was given his doctor's seal of approval for release. After thanking his caregivers profusely, the Saturday discharge finally arrived.

His FBI friend, Special Agent Kent Bryan, drove him to the West Palm Beach Airport and waited with McKay for his Bahamasair flight. Embracing at the small lounge near the gate, they made the usual promises to stay in touch.

McKay's flight to Jericho Island was uneventful. His newly liberated body stiffened on the sixty-minute flight and he hobbled painfully down the ramp at the New Zion airport. Beyond the glass doors of Customs and Immigration, McKay glimpsed Martha in a broad-brimmed straw hat and blue silk sundress. As he shuffled toward the exit, she seemed to him the most beautiful woman in the world. He drew strength from her as they hugged.

"How was the flight?" she said, hailing a taxi.

"It couldn't go fast enough," he answered, slipping into the cab's back seat.

"Welcome back, mon," piped the driver, grabbing the luggage. He turned to grin at McKay, a hint of gold in the ivory smile.

"Hollis, isn't it?" said McKay.

"Yeah, mon," said the cabby as they pulled away from the terminal. "You got your memory back. It's working good," he said, laughing. When they reached the ferry landing, Hollis leaped from the station wagon and hustled McKay's suitcase to the dock.

Martha tried to pay their fare, but Hollis dramatically insisted he would not take her money. It was his honor, he said. When their taxi left, the couple stood on the wooden pier, arms around each other. A white-hulled ferry plowed slowly toward them. As the craft kissed the ladder, Samuel Burton alighted and gently wrapped his arms around McKay.

"God be praised, Jeremiah. May God be praised. Welcome home, Brother."

Burton kissed Martha and hefted the policeman's bag into the ferry. He offered a hand as McKay carefully stepped aboard. Immediately, Burton reversed engines and pulled from the landing, spinning the wheel to port, both throttles forward. The throbbing diesels lulled his only fares into a pleasant, wordless union.

Burton radioed ahead. A small crowd had gathered by the time they docked. When McKay slowly climbed the ladder to the pier the crowd broke into applause. Lillian Burton met him with a bouquet of small red flowers and a long embrace. He shook hands and hugged his way through the entire assembly.

At last, a golf cart appeared with Abner Russell at the wheel. McKay and Martha got into the front while his luggage was piled into the rear seat. The harbormaster headed for the policeman's home, his passengers waving to those lining the route through narrow concrete streets.

"Glad to have you back, Mac," said the marina owner.

"I am truly blessed to be among the living, Abner."

"Crime has dropped dramatically in your absence." They laughed.

That night, McKay and Martha ate a candlelit welcome-home dinner on the Burtons' screened porch. The four of them talked late into the evening.

At one point, McKay raised a glass of iced tea to his hosts.

"One promise I made—aside from not touching alcohol again—was to make it a habit to be back in church starting this Sunday, Samuel."

That pleased the Burtons, and each said a silent prayer. The sounds of music and laughter from moored sailboats drifted across the harbor. McKay finally broke the spell.

"What's your sermon topic on Sunday, Samuel?"

A short pause. "The Prodigal Son," Burton said without smiling.

Silence—and then McKay roared, and the others joined him, laughter echoing across the harbor. For the first time in months, McKay watched the Faithtown Lighthouse sweep the anchorage with its powerful beam and his eyes filled with tears.

On a Friday in October, McKay returned from a lunch with Martha at her clinic to find a visitor waiting in the doorway of his small office.

"Good afternoon, Officer McKay."

Startled by the woman's presence, McKay awkwardly responded. "Hello, Mrs. Winthrop." He moved behind his desk piled with paperwork. "You'll have to excuse the mess."

"Oh, I didn't notice at all." She smiled tentatively and cleared her throat. "I've wanted to come for some time now, to apologize for the actions of my late husband. It was so horrible to hear what had happened to you and my husband's part in all that."

Embarrassed, McKay toyed with a pen, then dropped his hands in his lap.

She continued. "I'm leaving Kingdom Cay, you know."

He did know. The Winthrop estate had been part of the RICO seizure, but lengthy legal wrangling had finally severed it from the smuggling scheme. The property had sold to a wealthy faded English rock star due within the month along with his fourth wife and a baker's dozen of kids.

McKay had been pleased to learn his rescuers would be kept on at *West Wind*. He had met with them both shortly after his return to Faithtown and assured the Haitian he harbored no ill feelings for the man's part in his near drowning. He was also gratified to learn Elizabeth Winthrop had given both employees sizable gifts for their courage that night.

Even so, McKay felt ambivalent about standing here with this beautiful woman who had been married to an enemy.

"I do wish you well, Officer McKay. And I hope you won't object to my making donations to the school and the library in Jonathan Burton's name."

McKay was surprised. "That's generous. You needn't have done that."

"Oh, yes, I needed to. I don't know how else to atone for the past."

"The past is often better left alone," he said, averting his eyes.

"Yes, I suppose. Well, I must be going. Thank you for talking with me."

She stepped across the threshold and McKay followed. Elizabeth Winthrop held out her hand, that dazzling white smile again. "Goodbye, Constable McKay."

He took her hand and their eyes locked. "You sent the picture, didn't you?"

"Excuse me?"

"The picture of your husband with the dead boy he denied ever knowing."

Her expression did not change. She held the smile.

"The kid who was part of the yacht's crew," he reminded her. "His name was Virgil Livingston in case you had forgotten."

"Goodbye, Constable McKay," was all she said.

EPILOGUE

Dictionary Key never talked. He took the brunt of the prosecution for being implicated in the murders of Virgil Livingston and Jonathan Burton. He awaits trial on both charges since the actual killers have yet to be found. His Nassau criminal lawyers are among the best money can buy, and they are optimistic.

Hamilton Sawyer had insulated himself from the Island Imports drug smuggling scandal by layers of shell corporations and holding companies that hid his complicity. His influence with the ruling party put him beyond the reach of the law. Sawyer's Colombian investors accepted the temporary loss in revenue and regrouped. His law partner Isaiah Russell finally succumbed to a failing liver and was buried in a huge funeral at Sawyer's expense.

Sergeant Newton was disciplined and ordered transferred to Spanish Wells but opted to leave the Royal Bahamas Police Force rather than move. At the end of the summer, he and his family moved to New York City where they joined his wife's two sisters and their families. He works as a security guard for a private firm and his application for American citizenship is pending. Corporal Simmons, a marginally competent but unimaginative policeman, succeeded him in New Zion.

Zeke Cameron was never seen again, although rumors occasionally put him on Roger's Cay where his family still builds seaworthy boats. The Cameron's have family in Florida, and it is supposed he commutes between the two branches. He remains at large but police are confident they will bring him to ground soon.

Doctor Bernard Singh's role in drugging McKay was never discovered. He moved to Nassau where he lives in constant fear of being discovered for his part in the drug ring's activities. Sawyer promised the physician he could return to New Zion, but Singh is content to eke out a living on New Providence Island. He will be dead within the year, ruled a possible suicide by local authorities.

Former MP Lionel Parker claimed major credit for the Attorney General's Office in the break-up of the drug ring on Jericho Island. His position in ruling party circles has become even more prominent and he plans to run for his old Parliament seat in the country's next elections.

The Burtons survived the loss of their only child and continue the healing process that will take years, if ever, to complete. Samuel Burton's sermons have taken on a depth of emotion that surprises even him, and his church has added several families to the flock. Lillian still nurtures her garden, which provides fresh flowers daily for Jonathan's grave above the town.

Abner Russell's two sons now operate the ferry under Burton's eye.

Constable Jeremiah McKay accepted a promotion to sergeant with authority over Jericho Island on the condition that he did not have to move to the bigger island. He prefers the pace of Faithtown where he and Martha have grown even closer.

Elizabeth Winthrop reclaimed her maiden name—Lawlor—and banked what she was able to salvage in the wake of her husband's death before leaving Boston forever. Federal officials completed their RICO seizure of *The Green Turtle Two* and the office brownstone. After a six-month battle, Winthrop's widow bested the government in the courts over their attempt to seize her estate on Kingdom Cay. Her sympathetic role as that of the betrayed wife who had been unaware of her mate's compartmentalized life won her case.

Only weeks later did McKay's FBI contact, Kent Bryan, explain that Elizabeth Winthrop's sizable dowry of trust funds had been systematically looted by her husband. The crash of 1987 had begun the raid on her fortune. The 2008 housing debacle hastened the drain. For years, Winthrop siphoned off his wife's inheritance to stay atop Boston's Brahmin society with an elaborate Ponzi scheme that rivaled Bernie Madoff's in audacity, if not in size. The illegal financial conspiracy, combined with Winthrop's ill-advised leap into Wall Street's Byzantine world finished what was left of Elizabeth's funds. Then, like his grandfather's entry into the dark side of Prohibition, Winthrop had been seduced by the fantastic sums one could make from drugs. Eventually, he could not wean himself from the staggering amount of money to be had. The yearly run with his yacht was a natural vehicle that led him into an unholy alliance with New England mobsters. From that point on Winthrop was doomed. According to the FBI, if the Bostonian had not taken his own life, impatient young dons who now rule the Boston and Philadelphia organized crime families eventually would have killed him.

As a precaution, the FBI and Interpol tracked Elizabeth Lawlor when the newly minted widow moved her remaining fortune to London banks the following summer. She was seen in Paris, Rome, Vienna, and then Athens, where authorities lost track of her. She hired a car to drive her to Greece's eastern coast where she rented a small home on the Aegean Sea. A month later, her housekeeper arrived to find the reclusive American gone. A thank you note, and a thousand Euros was left behind on the kitchen table.

Today, Elizabeth Lawlor lives in a large villa clinging to a wooded hillside above the sea on the sun-drenched island of Skopelos. With its red tile roof, whitewashed stone walls and spectacular views of the Aegean, the spacious home rings with laughter and long romantic dinners. She shares this idyllic setting with her wealthy lover, Constantine, a retired sea captain who once went by the name Mikos.

Theirs is an enchanted life.

www.ingramcontent.com/pod-product-compliance
Lightning Source LLC
Chambersburg PA
CBHW070314260626
47160CB00003B/832